JUST IN TIME

JUST IN TIME

A NOVEL

Joan Lindstedt Jackson

SHE WRITES PRESS

Published 2017
Printed in the United States of America
ISBN: 978-1-63152-264-2 pbk
ISBN: 978-1-63152-265-9 ebk

Library of Congress Control Number: 2017946976

For information, address:
She Writes Press
1563 Solano Ave #546
Berkeley, CA 94707

She Writes Press is a division of SparkPoint Studio, LLC.

Dedicated to my brother who asked,

"How come you always get here just in time?"

1

Forty-eight-year-old Steve was lying in his bed upstairs, staring at the ceiling, talking to himself, replaying the events over and over. How his dad couldn't catch his breath. How he'd crawled on his hands and knees to his bedroom and Steve had to help him into bed. He was white as a ghost, and Steve told him he looked like he might pass. But his dad wouldn't let him call the ambulance until it was too late.

His older sister, Sylvia, had burst out sobbing on the phone after Steve told her. That Dad had passed away. Pulmonary embolism. She kept moaning and just couldn't believe it.

"Dad wasn't even sick. How could this happen? Just like Mom." And then she cried even harder.

Steve told her he'd done everything he could. Then took it back. "But maybe I didn't. I should've called 911 right away. But Dad wouldn't let me."

"It's not your fault," she'd said. "You did all the right things, Steve."

Still, he couldn't let go of thinking that somehow he was to blame. Now the whole family was here, probably to decide his future. He wished they'd all just go back to Los Angeles and leave him be. He could hear them talking in the living room below, but could not make out what they were saying. He was sure it was about him. He wondered out loud if they still would let him live in the house. "What if they sell it? Make me find an apartment? Or put me away?" Steve kept hoping it was some mistake, a bad dream, but he'd attended the memorial service that day and realized that life as he knew it was over.

Steve heard footsteps coming up the stairs then his younger brother, Scott, calling him.

"Yeah?"

The converted attic ran the length of the living room and their parent's bedroom on the first floor. It used to be Sylvia's when she was in high school in the sixties, and nothing had changed. Still one half bath, oval braided area rugs scattered on light oak flooring, pale blue walls (now dingy), and built-in bookshelves filled with high school memorabilia: yearbooks, Steve's trophies from his track star glory days, Scott's swimming medals, and pictures of Sylvia as cheerleader and homecoming queen in high school. The books ran the gamut of years, from *Make Way For Ducklings*, *The Boxcar Children*, Hardy Boys and Nancy Drew mysteries, to textbooks and novels.

Scott walked toward Steve's twin bed and stood at the end. He affectionately squeezed Steve's loafered foot a few times. "You been sleeping?"

"Not really, too much going on." Steve glanced at the shoe where Scott's hand was resting. "I forgot to polish my shoes today."

Scott took his hand away and laughed. "But you remembered to shower and shave."

Steve smiled at him. "Only when I have to. So what do you want?"

"Will you come to the living room for a minute? We want to ask you something."

"Do I have to?"

"That's why I came to get you," Scott said. "Nothing to worry about."

Steve eased himself upright and followed his brother to the living room. He plopped in the overstuffed chair where he always sat, the upholstered arms worn thin, darkened from body oil, much like his elbows where thickened patches of dry skin were permanently stained gray. Steve didn't like to bathe more than once a week and even then it took coaxing. But today he actually looked groomed and well dressed: camel corduroy slacks bunched from the leather belt cinched under his large belly, blue and white striped Polo dress shirt without food stains, and tasseled oxblood loafers. Blinking under his horn-rimmed glasses, he looked around at the faces peering at him. "I suppose you're wondering why I called this meeting." His dad's old line, and he sounded just like him.

Everyone chuckled.

"We were thinking that you'd probably want to stay here to live," Scott said.

Head tilted, his elbow resting on the chair arm, Steve twirled the hair on the top of his head with his index finger. "Yes. I want to stay here. It's my home. And yours. And Sylvia's." He gestured toward his sister. "We grew up here."

"We didn't think you'd want to live in Los Angeles, near us," Sylvia said.

Living arrangements for Steve were the first priority. He couldn't manage on his own, and none of them thought that he'd adjust well if he moved to Los Angeles. Even his psychologist said that although he'd probably adapt in time, the shock of moving to a totally new environment might trigger a setback at best, but at worst, a psychotic episode requiring hospitalization. Schizophrenics often become confused, disoriented, reclusive, and delusional with too much stimulation or change. It was agreed that it would serve him best to remain in his childhood home, where he'd been living with his parents the past fifteen years. Now that they were gone, Scott and Sylvia needed to find someone to live with him. Sylvia's husband, Adam, had come to the rescue when he suggested his sister, Nancy. She seemed ideal—that she'd even think to ask what Steve thought of the idea was more consideration than the family had expected. Steve was rarely asked what he wanted, unless it was food: creamed corn or peas, mashed or baked potatoes (always mashed), beef stew or spaghetti.

"I'd hate Los Angeles. How could I even drive there? I'd have to live with you." Steve mumbled to himself. "You probably wouldn't want me anyway."

Adam turned to Steve, "I was talking to my sister, Nancy. She needs a place to live and—"

"Nancy," Steve said. He vaguely remembered that Adam had a sister who lived nearby. "Isn't she your older sister?"

Adam nodded. "Right."

"We thought you'd need someone to live with you," Sylvia said. "Someone to do the grocery shopping, fix meals, clean, and pay some bills."

Steve stared at the floor. Seconds passed in silence while he processed what she said. "Yeah, I can't do those things."

"She'd be willing to move in with you," Scott said.

"Well, I've never met her, but I'm sure she's a nice person." He turned to his brother-in-law, "If she's anything like Adam." Steve and Adam had known each other in high school. His hands fluttered in front of his chest as he spoke. "Does that mean I could still live at home?"

"Affirmative."

"Wow, Scott, 'affirmative.' This is a meeting." Steve mumbled something unintelligible to himself.

"We need to call her back and let her know," Sylvia said. "I know this is sudden, but we need to decide soon."

Steve looked over at Adam who held the cordless in his hand waiting. One thousand one, one thousand two, one thousand three. "Oh. If that's the only way I can stay here. Where would she sleep? In Mom and Dad's room? That would seem weird—a stranger in their room, well, not exactly a stranger, but I don't know her. When would she move in?"

"We don't know yet," Sylvia said. "I guess as soon as she can. That way you won't be all alone."

"Can I meet her first?"

Sylvia suggested that Nancy come by for dinner the next day.

Adam called his sister back. She said she'd be glad to come tomorrow for dinner. "Hey, Steve, do you like dogs?"

Steve rolled his eyes. "Nancy has a dog? Is it a big dog? I hate big dogs. They scare me. The Baldwins' boxer chased me all the way home once when I was little."

"Maybe that's where you got your start," Scott joked. Steve was a state champ in track. Scrapbooks upstairs were filled with local newspaper articles from thirty years ago about "the gazelle who was definitely Olympic material." He was the talk of the town and college coaches from Florida to Massachusetts. Scholarship offers poured in and then went away. His test scores were too low.

Adam explained it was a small dog, a Pekinese. "His name is Sammy."

"Aren't they really ugly with buggy eyes? Don't little dogs bark a lot? I can't stand yapping. What if it urinates in the house? Or worse?" Steve wasn't comfortable using slang for bodily functions. He either skirted the topic altogether, simply excusing himself if he had to use the restroom, or used more polite terms. He lit a cigarette and stared at nothing.

"I'm sure he's house-trained," Scott said. "Maybe a dog will be nice to have around." Scott had heard dogs could be a calming influence for the elderly, but the mentally ill? Even though Steve had a soft heart for animals, Scott wondered if the dog would be safe with him day in, day out.

Steve relented. "What choice do I have?"

Scott excused himself. "Duty calls," he lied. He walked to the backyard and took a few deep breaths to calm down. To think how lucky Steve was that a family member would be willing to live with him (although Nancy had no idea what was in store for her), someone trustworthy and reliable to look after the house and cook his meals—it was such a long shot to find anyone at all and so soon. Yet Steve had no idea. So frustrating. He wasn't as patient with Steve as Sylvia was, and probably never would be. Maybe because Sylvia and Steve were so much closer in age, three years to his six. But she hadn't been around when Steve had his first psychotic break. She was married and out of the house by then, and Scott was starting high school. It was constant turmoil at home. He never knew what to expect when he walked through the door, so after school he stayed at his friends' homes or his girlfriend's as long as he could. As he described it, "We went from the Cleaver family to the Addams family." Scott took a deep breath and went back inside to join the family.

With Thanksgiving two weeks away, everyone helped (mostly Sylvia and Scott's wife, Amanda) to fix the traditional holiday meal, since none of the immediate family would be there to spend it with Steve. The weather was balmy for November, with an invigorating crispness in the air. While the turkey was roasting, they all decided to pitch in and rake leaves, a family chore during childhood, except for Steve who didn't like manual labor. "My meds make me sweat too much," he claimed.

Their dad had loved to do yard work, to be outdoors. Although sometimes he grudgingly raked the leaves—which could be three feet deep if he didn't stay on top of them—a big job since the yard was a quarter of an acre. He'd planted the pin oak trees, now over eighty feet tall, and the hemlocks that encircled the back patio when the house was built in 1950. He grew roses and peonies and photographed them all; their mother planted crocus, daffodils, and lily of the valley, and in summer hung baskets of red geraniums.

Nancy suddenly appeared in the backyard with a wriggling, panting Sammy in her arms. Sylvia decided that Steve was right—it had to be one of the ugliest dogs she'd ever seen. His breathing was so labored he sounded like he was snoring or had a cold, probably due to the flattened, Pekinese-squashed nose, a characteristic of the breed. Nancy was quite lean in her baggy, pale blue sweats and quilted pink parka with a fur-trimmed hood, and several inches taller than Sylvia, who was five foot five. Her short cropped haircut, resembling a cloche hat, accentuated the round, oversized glasses that magnified her jesting brown eyes.

She released Sammy, who ran around the yard in a fury, then she gave Adam a big hug and turned to greet the rest of the family, "Can I join in the raking? Haven't done this in forever!" Sammy ran through the piles of leaves, which everyone got a kick out of.

"Remember when we made leaf forts in the ditch by the road and hid when a car was coming?" Scott asked.

Scott's six-year-old daughter looked surprised. "But you could've been hit by a car!"

"Never thought about that. It was different then. We didn't even wear bicycle helmets."

"But it wasn't at night," Sylvia said. "Those were the days when you could burn them, too, like a big bonfire."

"Where's Steve?" Nancy asked. "Can't wait to meet him."

"He'll join us for dinner. Speaking of, let's go inside. It'll be ready in about thirty minutes," Sylvia said.

They set their rakes against the side of the house by the sliding glass door and settled in the family room. Conversation was lively and flowing, with much reminiscing about their dad. They shed tears, laughed about his habits—like how he carried a pill vial filled with peanut butter wherever he went and how easily he laughed at himself. They recalled his archive of family movies, at least fifty reels on 16mm film documenting their childhoods, with magically appearing titles, such as letters spilling from a child's hand, and dream sequences of department store Christmas scenes superimposed while Steve and Sylvia pretended to be asleep.

Adam said he'd missed his calling. "If he'd gone to Los Angeles, he'd have been a movie director."

Steve sauntered in. "You talking about Dad's movies? Maybe we could watch some tonight."

"Great idea! I'll set it up," Scott said.

Nancy stood and walked over to Steve. "You must be Steve."

He stuck out his hand and nodded. "That's me. And you must be Nancy."

"Do you want to meet Sammy?" she asked. "Oh God, I think I left him outside! C'mon, Steve, let's go find him."

Steve followed her to the backyard.

After about ten minutes, Sylvia and Adam got up and looked for them from the picture window. Steve and Nancy were standing at the far end of the yard and seemed engaged. Steve was bending down, petting Sammy.

"Looks good," Sylvia announced. "Let's hope he's on board for this."

"He'd better be," Scott said.

Steve and Nancy returned to the family room a few minutes later with Sammy in tow. They sat next to each other on the sofa.

Scott and Sylvia exchanged an expectant glance.

With uncharacteristic poise and self-assurance, Steve suddenly spoke up. "I have to get this off my chest. I have something to tell you about Dad." The room went quiet and all eyes were on him. "He made me promise not to tell you, but I guess I can, now that he's not around anymore. Last year, after Mom died, he told me I had to drive him to the surgery center to have his turkey gobbler fixed." Steve pulled at the excess skin at his Adam's apple.

They all looked at each other wide-eyed, mouths hanging open.

"What?" Sylvia asked, dumfounded. "Dad wanted plastic surgery?"

Scott burst out laughing. "I can't believe it. Why would he want to do that?"

"It's true." Steve's voice went up an octave. "I can prove it. The medical bills are hidden in his underwear drawer. I'll show you." He disappeared to the bedroom and returned with papers, handing them to Sylvia.

"Dad spent fifteen hundred dollars for his own vanity?"

"It's totally out of character," Scott said.

"He even tried to talk me into getting rid of all the fat around my neck. But I said no way am I letting them use a knife on me!" Steve couldn't wear ties, which only came up on the rare occasion when he'd accompanied his dad to church, because none of his shirt collars could button over his enormous neck.

Adam winked. "Maybe he had a female friend."

"Widow Briggs. That's what he called her." Steve looked at Scott. "You know, Frank Briggs's mom."

"He had a girlfriend?" Scott asked.

"No, not a girlfriend." Steve rolled his eyes. "He's too old. He went over to her house a few times to practice his trumpet is all. She played the piano, so they did duets for the church sometimes."

"Maybe he just wanted to feel better, or meet someone else," Sylvia said. "He was pretty depressed after Mom died. Sometimes he'd call me and get all choked up, saying how sorry he was that Mom never met his mother. They'd even planned a trip to Nebraska to meet her, but she died before they left."

"I don't remember that," Scott said.

Steve looked annoyed. "You guys interrupted me. I was trying to tell a story."

"Sorry."

Steve explained how worried he was on the drive home from the operation. "Dad was so pale and weak, and he could hardly talk." Steve winced as he related the jagged cut across his Dad's throat. "I thought it was all over. I was sure he was going to pass."

It was still hard to imagine their tight-fisted, eighty-two-year-old father, who didn't seem to care about appearances and what other people thought, was vain enough to spend money on facial surgery. Unless he really was trying to be more attractive for someone else.

"He must've really been depressed. And then to get caught up in that lottery scam this year," Scott said.

"I tried to tell him these guys who called every day were probably a bunch of scam artists," Steve said. "But Dad always knew better than me. He was so much smarter."

Dinner was ready, and they settled in the dining room, still chatting about their dad's little secret. Nancy sat between Steve and Adam. "I guess if you really don't want anyone to find out about your secrets, you'd better destroy the evidence," she said.

Steve marveled at the spread of food. He seemed comfortable and chatted easily with Nancy, which was unusual during a meal. Most often he ate by himself because he didn't want the pressure to make conversation.

As the plates were being filled, Nancy looked at Steve. "Do you want to tell them or should I?"

Steve had already started eating. He nodded to Nancy, "You can tell them."

"Well, I know you're all waiting to hear this," Nancy beamed. "Steve and I decided to be roommates. I can move in next week!"

Relief came over everyone, but mostly Sylvia. She was the designated trustee, as stated in their parent's will. Even with Scott's support, she'd be the one in charge of monitoring the household, and from two thousand miles away.

"Great news," Adam said. "I just knew you two would work it out." He stood and clinked his glass. "I'd like to propose a toast to your mom and dad who are watching over us now, smiling and happy that our families have joined together to take care of each other. And Steve, here's a wild thought, who'd have ever imagined back in high school that someday I'd be living with your sister and you'd be living with mine?"

2

Nancy had just learned she'd have to move out of her friend's guest house in two months. She'd always handled the curve balls thrown in her path, but this time she was striking out looking for a place to live. She had too much pride to sound desperate or too eager to her baby brother, who always seemed to have his life so together. With Adam, she kept her cards close to the vest, giving him the overview without the emotion. For her, this news was almost too good to be true—living rent-free with Steve. She'd told Adam she could probably move in about a week. (So much for not seeming too eager.) She didn't have much furniture, so it shouldn't take longer than a day. Anyway, she couldn't afford to take off work at the grocery store for more than that, since she wouldn't get paid. At least her thirty-year-old daughter, Lisa, and son-in-law would help her move—she could always count on them.

Things had been looking up two years ago, when Nancy had moved in with the love of her life, an honest, generous man who took good care of her (he gave her a new car), wanted to marry her (as soon as his divorce was over), and had a professional career (he was a mechanical engineer). And then her usual luck reared its ugly head. Her man got a brain tumor and died within four months. Before his divorce was final. So his wife got everything, even the car that was still in his name, and Nancy was penniless once again, barely eking out a living with her hourly wage at the grocery store.

Which reminded her, she needed to get cardboard boxes for packing. Today would be good; she'd meet Steve's psychologist (Sylvia's idea) and go to lunch on Sylvia's tab. A glimmer of hope peeped through the tiniest crack in the wall that always got in her way, the wall she couldn't climb over or go around, the wall that rose so high it blocked all the light. But not today. Today she actually felt like getting out of bed, even though the room was so cold she could see her breath. The damn space heater didn't work for beans. *At least I'll have heat again,* she thought.

At the last minute, Lisa was joining her mother to meet Steve and the psychologist. No matter how good things looked on the outside, Lisa wanted reassurance that her mom's safety wasn't in jeopardy. Her mom had a habit of leaping and asking questions later, then wondering why her life was in turmoil. When Lisa asked her if Steve had ever been violent, Nancy didn't know—it never crossed her mind to ask. After meeting Steve, Nancy couldn't fathom he'd be aggressive or capable of hurting anyone. He seemed like such a gentle soul, so deeply bruised by life's disappointments that he must've crawled inside and refused to come out again. Nancy could relate. She'd been feeling the same way for over a year.

———

It was almost noon, and Steve was still asleep upstairs. Sometimes he slept all day. Sylvia was making one of his favorite desserts, instant chocolate pudding, while she waited for Nancy and Lisa to arrive. Should she wake him up so Nancy's daughter could meet him? He was usually grumpy and non-communicative for the first hour, so she thought better of it. Maybe after lunch. She suddenly thought of his meds and wondered if he'd taken his morning dose. The pill tray sat on the dining room table, surrounded by a dozen pill vials that was like a maze she'd have to navigate—she needed to write down what they were, the proper dosages, and how often he took them. She walked to the table and looked at the plastic tray divided into seven rows with each day of the week printed at the bottom. Each row had several small square slots with hinged flaps containing the day's doses. Steve took his pills twice a day. She and Scott joked that 'flaps up' was a good sign, because Steve never closed the lid after he took his meds. She saw that the flap for the morning dose was closed; the pills were still there. She'd have to wake him up before leaving.

Nancy's singsong voice called out. "Yoo-hoo, anybody home?"

"Come on in, I'm almost done here," Sylvia said.

Sylvia suggested that Nancy show Lisa the backyard and let Sammy run around.

"He probably has to do his business anyway." Nancy was all smiles, the gap between her two front teeth on prominent display. She set him on the floor, cooing in a baby talk voice as they headed outside, "C'mon, does Sammy want to see his new home?"

Sylvia took the opportunity to run upstairs with the pill tray. "Steve?" She stood at the side of his bed. "Steve? It's time to get up."

Steve groaned. "I'm too tired."

"You haven't taken your meds today." She stood by his bed with the tray in hand. "Here."

"What are you, my nurse? I can't take them without something to drink." He usually took his meds with a couple of swigs of milk straight from the carton.

Sylvia hesitated.

He rolled on his other side away from her. "I'll come down in a minute."

"I made chocolate pudding for you. It's in the fridge."

"Thanks."

"Nancy and her daughter are here."

He groaned again. "What for? Is she moving in today?"

"No, not yet. Remember I told you that we're going to meet with Dr. Rita? And then we're going to lunch."

"Do I have to go?" he asked.

"No." Sylvia waited a moment.

"Take the tray back where it belongs. I'll take them when you leave," he said.

Since he slept in most mornings, the recommended twelve-hour span between doses was haphazard. Sylvia worried he'd fall back asleep, but what could she do? She went downstairs and put the tray back on the dining room table then she joined Nancy and Lisa in the backyard.

"What a great yard. I bet you guys had fun growing up here," Lisa said with a slight Ohio twang.

"Oh, we did." Sylvia told them how it used to be a gathering place for the neighborhood kids, how summer afternoons meant wiffle ball games, badminton, red rover, or hide-and-seek. "We used to erect tents with sheets draped over the clothesline and sit on the ground in our own private hideout and eat bologna sandwiches."

"Wonder Bread, I bet," Nancy said.

"With Miracle Whip," Sylvia laughed. "And potato chips and cherry Kool-Aid." She told them how in winter, with the snow piled several feet deep, they'd rush excitedly outside and flop on their backs to make angels, roll giant balls for snowmen, or pull each other on sleds down the snow-covered street.

"How was Steve when he was little?" Nancy asked.

"Normal," Sylvia said. "He was the family funny guy, easy going, and very popular in grade school and high school."

Nancy shook her head in disbelief. "It's so sad."

"Pretty scary," Lisa said. She had two young children. "Just when everything seems normal, you get slammed."

Sylvia suggested that they go back inside to show Lisa her parents' bedroom, where Nancy would sleep. They went through the family room, up three steps to the small kitchen (room for no more than three or four), and the doorway that opened directly into the dining room, which joined the living room at one end. It was a small house, a bungalow, and just a few steps to two bedrooms that were separated by a short hallway, with a bathroom in between. Sylvia couldn't imagine how her parents raised three children with one bathroom so tiny that only one person could fit at a time.

"Is there a cable TV connection?" Lisa asked chuckling. "Mom loves her soaps and *Perry Mason* reruns, plus a hundred other cable stations."

"I need to get it installed," Sylvia said. "Dad was still using rabbit ears."

"That would be great," Nancy said. "I'm deciding how to arrange my bedroom furniture. Do you mind if I take the pictures off the walls?"

"Of course not," Sylvia said. "You need to make this your home now. Hang whatever you want."

Loud barking could be heard from outside. "Oh my God, I did it again." Nancy ran out of the room laughing, "I left Sammy outside!"

Lisa rolled her eyes at her mother. "You'd forget your head if it wasn't attached."

Sylvia told them they'd better leave for the appointment. "What will you do with Sammy?"

"If I put his bed in the bedroom and shut the door, could he stay here while we're gone?" Nancy asked.

Oh brother, Sylvia thought. If the dog started barking, Steve would freak out. The house was small enough that anything could be heard from practically anywhere on the main level. There was no way the dog could stay there without Nancy. "Actually, Steve will need to get to know Sammy while you're with him. It wouldn't be a good idea."

"Where is Steve?" Lisa asked. "I was hoping to meet him today."

Sylvia explained that he was still asleep upstairs.

Nancy said leaving Sammy in the car was no big deal, that she wasn't thinking when she brought him along. They left for Dr. Rita's, who had her practice in her home only five minutes away.

3

Sylvia took the scenic route by the lake, which was a quarter of a mile down the street from their house. "It's not cold enough for ice yet, but by January the whole lake is usually frozen over."

"Can you ice skate on it?" Lisa asked.

"If it stays cold long enough, you can. We used to ice skate every winter. They open the boathouse and have a fire going to warm up. I've heard the garden club provides cocoa and cookies now."

"Would we be allowed to use it?" Nancy asked.

"As long as you're a resident, which you'll be soon enough," Sylvia said. "And you can swim and take row boats out in the summer. Just sign in at the boathouse—Lot 44."

Lisa remarked on the quaintness of the winding, tree-lined streets and the large historic homes surrounding the lake. "I never knew this place existed."

"Lots of people don't," Sylvia said. "And it hasn't changed since I was a kid. Silver Lake still has only about two thousand residents."

"No wonder Steve doesn't want to leave home," Nancy said.

Sylvia pulled into the driveway of Dr. Rita's two-story house. Dr. Rita greeted them warmly at the back door. White-haired, barely five feet tall, and shaped like a fireplug, she sort of waddled as she guided them into her comfortably furnished office. Sylvia introduced Nancy and Lisa, and they took seats on the couch across from Dr. Rita.

"I'm happy that Steve will have someone within the family to live with him." Dr. Rita smiled at Nancy and handed out three business cards. "Steve has become quite special to me. We've been working together for almost nine years. Please call me any time if you have questions or concerns." She looked at Sylvia. "Your parents were the exception to most I've known who've had to cope with the sudden onset of schizophrenia in late adolescence. They gave your brother the consistent, loving care and attention a person with this illness so desperately needs."

"I appreciate your saying that," Sylvia said. "I used to think they catered to him too much."

"Many think 'tough love' is the way to go and push them out the door—the exact opposite of what should be done. Your parents never did that or listened to anyone who might suggest they should."

Sylvia cleared her throat. "How do you think he's dealing with them both gone?"

"That's a good question. It's a little soon to tell, but people who suffer from this illness are emotionally flatter and unable to empathize the way many of us do. They often don't experience grief at the same level we would, but I'm sure he'll miss them greatly in the coming weeks and months as the reality sinks in. He adjusted rather well to the loss of your mother because he still had your father at home with him. In a way, he became a comfort to his father."

Sylvia still worried that Steve had gone through too much too soon—both parents dying essentially in front of him within eighteen months. She wanted Dr. Rita's assurance that Nancy would be the right influence for him, but she didn't know how to address that here. "How do you think he'll deal with Nancy moving into their bedroom?"

"Do you want me to move into the other room instead?" Nancy asked.

"Oh no. He understands where you'll be," Sylvia said.

"Sylvia's right. Steve is capable of adjusting to the change," Rita said. "He might seem a little anxious at first or reclusive, mostly because he'll worry about saying or doing something inappropriate."

"What do you mean, 'inappropriate'?" Lisa asked.

Rita laughed. "Steve's sort of a gentleman—prim and proper, if you will—so nothing of a vulgar nature, I assure you. He can be ill at ease when speaking and may use words that are too blunt then he senses he said the wrong thing and apologizes."

Sylvia turned to Nancy, "For instance, he told me I looked like I'd gained weight then quickly said, 'That was the wrong thing to say, wasn't it?'"

"He'll be fine," Rita said reassuringly. "The change will probably mean he'll want to sleep more, but it has nothing to do with you personally, Nancy. Overstimulation wears him out also. His father wasn't much of a talker, and they led a fairly quiet life, so it's important that the noise level, like phone chatter and frequency of visitors, is kept to a minimum."

Lisa looked at her mom. "Mom's a talker. So what happens if he's over-stimulated? Does he ever get violent?"

Nancy sat up straighter. "I'll be at work five days a week, so he won't have to worry about me!"

"Steve hasn't had a history of violence, but those with severe paranoia who aren't on medication can be so delusional they might become violent," Rita said. "Their sense of reality is distorted, and they may see others as a threat."

"How can I be sure he's taking his medication?" Nancy asked.

Sylvia explained the pill tray (flaps up) and the importance of checking that it's filled, as well as reminding him twice a day to take his pills. She said that Steve keeps track of what he needs with the pharmacy and takes pride in monitoring this himself. Sylvia didn't mention how recently he'd started taking on this responsibility—just within the past year after their mom died.

Rita asked Nancy if she had a consistent work schedule so Steve would know what to expect with her comings and goings. Unfortunately, her schedule changed weekly, but she said she'd do her best to request more routine daytime hours and would write it down on a calendar so he'd know ahead of time. Sylvia brought up his poor eating habits since their mother had died. Their dad didn't cook anything but pancakes, and he brought leftovers home for Steve from restaurants. She asked that Nancy prepare balanced dinners and make sure there was food in the house. Lisa joked that her mom's specialty was Hamburger Helper.

Nancy put her hands on her hips. "I make a pretty mean pot roast, young lady."

"But what will you do with Sammy when you're at work?" Sylvia turned to Dr. Rita, "Sammy is Nancy's Pekinese."

"How wonderful. He'll have a dog to keep him company."

Sylvia would have to trust Dr. Rita on this one.

"I fill his food and water bowls and take him outside to go before I leave for work. He's used to it, so he'll do fine." Nancy's tone was typical of Midwestern good cheer and eagerness to please. "And Sammy loves people."

Rita suggested a follow-up appointment for Steve and Nancy after Nancy got settled. When the session ended, Sylvia had the feeling there was a lot more to discuss but figured there'd never be enough time for her to feel completely at ease before flying home. She could always call Dr. Rita to ask her impressions. At the moment, she just hoped Steve was up and had taken his meds. They decided to stop for fast food and eat at home since Sammy was with them. When she pulled into the driveway and hit the garage door opener, she saw that his car was gone. "I guess we missed Steve."

4

They pulled into the garage and got out of the car. Sammy bolted toward the driveway with Nancy running after him. "You crazy dog. If you don't behave, I just might let you keep going!" He barked and ran in circles like he wanted to play, and Nancy went along, teasing him, darting in different directions, giggling like a school girl. Her fun nature and silly antics made Sylvia think of her own mom: playful, a little ditzy even, but she was good-natured and had common sense when she wasn't feeling overwhelmed. Sylvia didn't have much to go on yet, but Nancy's immediate regard for what Steve thought about her moving in was a positive sign that her heart was in the right place. Maybe Steve would feel right at home with her.

"This could go on for a while," Lisa said. "That dog has her wrapped."

Nancy called out, "He just needs to run off a little steam. We'll be right there."

Sylvia had the lunch bags from Wendy's in her hand. "No problem. We'll go in so the lunch doesn't get cold." She went straight to Steve's pill tray in the dining room and saw the flaps were up—he'd taken his morning dose. The tray and pill containers took up one end of the dining room table so they settled in at the opposite end. Sylvia went to get plates from the kitchen.

"We don't need plates, do we?" Lisa asked. "Mom usually uses paper ones anyhow."

"Uh, sure, I guess so. If you want paper plates, I think we have them."

"Naw, don't go to any trouble on our account. We'll just eat out of the wrappers." Lisa picked at her fries, then gestured toward a sorority photograph of Sylvia that hung framed on the wall at the end of the dining room—bare shouldered, the same broad smile, bangs sweeping across her forehead, and classic, straight auburn hair that hung chin length, tucked behind her ears.

"Eons ago, in college." Sylvia made a mental note to ask Steve what pictures he might want on the walls—any of him were noticeably absent. When their brother Scott had become an international model ten years ago, their mother hung him all over the house. She cut pictures out of magazines and taped them on curtains, doors, and mirrors, and if she was able to get a glossy, she had it blown up and framed. Scott had told her he was embarrassed. No matter how many times each of them tried to tell their mom, she scoffed at the idea that this might make Steve feel even more invisible and worse about his life. After she died, Sylvia, Scott and their dad took them all down.

"You don't look that different except your hair has blond highlights now," Lisa said.

Sylvia said she appreciated the compliment and thought how her life had turned out nothing like she would've imagined back then: love affair, divorce, financial ruin, single parent for twelve years. Her twenty-two-year-old son was a drug addict. She didn't even know where he was right now. But of course, Lisa knew none of this. "I'll probably be hiding the gray until the day I die."

"Weren't you a queen or something?"

Sylvia grabbed a couple of placemats and handed one to Lisa. "Homecoming, in high school."

"And Uncle Adam had a crush on you, but you didn't know he did?"

"That's what he says. I'm a year older, so I didn't pay much attention—only into upper classmen, you know." Sylvia and Adam became reacquainted after attending a multi-class high school reunion, her twenty-fourth. They fell in love and after a three-year, long distance relationship, they decided to marry. But Sylvia had to relocate, leaving her precious Oregon to move to Los Angeles where Adam lived. It was a difficult decision since her son, Trevor, was still in high school and her daughter, Alice, was in college at Oregon State. Then tragedy struck. Several weeks before the wedding, Sylvia's ex-husband, Tom, her kids' dad, was killed in an automobile accident. The excruciating turmoil of her children's pain (and her own) threw doubt on their plans to move forward with the marriage. Sometimes Sylvia felt like she was paying the price for following her heart instead of her head, a lesson she thought she'd learned from her torrid love affair almost twenty years ago. Except Adam was truly a kind-hearted, loving, generous man.

Sammy came running into the dining room. Steve brought up the rear.

"Look who I found!" Nancy announced, extending her arm toward Steve.

"I wasn't lost," Steve said. He bent down to pet the dog, "Here, Sammy." Sammy's bug-eyes fixed on him, tongue hanging to the side of his mouth, all out of breath. "Good dog. Good Sammy," he said quietly, stroking his back. Sammy slipped out from under Steve's hand and reached his paws up on Lisa's leg, begging. Steve abruptly stood up like he forgot something. "I'm sorry," he reached his hand out, struggling to remember her name. "You must be Nancy's daughter."

Lisa quickly wiped her hands on a paper napkin and shook his. "Yes, I'm Lisa. Nice to meet you, Steve. You sure have a nice home here."

"Thanks, I think so," he said. "Been here all my life and hope to keep it that way. That is, if my sister lets me." He shot a half smile at Sylvia. "Nancy and I can probably work it out."

"We sure will," Nancy said. "This is your home and I'll take care of whatever needs to be done here. I'll even cook for you!"

"Sounds like a good deal to me," Steve said.

"You might change your mind after you've tasted her cooking." Lisa's wisecrack meant no harm. There was no way she'd know that one of Steve's biggest worries was feeling like he had to eat someone else's cooking when he didn't like it, that it might make him sick. Always a picky eater, he avoided eating at friends' houses when he was little, and he ate only Rice Krispies on family trips.

Nancy and Lisa went back and forth awhile, poking fun, razzing each other. Steve shifted his weight uncomfortably several times, from one foot to the other, looking at Nancy then Lisa as he tried to follow their banter. His shoulders slumped visibly. The exchange was becoming tiresome for Sylvia, too, and she wondered if they really understood the therapist's recommendation to keep the chatter to a minimum.

"You don't have to cook for me," he said quickly. "Dad never did."

"I'm kidding. Mom can cook anything out of a box," Lisa laughed at her own joke.

Steve looked puzzled. "Out of a box?"

"Potatoes au gratin, macaroni and cheese, Hamburger Helper—"

"Hamburger Helper? I love the, what's it called . . . " He looked down at the floor for several seconds. "Stroganoff. That's it."

Sylvia could see that he was trying hard to keep up and instinctively started to put her hand on his arm but pulled back, remembering he was usually uncomfortable with touch. She turned to face him instead. "How about I give Nancy a list of your favorite meals, like spaghetti with meat sauce, chili, Shepherd's pie, and some of Mom's recipes?"

With a sigh and a nod, Steve's relief was apparent. "That'd be great, Sylvia." He started to head toward the stairs. "I'll leave you guys, so you can eat."

"I brought you a burger and fries, too," Sylvia said.

Steve brightened, "In that case, don't mind if I do." He stood by his sister while she dug in the bag for his meal.

"Why don't you pull up a chair, roommate?" Nancy offered.

"I think I'll just go eat upstairs." Conversation during a meal was often difficult for Steve. He might worry that his mouth was full when asked a question then chew too fast so he could say something to be polite. Sometimes he choked trying to get the words out before he'd finished his mouthful. Besides, he'd probably never be able to follow the conversation. Women seemed to talk at the same time. Steve looked sheepish, "But I'll come back down when I'm finished." He escaped to his room.

Lisa commented on Steve's kind manner and how glad she was to know that her mom could live here and that Dr. Rita was so helpful and close by. "I know I haven't been around him much, but Steve acts pretty normal to me. And he seemed fine with Sammy. What really happens if he doesn't take his medication?"

Sylvia thought it best not to mention his occasional angry outbursts when he leaned into your face with fearful, darting eyes as he turned his head to the right and left as if searching for someone who might sneak up behind him. When he raised his voice, refusing to do whatever was asked of him—like dump his ashtrays teaming with cigarette butts, or make his bed, or pick up his clothes piled three-feet high on the floor. Upstairs, he might rant at no one in particular or at the committee in his head. If his fears got the better of him, he might curl up in a ball in bed, hiding under the covers, saying, "They're after me." She decided to tell them the truth, just not all of it.

"If he misses his meds, he becomes more reclusive and won't talk to anybody. Or he'll talk about God and the Bible and say God talks to him. He'll hear voices more often and more strongly. He says he doesn't hear them at all anymore, since he's afraid his psychiatrist will put him in a psych ward if he tells the truth, but the meds don't get rid of the voices completely, they just subside." She explained that he still has running conversations by himself—as if he's talking on the phone. "Without the meds, he can appear lost or in a daze. Because there's so much going on in his head, he can barely decipher what you might be saying to him, especially if he's in a group. This is probably why he keeps to himself so much." Dr. Rita had told Sylvia that he doesn't trust that he'll understand what's being said or, even worse, that he can speak clearly enough to make himself understood.

"How did this happen to him?" Nancy asked.

"We don't know—doctors don't know what causes it. Like I said, he seemed fine all through childhood, but he did stutter until he was four or five," Sylvia chuckled. "I was the only one who could understand him. Also his hair fell out in patches when he was in second grade. The doctor said it was nerves, so my parents switched teachers and it went away. Other than that, he was always well liked, a good athlete, and, by high school, a huge track star. He was even voted prom king." Sylvia told them how scholarship offers poured in at first, but his test scores were low and his grades average. "When all but one of the offers went away, it crushed him. Steve started saying how dumb he was. He took the one remaining offer from nearby Kent State University, and, after one year, he transferred to Ohio State and Big Ten track. By the time he was twenty, it became obvious that he needed serious professional help."

a reminder of him during better times, to put positive energy around him rather than hopelessness, which was what the whole family felt when he had his first psychotic break.

⎯

In the fall of 1969, Steve had told his Mom, Vivian, and his Dad, Matt, that he didn't want to return to school for the winter quarter. They saw that he'd been struggling and agreed. They took him to a psychiatrist for evaluation but nothing concrete came of it—he just needed a break, they were told. Then the track coach at Ohio State came all the way from Columbus, a two-and-a-half-hour drive, to encourage him to return. The enticements were tempting: a reduced course load, a friend from the track team for a roommate, and assisting a physical education teacher in an elementary school. His parents let him decide, and Steve went back to school. He managed to continue through summer school, even holding down a part-time job delivering Coca-Cola. The truck driver was a religious fanatic, preaching gospel and the sins of any form of non-church related entertainment. When Steve came home, he was unrecognizable. He ran around the house, up and down the stairs, ranting "He won't save me." When his mom asked who, he kept running, repeating, "Jesus, Jesus won't save me."

Steve spent thirty days in a psychiatric ward in a hospital in Cleveland, but there was no clear diagnosis, just the loosely held term, "nervous breakdown," commonly acknowledged as a short-lived condition, a one-time occurrence. The psychiatrist had prescribed an antidepressant and simply said that, due to his anxiety, "Steve hasn't learned how to live." He was sent home to gradually resume a normal life. Steve said all he remembered about the hospital was that his dad had tricked him into going and he never understood why. The slipping mind often has no tools to recall the events or odd behaviors that others witness, and Steve had been shocked to learn that a simple doctor visit was never the intention. To him it was a setup—his father had just left him there.

Within several months of his return home, Steve had taken a messenger job at a local bank. He drove a company vehicle to deliver bank documents to other branches. After three months, he quit, telling his parents, "I hate living in a car." He said he should go back to college to get a degree, but he didn't know what he wanted to be. A physical education teacher? A coach? He figured he wasn't smart enough to be anything else, and apparently, to him, those options didn't seem respectable enough. They weren't "professions." Still, Steve wanted to give it the ol' college try. His parents went along with him, and he enrolled in two courses at the local university.

Steve would sit for hours at his desk upstairs, staring at the pages of his college textbooks, the hundreds of words, but they became jumbled on the page and didn't make sense. He read and reread the same paragraphs over and over. Soon, the words started moving then leaping off the page, hitting him in the face. He had to keep the books closed to protect himself. Sometimes he could hear the muffled voices of the words telling him to open the book and let them out. He put a pillow over his head but still heard them. He struggled to keep up with what they were saying, to formulate answers to their questions, but they were relentless and never gave him enough time to respond. He couldn't sleep for the voices, so he went to the basement and played his record albums over and over—Jim Morrison, The Doors, Little Richard, or James Taylor—to try to drown them out. He started singing along and discovered that if he sang loudly enough, he could keep them at bay. When his parents couldn't take the nightlong music marathons anymore and told him he had to stop, Steve became angry, insisting, "God made me a rock star. I have to do what He says!"

The "nervous breakdown" had lasted over a year, and Steve was much worse. Matt had read about a mega-vitamin theory that was attracting

done to evaluate the mega-vitamin doses. They returned home with a bag full of vitamins, and Steve willingly took some twenty vitamins a day for several weeks. He became extremely gaunt, weak, and, finally, couldn't keep food down. He dry-heaved to the point where he needed to be hospitalized.

Schizophrenia was the ultimate diagnosis, and the search for institutions began. The Meninger Clinic in Kansas, one of the most renowned, treated schizophrenia through talk therapy without medication, an approach later considered ineffective. Steve's parents had determined that it was too far away. Harding Institute in Columbus, Ohio, was considered one of the top three in the nation, and was, of course, much closer to home. By this time, Steve had lapsed into catatonia. He stared, never spoke, and moved only with guidance and an encouraging word. After two and a half years at Harding, his improvement was remarkable—a major rebound. Although fragile, it seemed that Steve was back. The medical staff had recommended he stay longer, but the insurance had run out. At three thousand dollars a month, Steve's parents couldn't afford to keep him there.

He moved into an apartment in Columbus with a roommate from Harding, with supposed out-patient treatment through the institution. The roommate drank alcohol, became unruly, and then disappeared. Unable to reach Steve on the phone, his parents became concerned.

They drove to the apartment only to find Steve curled up in bed, his pill vials full, and his dwelling a bug-infested rat's nest. They cleaned for several days, moved out his furniture and his clothing, paid the remaining month's rent, lost the security deposit, and took Steve home once again. There he gained weight, grew a beard, chain-smoked, and walked for hours through the safe haven of their quiet lake community, head down, mumbling to himself. The handsome, engaging, lean, athletic wonder had become the local madman, the center of hushed gossip. *What could've happened to him? He seemed normal growing up. Probably drugs. His parents must've pressured him. Maybe he's dangerous and should be locked up. Best to stay out of his way.*

Matt and Vivian had kept the diagnosis to themselves. They were initially ashamed and guilt ridden, certain they had caused it, until the psychiatrists assured them otherwise. But how could anyone else, even their friends, understand? Schizophrenia—derived from the Greek *schizein*, to split, and *phren*, mind—had become misleadingly popularized as "split personality," usually imagined as a version of a horrifying Jekyll and Hyde. Though Steve's parents learned there is no category or phenomenon in psychiatry called split personality, try telling that to your next-door neighbor. If there is any "splitting," it's within one single personality where the individual's thoughts, feelings, and emotions are seriously and confusingly disconnected from each other in a random chaos. Schizophrenic individuals, far from having split or multiple personalities, actually have a great struggle maintaining the coherence and integrity of even a single self. This knowledge, however, would not necessarily be reassuring to the neighborhood, which had surely witnessed his ranting and raving in the driveway or a police car taking him away. And Steve always looked angry—his appearance alone would make anyone wary.

Fifteen years, in and out of various institutions, were a muddled array of potential cures through shock treatments, strict dietary regimens (no sugar or carbohydrates, which he craved, and lots of vegetables, which he never liked), medication changes, and more attempts at apartment living or halfway houses (short-term stays since he'd eventually just walk home). His parents had become involved in the county chapter of AMI, Alliance for the Mentally Ill, attending the weekly support group, and discovered that some parents were coping with a combination of mental illness and drug addiction or alcoholism. This "dual diagnosis" was rather common—a problematic, "chicken or egg"

Still, Matt and Vivian did make new friends within the support group, friends who could commiserate. Plus they had found out about available county resources like Community Support Services (CSS), paid for by the government. As mentally disabled, Steve qualified for Medicaid and Social Security Income. Part of the "tough love" message had begun to take hold. Maybe some of the burden would be lifted or at least shifted? Maybe they could make him get involved in CSS as a condition to live at home, but only through gentle prodding, never as a harsh ultimatum. They knew their son. Through the vocational department at CSS, he could work part-time with a supervised team and earn minimum wage. He'd be assigned a case manager to meet with on a regular basis, go out for iced tea or lunch, someone who'd organize a work program, someone to be his advocate. Things were looking up.

By the mid-eighties, Steve had a case manager he seemed to like, worked three evenings a week as a janitor with a group of his "peers" (the mentally ill and/or addicts in recovery), which he hated. But to please his parents, he went. And he was taking his meds more regularly. Maybe Steve had turned the corner.

Heavy footsteps came from the stairs behind. Steve opened the door and entered the dining room. Sammy approached him and Steve almost stepped on him. "Geez, I didn't see him," he laughed nervously. "At least he didn't bark at me. Does he bark a lot?"

"Only at strangers who come to the door," Nancy said.

"So will he bark at me? Aren't I a stranger?"

"Not anymore. He knows you belong here, so you're okay."

Steve squatted on his toes, knees wide, and petted Sammy. "I think he likes me."

"He does! He can sense who to trust right away," Nancy said.

"Let's show Nancy and Lisa around the house," Sylvia said to Steve. "I want to go over a few things that Nancy will need to know."

"You don't need me for that, do you? I want to go to Friendly's." Steve went several times a day, for two hours at a time, to his favorite restaurant chain known for its ice cream, where he drank iced tea, smoked cigarettes, and chatted with the waitresses who knew him by name. His Cheers bar without the alcohol.

"Just stay for a few minutes," Sylvia said.

"For what?" he asked.

"I wanted to show Nancy your pill tray and . . . "

"I do my own meds." Steve peered at his senior photo in Nancy's hand. "What are you doing with that?"

"I wanted to see if you were as good lookin' as Adam said you were." She handed the photo back to Sylvia. "He was right. And you still are!"

Steve rolled his eyes then looked at his protruding belly. "No, I'm not. I'm fat now. Can we talk about something else?"

"About your meds—I just want Nancy to remind you to take them and to fill your tray."

"I know I have to take them."

"In case you forget though, or fall asleep. It's important not to miss," Sylvia said.

"I hardly ever miss," he said.

"How about if I leave you a note when I go to work?" Nancy asked.

"I like notes," Steve said. "I write myself lots of notes so I won't forget things or when I take a phone message because Dr. Rita told me it would help me remember."

"Me too," she said. "It's the only way I can remember anything. Maybe we can write a grocery list, too, so I know what to get."

"As long as you do the shopping. I hate shopping."

more elated by the minute, just thinking about not having rent to pay, or utilities, or phone. Since she was buying food for Steve and cooking, maybe she wouldn't have to pay for groceries either. She held up a french fry for Sammy, which he snapped right up.

"Let's show her the basement," Sylvia said. They all went downstairs. Notepad in hand, Sylvia began in the laundry room, explaining the broken water level in the washing machine and how it would overflow if you didn't know what to do.

"Dad never let me do my laundry," Steve said. "I tried once and water was all over the floor."

"I have a new washer that my old boyfriend bought me," Nancy said. "When I move in, Lisa's husband can install it and get rid of this one," she turned to Steve, "and I'll teach you how to use it so you can do your laundry."

Oh brother, Steve thought. *I don't want to learn how. What if I break her machine?* "I don't know. I'm kinda slow. It might take me too long to learn. Don't you have to separate colors and stuff?"

"We'll take as long as you need," Nancy reassured him. "Don't you worry about it."

Sylvia showed them the rest of the basement, the fuse box, furnace, and water heater. They decided that Nancy could move all of her belongings in the main area, a large, linoleum-tiled rec room. They went back upstairs, and Sylvia explained a few more things like the thermostat and switching it to cool for the air conditioner in summer. She was glad it was winter and didn't have to think about lawn care, weeds, and trimming the bushes. They sat in the living room, and she showed Nancy a list of who to call for household repairs.

"My husband's a pretty good handyman, if anything needs fixin'," Lisa offered.

"Speaking of need," Nancy interrupted. "I was wondering if you've thought about selling your dad's car, because I don't have one."

Lisa looked at her Mom, "I told you I'd let you have your old one back."

"Oh no. I'm no Indian giver," Nancy said.

"I haven't had a chance to think about it yet, but I don't see why not," Sylvia said. "What do you think, Steve?"

He hated to think of someone else driving his dad's car. His burgundy Chrysler with matching leather interior. Dad loved that car, got it for a song, he said, from the bank like he always did. Never bought a brand new car—said it was a waste of money.

"Steve?"

He shrugged. "Do what you have to, Sylvia."

"It seems like a waste to have a car just sitting in the garage, don't you think?" Sylvia asked.

"Yeah, it would be a waste I guess."

"Why don't you give me a price," Nancy said. "I can't pay for it all at once, but if you'd be willing to take a monthly payment, I think I could swing it."

—

More and more, the situation was becoming a win-win. It was apparent that Nancy really wanted this to work and so did Steve. They discussed particulars, like setting up a joint checking account for Steve and Nancy, to pay for groceries and necessary repairs. With Nancy's help, maybe Steve would learn how to write a check again. He had a monthly Social Security benefit deposited directly into his savings for personal expenses: cigarettes, gas, fast food, and, of course, the iced tea that he drank by the quart at his local spots. Since he didn't know how to use an ATM card, he got cash the old-fashioned way. He went inside the bank branch, where the tellers knew him, and filled out a

her brother was showing, as if he was slowly realizing that with both parents gone, without them to rely on and take care of him, he'd have to rely on himself more than ever before. Nancy was there to walk him through the transition, to be his safety net, but ultimately he had to gain some independence and self-reliance, and little by little, maybe learn how to live as a man, perhaps for the first time in his life. Was she being too optimistic? Or in denial that he could continue to get better, well enough to be on his own someday?

She was beginning to understand how her mother had become hopeful after a few "good" days, thinking he was over the hump, hoping the worst of his illness was behind him. Up and down, up and down. She remembered her mother's tearful phone calls: Steve won't take his meds; Steve hasn't talked to us for days; Steve won't come downstairs; Steve won't take a shower or change his clothes or smoke outside. Wasn't Sylvia doing the same with her own son? After a few days, then weeks, and finally a few months of sobriety, she started thinking his drug use was behind him, that he wasn't like other addicts. Then he'd relapse and go missing again, and she'd fall into despair. Her son's ups and downs had swallowed her whole. Maybe her brother's lifelong illness would help her to accept her son's, and she could start living again? She was learning how to hope but not to expect. There was always hope, and she'd never stop hoping for a better life for both of them.

5

Nancy moved in a week later, as scheduled. She transformed their parent's bedroom on the first floor from the sixties-style Mediterranean décor with burnished brass mirrors and family photos in antiqued wooden frames, to a version of early American, with a faux brass bed, cross-stitch printed quilt, and plastic flower swags along the top of window sheers shirred on wooden rods. Ceramic animal knickknacks and perfume bottles covered every square inch of surface space. Where stacks of books used to sit on the bedside stand, there was now a video game console. Sammy's dog bed was tucked under Nancy's, and his food and water dishes sat on a plastic placemat next to the closet. The room was jam-packed. The rest of her furniture (along with Steve's parents' bedroom set) and a dozen or so Hefty trash bags stuffed with her other belongings filled the rec room portion of the basement, making it necessary to weave around or step over to get to the fuse box on the far wall.

Nancy was gone a lot. Her commute to work was forty minutes, one way. If her shift started at noon, she wasn't home until almost nine, but a Crock Pot supper would be simmering all day, ready for Steve by dinner time. Other days, she might start at eight and be back by five. She left daily reminder notes for Steve, because she didn't know her schedule enough in advance to put it on the large desk calendar Sylvia had set on the kitchen table. Even so, Steve began calling her at work several times a day to make sure nothing had changed, or she might call him before leaving, asking if he wanted something from the store, or to say she'd be late because she needed to babysit for her grandchildren, which she often did on her days off.

Steve wasn't used to so much distraction. Or to being left alone for so many hours at a time. And now he was in charge of letting Sammy out several times a day. Already the carpet was soiled throughout the house from his numerous accidents, which Steve dutifully reported to his sister, "I gagged and almost vomited when he did number two! I

one leg in an auto accident when he got drunk and hit a tree, although Nancy never believed that her son was drunk. "It was two in the morning," she'd say. "He just fell asleep at the wheel." He wore a prosthetic from the knee down, but he needed crutches to walk. He couldn't find a job, so he watched his two toddlers while his wife worked as a waitress and bartender.

Steve changed his mind every other day about going, *I don't know them. What will we talk about? I can't stand little kids. They can't sit still. They cry at Friendly's and make me nervous. If I go, I probably should get presents for them. I'm not going.* He'd think about a nice big dinner and decide to go then he'd wonder if he'd like their food and decide to stay home, play it safe.

"You worry too much, big guy," Nancy said. "You don't need to bring presents, and you can see how you feel on Christmas day and decide then."

Nancy tried to help Steve lighten up, but there were just so many things for him to sort through. He'd have to ride with her and the son with the missing leg and his two little kids, since he might get lost if he tried to follow them in his car—it was all the way to Canton, a half an hour away. But if he rode with them, he'd be trapped. He couldn't leave until they did, which could be all day and evening. "Will they let me smoke in the house?"

"No, but you can smoke in the garage or outside. With me." Then she told him the dinner menu: roast turkey, ham, mashed potatoes and gravy, corn, green beans, Pillsbury crescent rolls, and enough for seconds and thirds.

"Sounds so good," he said. "Can Sammy come?"

"He can ride in your lap in the car if you want," she said.

Two days before Christmas Steve made his decision to go, and he didn't waffle. He even laid out his dark brown cords, light green oxford shirt, and red cable knit sweater. After all, it was Christmas. Nancy's family was warm and engaging, and he found the usual male conversational bond with her sons: sports. Steve could quote names, dates, and statistics as far back as the sixties, and they seemed to really want to know about his running days as the local track star. The kids would've driven him crazy (except he already was), so Steve escaped outside throughout the day. Nancy couldn't find him at one point and asked if anyone knew where he'd gone. Finally Lisa spotted him lying down in the snow by the garage, leaning on one elbow, smoking and quietly mumbling to himself. Odd as it was, no one seemed concerned. They just left him alone until he was ready to rejoin them.

After the holiday, Steve slept for almost two days straight, barely up long enough to eat or smoke. Sammy had more accidents, but Steve was used to them now. He was too tired to clean up after him though. *Nancy'll do it when she gets home,* he told himself. *It's her dog anyway.*

As winter wore on, the skies were gray for days on end and the temperatures dropped into the teens much of the time. Freezing rain covered the roads off and on, or enough snow fell to make it difficult to get out of the driveway. Nancy found someone to plow it for thirty dollars. Steve showered less, chain smoked, and wore the same clothes a week at a time. His plaid flannel shirt was torn at the elbows, and his hair was growing over his ears. Nancy wanted to help him but didn't know how. She figured he was lonely and depressed and that his parent's deaths were finally catching up with him, especially if he thought he was responsible somehow. After all, he was the one who first found his mother collapsed on the kitchen floor and called 911, then made the same call for his father when he struggled for breath and, unable to stand, crawled on his hands and knees to get into bed. Each died in the ambulance on their way to the hospital.

When Sylvia called weekly to check on them, Nancy painted a rosy picture. She didn't want to alarm Sylvia or lead her to think the living

he didn't like to talk while he ate, and she remembered that he'd said he preferred to eat alone. He'd probably feel more comfortable without her sitting there. But the final straw was his runny nose dripping onto his food—she was gagging and had to leave the room. Besides, she had all her TV shows to catch up on or video games to play, something to pass the dreariness of her days. Soon Steve took his dinner upstairs to his room, so they never ate together.

Steve was spending more and more time in his room, which made her worry that she wasn't capable to care for him. Until one day she had an idea for him. "Maybe you'd like to move into the downstairs bedroom. Sammy might not be so lonely and could find you better."

"I might like that, and since Sammy can't climb the stairs," Steve said. Sammy was too small to manage the steep steps. "But what about my clothes?"

"We can move them down," she said. "We could start right now."

"Maybe later," Steve said. "It's so much work. I'm too tired."

"Just leave it to me," Nancy offered. He agreed, and she went ahead without him. If he didn't like it, he could always go back upstairs, but she had to try something. She made up the bed, transferred some shirts and pants to the downstairs closet, put his underwear and socks in the small dresser, brought his toothbrush, comb, razor, and shaving cream down to the bathroom between their bedrooms. That night he slept in his new room, never to return upstairs again. Every night she called out, "Good night. Don't let the bedbugs bite!" And he began saying it back to her.

Sometimes Nancy talked Steve into watching a movie with her on video—she had quite a collection of VHS cassettes: all of Doris Day and Rock Hudson, most of Katherine Hepburn and Spencer Tracy, Abbott and Costello, Disney movies like *The Lady and the Tramp*, *Snow White*, and *Bambi*, and more current ones with Meg Ryan, Tom Hanks, or Sandra Bullock. Even though he usually didn't sit through an entire movie, Steve seemed to feel more and more at ease sitting on her bed, eating popcorn, drinking Coke, and smoking cigarettes with Sammy sandwiched between them. Relieved, Nancy figured they might make it through the winter after all, even with a few laughs.

At the end of February a letter came to Steve from Dr. Rita. She had taken ill and recommended someone else for Steve to see in the meantime. He didn't tell Nancy or his sister, instead tucking the letter into his metal strong box on the upper shelf in his closet, where he kept important papers or mementos: birth certificate, social security card, tassel from his cap at high school graduation, baptism certificate, several black and white photos of himself laughing as a baby (to prove to himself he was happy as a child), and grades from his three years in college (to prove that he did fairly well). Steve figured Dr. Rita would be well soon enough, and he'd wait for her to recover. He didn't see her that often anyway, maybe once a month. Dad didn't see any need to pay her for more than that. *Why should I even have to go anymore?* Steve thought. *I take my meds.* But his cover was blown one day when Sylvia called.

"I haven't talked to you in so long," she said. "I keep missing you—you're always 'at the office!'" Nancy was the one who coined the phrase for his hours away at his local haunts. Going to the office? Have a good day at the office! Yep, he's at the office again.

"But I don't really work—I just sit there and drink iced tea," Steve said.

"That's what a lot of people do in offices, except they sit all day and drink coffee," Sylvia said.

He chuckled, "You'd know. You work in an office. Is that what you do all day? I've never worked in an office, and I hope I never do."

"If I'm not busy, I can waste a lot of time yakking on the phone," she said.

"Dad said that about Mom, always yakkin'. I don't like talking on the

ventured.

"She's so happy all the time. And she cooks for me. I like her spaghetti, but she ruins steak. I don't tell her that though."

"That's good you're eating regular dinners."

"Except I'm getting fat. Dr. Keller told me to walk to lose weight, but I hate to walk." Steve's weight hadn't changed in twenty years. He hovered around 220 pounds but carried it well—he looked heavy, not fat, but forever compared himself to his track era thinness.

"And not eat burgers and fries?" Sylvia asked.

"I hardly ever go to McDonald's anymore," which meant he hadn't gone for a day or two. His sense of recent time was negligible.

"Speaking of doctors, how's Dr. Rita?"

A long pause. "She's okay," he said quietly.

"When did you see her last?" Sylvia realized he probably wouldn't know as soon as she asked it. "I haven't seen any cancelled checks for her."

"Oh. Well . . . she's been on vacation." Steve sneezed, then coughed hard.

Sylvia waited.

"I guess I have to tell you the truth. She's sick."

"Maybe I should call her," Sylvia said.

"No, you don't have to. I'm sure she'll be better soon. I'm fine. I don't need to see her."

"It's pretty important, Steve."

"I never saw her that much when Dad was alive," he said.

"I'll call her and see how she is anyway," she said.

"She sent me a letter."

"What did it say?"

Steve finally told her the whole truth. Sylvia said he needed to call the other therapist Dr. Rita had recommended, but he refused, so she said she'd call for him. He dug his heels in and wouldn't give her the name or phone number. Once he made up his mind, there was no way to change it. Sylvia didn't know what to do. Working directly with Steve was still new to her. When her parents were alive, she usually heard about him through them. When she did talk to him on the phone, they only had light conversations during which he rushed to get off, handing the phone over to their mom or dad. *Should I get Nancy involved?* Sylvia wondered. Steve said Nancy didn't know about the letter, but wouldn't she notice he wasn't seeing his therapist? If so, why didn't Nancy tell Sylvia?

Her son's troubles were the most Sylvia could handle at the moment. She'd finally heard from him when he'd wrecked his car. Thank God he wasn't hurt. Slowly, one step at a time, she was attempting to make him responsible for his actions, to stop picking up the pieces, stop being the mommy who babied him, enabled him, and overprotected him. It was the only way to save him, she was told, "Stop being a mommy or he'll die." So she put his car insurance in his name while the car was being repaired. She didn't think he should have a car at all, but he'd had it since high school, and it was paid for. And he was persistent. "How will I work?" he'd asked. He was delivering take-out food from restaurants all over LA. "And where will I sleep?" On the advice of drug counselors, Sylvia had kicked him out a year ago because he was using. It seemed heartless to take the car from him now. At least she and her husband wouldn't have to bear financial responsibility the next time he had an accident. Besides, he told her he was considering going back to rehab. This time she didn't offer to find a treatment center, to set up a detox, or to take him. She kept her mouth shut and waited, which was progress, but it was all so hard.

When Sylvia told Nancy about Dr. Rita's letter, she sounded shocked (with an undertone of guilt) and apologized for not paying enough attention to notice he hadn't met with her. She confirmed that he was still taking his meds regularly, seemed more withdrawn but overall okay. Sylvia asked her to keep an eye out for the letter, but figured he'd

case manager worked for the county, the psychiatrist didn't consult with psychologists, and the internist had no contact with the mental health community. Sylvia, already overwhelmed, shoved it under the rug. She'd deal with it in June, once she was back in Ohio.

At the end of April, Nancy called Sylvia, "The letter from Dr. Rita was sitting open on the dining room table. It was dated in February! I wonder why he left it out."

"We'll never know the answer to that," Sylvia said.

"I have names and numbers of two psychologists, a man and a woman."

Sylvia took down the information. "I'll call the woman first. If Steve does agree to see someone else, I doubt that he'd consider a man."

"I wonder why," Nancy said. "You'd think he'd be able to relate to a man better."

"We'll never know the answer to that either. All I care about right now is finding out about Dr. Rita."

Sylvia reached the woman, Dr. Nora Ingram, the next day.

"I'm so sorry to be the one to tell you, but Dr. Rita passed away in early March. She's had heart problems for years. I'd be happy to meet your brother whenever he's ready, but he might need some time."

Sylvia had to sit down. What a blow. Another unexpected death, and within a few months of their dad. How would she ever tell Steve?

6

Steve woke up in the middle of the night. He had to go to the bathroom. The bedroom door was ajar and he saw a flickering neon glow on the hallway wall. It was spooky and he was afraid to get up. Low voices and light laughter—was it Nancy's television? She always fell asleep with it on. On his way to the bathroom, he slowly pushed her door open and peeked in her bedroom. She didn't stir. Sammy, curled up on his bed, looked up at him with those bug eyes. They gleamed. He looked like a demon dog. Steve quietly pulled the door shut and went to the bathroom. He couldn't get the dog's eyes out of his mind. He flushed the toilet and went back to his room.

He had fallen asleep in his clothes again, but it didn't matter to him. He turned on the bedside lamp and lit a cigarette. Leaning on his elbow, he puffed away, one after another. *Mom and Dad never had the TV on all night. Nancy watches it all the time. It's so annoying. Maybe I should shut it off. Better not. It's her room now.*

Steve got up and trundled to the kitchen. He opened the refrigerator and grabbed the plastic gallon jug of milk. He took a few swigs, then realized he hadn't taken his meds. He went to the dining room table where he kept his pill tray. *What day is it?* He stood there thinking for a few minutes then decided Wednesday was last night, that he'd missed the dose, and poured the handful of pills into his hand. He went back to the fridge and took another swig of milk to wash them down. He was hungry and fixed a large bowl of Neapolitan ice cream and took it back to his room. Nancy always bought his favorite. Sometimes it was marble fudge or chocolate chip mint, but mostly it was Neapolitan. The digital clock said four p.m. He knew that wasn't right, but didn't know how to reset it for a.m. Friendly's wouldn't be open until six thirty. He finished his ice cream, set the bowl on his nightstand, lit another ciga-

his duty. She didn't have a plastic bag, so she left it and hurried back inside, Sammy trotting along behind. She grabbed a cold can of Coke from the fridge and headed to the bathroom to get ready for work.

On her way to the garage, she decided to leave Steve a note and went back to the dining room table, where she always left her notes for him.

"Hi, Steve, Sorry I missed you! I'll be home early today, around four or five. Remember you have work tonight! Chuck roast is in the Crock-Pot—it'll be ready before you go! PS: Don't forget your morning meds!" She dashed out the door with a second can of Coke, started the car, and turned on her favorite cassette, The Carpenters, which always reminded her of her sister who loved them, too. They used to sing in the city chorus together, mostly show tunes, but she died of lung cancer four years earlier and it had taken Nancy almost that long even to want to sing again. Her sister was her best friend, her pal and confidant, and they had seen each other several times a week. They played bridge every weekend and watched movies. And they smoked like chimneys. Then she got a cold that wouldn't go away. After the diagnosis, she was gone in three months. Nancy quit the chorus even though she loved it. It was just too hard to be there.

She began to sing along: *"I'll say good-bye to love, No one ever cared if I should live or die . . . So I've made my mind up, I must live my life alone . . . "* But Nancy hadn't made her mind up. She would find somebody again. Anything was possible, even at her age, pushing sixty. She needed a man in her life to make her feel alive again. There was the guy in the meat department, but she thought he was probably gay. Just the same, he was fun and they had a lot of laughs together. And the fella in the deli was kind of cute and seemed flirtatious, even if he was pot-bellied and bald. He was nice, she knew that right off. You never know where love might happen. You could meet somebody anywhere: a parking lot, the post office, a gas station. Her best chances were probably right in the grocery store, where she spent eight hours a day, mostly in the prepared food department. Lonely, single men, usually divorced, bought dinner every day to take home and heat up. And she acted like a waitress, making suggestions, recommending the most popular meals, or even those she loved to prepare, just to show she could cook. Since she was rotated in the store to the various departments, she tried to get that position as often as possible. It was a lot better than in the back where she was out of the public eye. Anyway, her antennae were up, and she kept a look out at all times.

—

When Steve got back home he saw Nancy's note. *Work! I hate going there. How can I get out of it?* he wondered. He made two chip-chop ham sandwiches with Miracle Whip on white bread. He dug into the bag of potato chips and started chomping away. Broken bits of chips sprinkled down the front of him, but he didn't notice. He set the open bag on the counter and took the paper plate of sandwiches to his bed. Reclining, he leaned on his elbow and ate. He liked paper plates. It was so much easier than rinsing dishes (he rarely washed them) and leaving them in the dish rack. *Mom never used paper plates. I bet Sylvia won't let me either,* he thought. Sylvia was coming home pretty soon. He couldn't remember if it was in two or three weeks, but he wanted to see her. Then again, maybe not. He still hadn't learned how to do his laundry, and it sat piled high in the basement laundry room. She'd probably be mad. Maybe Nancy would do it for him before Sylvia came.

And Sylvia would want to go with him to his psychiatrist. He'd rather go alone. And Dr. Rita. He wished she were better so he could see her. She'd taught him to write down his thoughts and said maybe she'd make a book out of them. And she thought he could go back to college. Just one course to start. When he was ready.

it did him if he felt worse about himself working as a janitor with a group of drug addicts from the south side of Akron. They bummed rides and cigarettes off of him, and he was hesitant to refuse. Steve was probably an easy target. Most of them were black, which made him feel uncomfortable, like he didn't really belong.

Nancy knocked lightly on Steve's door. In her most light-hearted voice she called to him. "Steve? It's time to go to work. And dinner's ready."

He groaned and rolled over. "I don't feel well. I have a stomachache."

"Maybe you just need to eat. C'mon, give it a try. You didn't go last week, remember?"

"Do I have to?"

"Well, it's probably too late to cancel now."

He finally got up, ate, and left without another word.

To get downtown, Steve had to take the expressway, which made him nervous. Everybody drove too fast. He hugged the slow lane, barely hitting fifty. Everyone seemed to pass him. He finally pulled into the courthouse parking lot and ambled over to the waiting group of guys.

Larry, the supervisor, looked up. "Steve, glad you made it tonight."

"I'm not glad," Steve mumbled.

"What's that?" he asked

"Nothing."

They filed into the building, and Larry designated the duties to them. "You'll work in pairs, like always. Steve, you and Howard will vacuum the judge's chambers tonight then the courtroom."

"The courtroom?" Steve asked. "It's huge. We'll never get it done in two hours!"

"You'll just have to hustle," Larry said.

Steve shook his head, "Three guys couldn't get it done."

Larry stood with his hands on his hips, "Maybe you'd rather clean the bathrooms."

"No way." Steve turned on his heel and followed Howard down the hall to the supply closet where they took out two commercial-sized vacuums.

"At least it's a job," Howard said.

"You like this?" Steve asked.

"Don't even ask myself that, just do the work, keeps me off the streets," he said.

"You do drugs?"

"Used to. Two months clean."

"So you don't now?" Steve asked.

"No, but I'm thinkin' on it every minute."

They entered the chambers and turned on the lights.

"The carpet's not even dirty!" Steve exclaimed. "There's nothing to clean."

Howard howled and slapped his knee. "That don't even matter. Just givin' us something to do." He suggested that he do the chambers, and Steve start in the courtroom.

"Oh, sure. I get the biggest job!" Steve said.

Howard smirked. "I'm comin' in there to help when I'm done here!" He shook his head and started his machine.

Steve went into the courtroom and started at the front. Back and forth, back and forth. He was breaking out in a sweat, beads trailing down his face. He wiped his forehead with his hand, then on his pants. The steady whir of the machine rang in his ears. Larry came in.

"Hey, Steve," he shouted over the noise. "You've got to make even strokes up and down on the carpet." He took the machine from Steve, "Like this."

"I guess so," Steve nodded. It wasn't that far out of his way since they were already downtown. He unlocked his eight-year-old, white Dodge Spirit, and they climbed in. Howard pointed out the lefts and rights as they wound their way through downtown then to the south of Akron. The bad part of town. The "other side of the tracks" where the Negroes lived, except now they were called Blacks or African-Americans. Steve didn't know what to call them.

"Which street?" Steve asked.

"Howard Street," Howard said.

"I know where that is," Steve said. Howard Street was the one street known to whites as the heart of the black neighborhood. Since Steve was a kid, it had a scary, "stay away from there" danger about it. "Howard on Howard?" Steve snickered and turned to him sitting in the passenger seat, "Must be confusing."

"Used to be for some, but my momma said that's cause you'll never forget where you live. Damned if she wasn't right about that!"

"I'm glad mine didn't name me Hastings." Steve mumbled, "Hastings on Hastings."

A few streetlights that looked like they'd been there since the fifties cast a dim light on the cracked sidewalk. The house had a front porch with an old porch swing that reminded Steve of his grandmother's home in another somewhat rundown section of the city.

"Do you want to come in for a beer?" Howard asked.

"Oh no, I don't drink. I should get home anyway," Steve fluttered his hands as he spoke. "Can't drink with my meds."

"I'm on meds too, but I drink beer anyway. Just wanted to offer it since you gave us a ride. You want something else? Like coffee or iced tea?"

Steve sat a minute. He was really thirsty but didn't have enough money on him for the vending machine at the courthouse. But he wasn't sure if he felt safe. Could they do something to him? He didn't have any money to steal. But he had a car. Could he leave his car on the street? "I am kinda thirsty."

"Hell, c'mon in then."

Steve hated that he swore so easily, like every other word. "Where should I put my car?" he asked.

Howard pointed to a gravel driveway with a strip of grass down the middle, "You can pull it in here."

Steve bumped the back tire over the curb as he awkwardly angled the car into the drive.

"Don't think you'll be gettin' a job parking cars anytime soon," one of his buddies called out.

Steve struggled to remember their names. Leroy? Lerner? *Why are their names so different from ours?* he wondered. He thought of the black guys he ran track with back in the day. Lots of presidents names: Lincoln, Washington, Cleveland, Jefferson. Did they really think they could end up president some day? Never in a million years. Following them up the steps, he took a deep breath. Steve looked around as he entered. "You have a nice house," he said to be polite. The living room on the right was small with room only for the sofa, coffee table, two chairs, and a console TV, like the first one Steve remembered having.

"This isn't mine. It's my parents," Howard said.

A woman called out from upstairs. "That you, Howard?"

"Yeah, Momma, we're back."

Howard waved them all to the kitchen in back. He grabbed three

Pilsners from the fridge. "I guess we don't have iced tea." He looked at Steve, "How about a Pepsi?"

"That's great." Steve could tell that he sounded a little too eager to please. He took the can from Howard and gulped it down fast. A belch worked its way out. Nobody reacted.

Steve shuffled his feet and felt like he wanted to go. He finished his soda, "Well, I guess I'm off."

"Wanna drop us at the bar? It's about a mile down the road."

"I really should go," Steve said.

"It's on your way," Leonard said.

"How would you know that?" Steve asked. Then he thought it came out wrong, like it always did when he hung around too long. He could make somebody mad. "I didn't mean it that way, I mean, you don't really know where I live so when you said . . . oh, never mind. I can't talk right."

"Shoot, man, you worry too much," Howard said.

Leonard stuck out his chin a little. "Ever been to a black man's bar before?"

Steve shook his head. He pushed the bridge of his glasses to bring them closer to his face. He should never have come inside. He just wanted to go home. He played with the keys in his pocket.

"Maybe you should come with us. Always a first time," Leonard said.

Howard told Leonard not to bother Steve. "Let's go," he said. "Steve's gotta get home."

Steve thanked him for the Pepsi, mumbled a good-bye, and rushed out the door. He started his car and bumped it again over the curb as he pressed a little harder than usual on the accelerator. He wasn't sure, but he thought he heard them laughing. He didn't care. The streets were unfamiliar and he was lost, but he just kept driving. He'd find his way home again. At least he was out of there.

7

with the finalizing of the estate settlement. Fortunately, she and her brother, Scott, had no disagreement on the purpose of the estate monies—to take care of Steve. Because of his mental disability, Steve would receive forty percent and she and Scott thirty percent each, as stated in their parent's will. At the moment, the money was still in one stock portfolio, but upon disbursement, the investments needed to be adjusted to generate enough dividend income to cover all Ohio expenses: house maintenance, utilities, Steve's car and health insurance, his dental and psychological care, and groceries. With his Social Security benefit, Steve could pay for his gas, cigarettes, iced tea, and fast food meals. Steve's stock portion wouldn't generate enough dividends, so Sylvia and Scott would need to regularly supplement his support from their respective accounts, once the monies were disbursed. Unfortunately, since they'd need to use every dollar of dividend income to support Steve, the dividends couldn't be reinvested, and the portfolio couldn't increase in value. The situation was precarious. If the market didn't hold steady, they'd be sunk.

Their father had managed to pay off the mortgage years ago, and they were thankful for that. Still, the house was almost fifty years old. The light beige carpet was badly soiled—darkened pathways, almost black in color, trailed through the dining room to the two downstairs bedrooms and bath, and smudged the edges of each step to the upstairs.

The walls, once eggshell, were dingy gray, sheer curtains were shredding at the windows, the Formica counter tops in the kitchen were lifting at the corners, and the dishwasher leaked, so it sat unused. Nothing had been upgraded in twenty years. Like Sylvia's own life, everything was unraveling.

Nancy rearranged her schedule so she could pick Sylvia up at the Cleveland airport. On the forty-minute drive home, Nancy chatted away about how well Steve was doing, with the exception of going to work.

"I never expected him to like going, but I didn't think he'd resist. Isn't he scheduled for three times a week?" Sylvia asked.

"Yes. Two to four hours each night, but he barely manages to go once a week."

"So how does he get out of it?" Sylvia asked.

"He says he's sick to his stomach. I've heard him throw up, but I figured it was nerves," Nancy said. What neither of them knew—and what Steve admitted much later—was that he often stuffed himself with three or four McDonald's hamburgers an hour or two before work and then purged to fake illness.

"I know I haven't been around long, but I'm not so sure the work is good for him," Nancy said.

"He's been working there for at least five years, so I don't know why it would bother him so much now," Sylvia said. "He needs to do something outside the house."

"But if he hates it so much and the guys he works with make him uncomfortable, I'm wondering if it does him more harm than good. Especially if he's getting sick over it. Maybe it makes him feel even worse about himself."

"I never thought about it that way. I just accepted what Mom and Dad had set up for him. He always refused to go to support groups or social functions for the mentally ill, because he didn't want to see himself as one of them. Maybe you're right. It might make him feel worse about himself," Sylvia said. "You're good, Nancy. You should've been a shrink."

"Just common sense and observation. After all the hard knocks I've been through, you start to pay more attention."

Sylvia nodded. For her, always anticipating another shoe that might drop, it was more like being on "high alert" than just paying more attention. She told Nancy she'd contact Dr. Nora again the ~~~~~~~

~~~~~ ~~~~~, she had to find a gardener. The grass was higher than her ankles and weeds were taking over the flower beds as well as sprouting throughout the gravel driveway. At least Scott was coming soon to help her. They had appointments with Steve's psychiatrist, the attorney, and social worker. Scott was only staying four days, but she'd take whatever he could arrange.

—

The last time Scott had come to Sylvia's aid was a year ago, when she'd gone home on the first anniversary of their mother's death to hear her dad play a trumpet solo at the Sunday service at their church, in honor of her passing. Overwrought from her son's drug relapses, car accidents, and disappearances, Sylvia needed to get away for a while and, desperately, had been looking forward to the peace and quiet at home with her dad, and even her brother. When she arrived, her dad had opened a new bottle of Gilbert's and asked if she wanted "a snort"—gin with Bitter Lemon, his favorite summer drink—which she did.

While he fixed their drinks, she wandered through the living room to the family room, half expecting to hear her mom's cheery voice sing out her welcome before bounding over for a big hug. Sylvia stood behind the desk, staring out the picture window at the expanse of green that canopied the backyard, the cardinals, her mom's favorite bird, darting from one tree to another. She tried to absorb the loud, unsettling absence. Glancing down at the desk, she saw a large foot-high pile of unopened mail. Beside it, an empty bottle of gin. She looked around the room—stacks of magazines and newspapers sat on the floor next to her dad's La-Z-Boy, even more on the coffee table and in front it. She went back to the living room—more of the same. The general mess was out of character for her dad.

No sooner had he handed her the drink than the phone rang. She answered it. An overly friendly man asked for her dad. The conversation she overheard seemed odd, as if her dad was speaking to someone he didn't know very well, yet was happy to hear from, like a new friend. He'd settled into his leather recliner with his drink, a signal that he'd be in conversation awhile. "Yep, it sure is nice to have my daughter home—she lives in LA now. Used to be in Oregon but got married to a guy from high school and moved." He went into more detail, their plans during her stay, his golf game, and seemed genuinely glad that someone had taken an interest in him.

Since he was on the phone, Sylvia went back to the family room to glance at some of the unopened mail. Many had return addresses in Florida or Canada, with professional looking names of investment houses. The envelopes had an official appearance too, as though a government document or a check were enclosed. She opened one. A form letter requesting one hundred dollars for a lottery in British Columbia tripped her suspicion. When Steve came in, she'd asked him if he knew anything about it.

"Dad says he can make a lot of money. These guys call all the time," he said, exasperated. "I told him they didn't seem on the up and up, that maybe they just wanted his money." He fiddled with his hands, "But why would he listen to me? He's so much smarter and experienced in business. He'd know better than me."

"You're very smart, Steve. And I think your hunch is right." Sylvia couldn't imagine their dad getting sucked into giving money away, or rather, gambling. "How long has this been going on do you think?"

Steve had looked up at the ceiling and put his hands on his hips.

"Not that long—a couple months? Maybe since March. I'm not sure." He turned toward the garage and opened the door, "Look in here." A dozen or so shipping boxes, each about the size of a microwave, sat next to the garbage bins.

Sylvia looked inside a couple of them. They were filled with cheap

Steve chuckled in a wheeze through his teeth, "You're right—he always says that."

"Is he drinking a lot?" she asked.

"Not that much, but I did take the car keys from him once because he was so tipsy. Maybe I did the wrong thing." Steve looked away and took a deep breath, "But he wasn't walking straight, and he was slurring his words. I was worried that he might get in an accident." He looked at his sister wide-eyed, eyebrows raised. "And he was going out for more gin!"

Sorry that her brother had been dealing with this alone, she couldn't decide which was more surprising: that her dad was drunk or that Steve had the courage to take away his keys. "Steve, you absolutely did the right thing. I'm so glad you were here," she said. She hadn't seen Steve this lucid in a long, long time. Was it possible that he was the one taking care of their dad more than the other way around? Maybe he finally had a sense of purpose in life. "Did he argue with you about it?"

"A little at first, but I stopped him from going into the garage."

She touched his shoulder and he didn't back away, "Good for you. That must've been difficult."

"Yeah, it was. Anyway, I think you got here just in time," he said.

"I think so, too." She made eye contact with him, "I think Dad might have a drinking problem, Steve."

"No way, not our dad," he said as if the idea were absurd. "He's just depressed since Mom died." Steve started to laugh to himself and mumbled that maybe Dad should be on meds like him, then he said, "I'm tired. I'm going to take a nap."

Syliva thought their dad probably was depressed, but that didn't mean he hadn't developed a drinking problem. She thought back to phone calls when she could hear the tinkling of ice cubes as early as noon. He'd talk about their mom and how nobody called him anymore. "Everybody liked her better," he'd said. Choked up and weepy, he'd confessed that one of his biggest regrets was that she never met his mother, who died before they got married. Sylvia had tried to comfort him, but losing his partner of fifty-five years was too much. His sorrow was palpable, and if he was overindulging, she couldn't blame him. Still, she'd have to talk to him about the lottery and maybe the drinking, but she dreaded the thought. She needed to gather more information, something concrete to open up the discussion. Their dad was a gentle soul with a crusty edge, but he'd listen to her. That she knew.

The next morning, she'd gone to the kitchen cupboard where he kept his booze and her heart sank. Not even twenty-four hours had passed since her arrival and the new bottle of gin had only an inch or two left in it. When he left to play with his orchestra group at a nursing home, she took advantage of his absence to look through his checkbook. Sure enough, numerous checks were written to lotteries or sweepstakes. Nothing was over one hundred dollars, but there were dozens of them. The entries started in February and increased almost exponentially each month. Here it was June. She roughly totaled them in her head— easily eight thousand dollars. When she found a post-it note on his nightstand with the handwritten amount of fifteen thousand dollars and an address in Quebec, she panicked. The stock account statements! She searched through his neatly organized files that he'd kept since the seventies, and flipped through the pages of the current year. And there it was—a withdrawal in May for that very amount.

Their dad wasn't a wealthy man, but he'd provided a comfortable life. His stock portfolio amounted to six hundred thousand, and his monthly pension was four thousand. Sylvia tallied his losses at thirty thousand dollars—an enormous sum, but not his entire fortune, at least not yet. Feeling guilty about exposing her dad's secret, Sylvia hesitated, but then decided she had no choice. She'd called his doctor, his stockbroker, and the family attorney, who recommended that sl contact the state attorney gen- "

... Sylvia was

... her father down to explain that she'd discovered what had been going on and the amount of money lost. He hadn't tallied it, he'd said, and he seemed surprised by the sum. He was contrite and ashamed and looked down at the floor as he spoke. "Your mother always entered the Reader's Digest Sweepstakes, so I wanted to keep it going after she died. Sort of to honor her," he said quietly. She told him Scott was to arrive late that night, and a representative from the attorney general's office would meet with them the next day at the house.

When the representative arrived, they all sat in the family room, quietly listening while he explained that Ohio was a primary target for scam artists preying on the elderly in international lotteries. He said the house phone number, the one they'd had since the house was built in 1950, would have to be changed. He added that it was unlikely they'd get the money back. "Best to consider it gone. Expensive lesson," he said. The worst of it was their dad still had the idea that he could recoup his losses. That evening, he'd even flashed his fancy looking watch (a cheap copy) at Scott, saying he'd won it in the lottery. Scott had retorted, "Oh, you mean the thirty-thousand-dollar watch?"

Their dad had actually laughed out loud at his own stupidity. Though he made no promises to stop spending money, he did agree to see a geriatric therapist because "my daughter wants me to." He told Sylvia he could stop drinking anytime. "I used to be a teetotaler, you know. I'll quit if you think it's too much." Because of her son's spiral into drug addiction, Sylvia had learned from the treatment centers and family meetings that an alcoholic had to accept that he had a problem, that quitting to please someone else never worked. She hoped the therapist could help him. At least he'd been willing. True to his word, he never sent money again and he continued to see the therapist until he died several months later.

———

Sylvia stood in the driveway, staring at the front yard of her childhood home, thinking about how much her dad used to love caring for the roses, the lawn, all the yard work, when she felt a tap on her shoulder.

"Are you all right?" Nancy asked gently.

"I was just missing my dad." Two of Sylvia's fondest memories with her dad happened the prior summer, during the thirty-thousand-dollar loss era: their round of golf on a lush, public course laid out over rolling hills, surrounded by forest; and their day trip to the Rock and Roll Hall of Fame (music he never enjoyed) in Cleveland. They laughed, talked about happier times, and simply enjoyed being together. Perhaps they remained her fondest because they also were her last. Five months later, Steve had called with the heartbreaking news.

As successor trustee, Sylvia was the main contact for estate business and Steve's care, but she ran everything through Scott. And like the last mess with their dad's lottery scam, Scott would drop everything to come to her aid. He was her back up, her unwavering support, and much like her dad, she could count on his guidance in all decisions. He also added levity when she needed it most. The next day, she picked Scott up at the airport and jumped into the issue at hand.

"I think we should tell Steve about Dr. Rita right away."

Scott said he thought they should give him some good news along with the bad, "How about if we tell him that he doesn't have to work at that job he hates so much?"

They talked it over and decided there was no good reason for him to continue. Nancy was right—just because their parents insisted Steve work, he didn't need to continue if it was more of a detriment than a help to him.

"Maybe we could ask him to do something for us if we let him quit," Sylvia said.

"So we give him bad news, good news, and then bad news?" Scott

"Once he knows Dr. Rita is gone, he might open the door a crack," he said.

"True," she said. "Also, if we say he doesn't have to answer right away, he might agree. When he thinks he has time to decide, he's more acquiescent."

"But we don't have time, so I'd rather push for an answer on the spot."

"Like minds sure make decision making easier," Sylvia said.

Scott suggested they choose the right moment, like before he headed to "the office" for his iced tea run, when he was kind of upbeat and Nancy was at work. Later that afternoon, Steve asked if he could go to Friendly's. Sylvia said they had to talk to him first.

All he had to do was look at his sister's face. "What's the matter? Did I do something wrong?" Steve felt outnumbered.

"Not at all," Sylvia said.

"You're doing just fine," Scott chimed in.

Sylvia took the advice of the new psychologist, Dr. Nora, who said to keep it simple and say it straight out. "I'm afraid we have some bad news about Dr. Rita."

"I was just wondering about her today," Steve said. "Won't she see me anymore?"

"She's had heart problems for many years, and I'm sorry to have to tell you this, but she died."

"No way. I don't believe it," Steve plopped heavily into his favorite chair with the grime-covered arms. "She was fat and sometimes she was breathing heavy. I asked her about it once, not the part about being fat, the breathing part, and she told me she already had two heart attacks. Maybe it's true. When did she die? There must be some mistake. Who told you?"

Scott explained how they found out. He and Sylvia were careful to acknowledge Steve's feelings, telling him how sorry they were, recognizing how much he liked her and would miss seeing her. Nine years is a long-term relationship.

"First, Dad. No, first Mom, then Dad, and now Dr. Rita?" Steve leaned forward, his head in his hands. "Why does everything happen to me? Why does everything go wrong? You're not going to make me see somebody else, are you?"

"No, but we want to ask you to do a favor for us, while we're both here," Scott said.

Steve groaned without looking up. "What now?"

"Meet the psychologist Dr. Rita recommended." Scott's tone was light-hearted, "Just once, and you can decide if you want to see her again."

Steve asked about her, and Scott told him her name and that she'd gone to school with Dr. Rita. She'd come to the house the first time, and if he wanted to see her again, she lived only ten minutes away. Like Dr. Rita, her appointments were in her home.

"I don't want somebody else." Steve removed his glasses and rubbed his eyes with both hands at the same time, in loose fists, pinkies extended, in the same way since he was a toddler. "I hate change. Dr. Nora. She sounds old."

"We know this is a shock for you," Sylvia said. "We also have another idea."

"Oh great," he said. "Make my day. Didn't Clint Eastwood say that in a movie or something? Before he was going to shoot somebody?"

Scott laughed out loud. "You don't miss much, Steve. We think this idea you'll like. Actually, it was Nancy's idea."

"What does she know about me?"

"We'll let you quit working at Clean Sweep if you agree to meet Dr. Nora," Sylvia said.

"Quit work?" Steve beamed. "I didn't know I could. You mean I'd never have to go again? No more vacuuming? Driving at night? Being with those landlife...?"

it down, so he could remember better. He said it was Dr. Rita's idea to write everything down. "She also told me not to walk around with my head down because it made people nervous. I guess my journal won't get published now. Can you call Ted Snyder, my social worker, to tell him I'm quitting the job? I don't want to tell him."

Scott said he'd take care of it.

"No more Clean Sweep. You two did make my day. Can I go to Friendly's now?"

8

The next morning, Scott and Sylvia met with Steve's psychiatrist, Dr. Pandi, whose role as a medical doctor was to determine Steve's appropriate medications and dosage. A monthly session to monitor his stability was the norm. Psychologists, like Dr. Rita and now Dr. Nora, were certified for talk therapy, not for prescribing medication. Dr. Pandi was a stout, middle-aged, dark-skinned Pakistani woman who, despite having lived in America for over thirty years, spoke broken English with a thick accent, garbling and rolling her consonants in a cadence that made her sound like she was underwater. "Steve is doing better after your mother pass away but will never live independently. Your father was good for him, because he is more calm and quiet. Your mother could be moody and nervous and upset with Steve."

Scott thought of their mother's tendency to say the first thing that came into her head. Living with Steve took more patience than most people would have, but on the days Mom's ran out, calling him "a big load who just sits around all day," probably did more damage than if she'd kept her mouth shut and left the room. Scott was certain their father never spoke to him like that.

"Why was his antipsychotic dose reduced from ten milligrams to five?" Sylvia asked.

"Steve wasn't taking it regularly, so he had pills left over at the end of the month," Dr. Pandi explained. "In case he overdose, I could have problem with liability. You want me to increase back to normal dose?"

They both nodded in agreement to increase it. Was it odd that she'd change his dosage without seeing Steve first? One had to assume that after eight or nine years as her patient, she'd know that his original dose of Prolixin was fine. Nevertheless, Scott was relieved that changing the dosage was so easy.

She also told them she'd tried to get Steve to join her group therapy sessions, but he wasn't interested because he didn't think he was as sick as her other patients. "But schizophrenics always think they are not

'Her attitude is terrible. How could she say, 'Steve will never get better?' If she thinks that's true, Steve would definitely pick up on it. And he's been seeing her a long time." Here, Scott was more like his dad—he wasn't so sure Steve ever would get better—but Sylvia, like their mom, always held out hope.

When they got home, Steve was on the patio, smoking. Head down, he looked at them sidewise. "So how was Dr. Pandi? Am I going back to the psych ward?"

"No, but she increased your dose of Prolixin back to where it used to be."

"You mean ten milligrams?" Steve asked. "So I won't hear voices anymore?"

"Do you still hear voices?" Scott asked.

"If I do, do I have to go to the psych ward?"

Sylvia told him he wasn't going to the hospital and that they knew he still heard voices, but he'd hear them less with the dosage increase.

He said he was okay with that.

"Do you have trouble understanding Dr. Pandi?" Sylvia asked.

"I hardly know what she's saying, but Pandi just prescribes my meds. I talk to Dr. Rita more anyway." Steve looked up at the sky. "Oh yeah, Dr. Rita died. Am I supposed to see . . . um . . . Dr. Nora today?"

Scott reminded him that she was coming at five o'clock.

"I better write that down," he said. "Maybe I'll like her. I do kinda miss talking to someone, and if she's nice and likes me, maybe I'll start seeing her. And if Dr. Rita recommended her, she might be okay." Steve stubbed out his cigarette in the ashtray then pressed the heels of his hands into his eyes and let out a long sigh. "I'm dying tired."

They all turned when they heard scratching and yipping at the screen door.

"Sammy, I almost forgot you." Steve's voice changed to a high pitch, and he jumped up to let the dog out. "I hope he didn't do number two in the house. Maybe Nancy already took him out before work." He patted his knee, calling to the dog as he led Sammy to the front yard.

"I think the dog is good for him," Sylvia said.

"For the moment, anyway. It could all change tomorrow." Scott got up to get something to eat. "Let's go down to the lake."

"I'm up for that. Maybe Steve'll want to go too," she said.

"Doubtful."

Steve didn't want to go. He said he was too tired, they'd have a better time without him anyway; it was too hot, and he never went swimming because of his stomach. "You're both in such good shape. Look at me." He grabbed his middle. "I'm so gross." Steve could come up with a million plausible reasons for avoiding anything he didn't want to do.

"We want you to come," Sylvia said. "Nobody cares about your stomach—you could wear a T-shirt if it bothers you."

"I'd look stupid," he scoffed.

"We could all go in a rowboat to the other side of the lake where nobody would see you and you could jump in and cool off," Scott suggested.

Steve refused, saying it was too hot to ride in a boat. "Besides, I'm not supposed to be in the sun because of my meds. I could have a heart attack. Mom died of a heart attack—arrhythmia, wasn't it? And Uncle Johnny too, and he was only sixty! Her whole family had heart attacks. Nope, too risky."

Even if most people wouldn't consider his life worth living, Sylvia knew that living mattered to Steve. Or maybe the idea of dying, entering the void, the unknown, frightened him like everyone else—probably more because of his experience. He must've thought he was dying during electric shock treatments or a particularly scary hallucination or when God spoke to him. He was always the first one to fasten his seatbelt in the car, but he worried for others too. Now that their parents had passed away, and Dr. Rita, he might be even more afraid, sure that

they've always dreamed about before it's too late. Steve had no dreams, only fears.

Since it was close to dinnertime, Sylvia and Scott decided to go to the grocery store instead of the lake.

Scott went to Steve's room to tell him where they were going. "And it's almost five so Dr. Nora will be here soon. Maybe you should get up to let her in."

Just then, Sylvia called out. "She's here!"

The doorbell rang and Steve rushed to the front door. He greeted her like a gentleman, introduced himself and shook her hand. He ushered her into the living room and turned to introduce Sylvia and Scott. Then he offered her something to drink. Dr. Nora was his guest. So far, so good.

Dr. Nora looked to be Steve's age, which surprised Sylvia. She'd assumed she'd be close in age to Dr. Rita, since they'd gone to graduate school together. Was it a good thing? Maybe. She was trim, dressed casually in dark blue slacks, a flowered blouse, and loafers. Her light brown hair was chin-length and softly curled. She wore no make-up.

Dr. Nora smiled at Steve. "My husband says he went to high school with you, Steve. Rick Ingram."

Steve glanced at the floor then looked up in surprise. "I remember him!"

"Small world," Scott said.

Sylvia and Scott exited gracefully to leave them alone.

—

Upon their return an hour later, Dr. Nora had already gone. Steve told them he was going to take it slowly. He'd see her in two weeks for a half an hour, which would only cost thirty-eight dollars. He liked her. He liked that she was his age. He said he asked her, then realized it probably wasn't polite, but she told him anyway. He liked that she laughed easily and that she ran a half-way house once, so she understood why he hated group living. He was glad he had someone to talk to again.

Sylvia followed up with Dr. Nora to verify Steve's interpretation of their session (sometimes he confused what was said with what he was thinking) and to ask if there was anything else she should do while she was in town. Dr. Nora was very encouraging about Steve's positive, open attitude and his willingness to see her on a regular basis. She also mentioned that she gave Steve a sort of assignment to think about—a list of places where he could do volunteer work. She said he needed to do something productive outside the house, something to replace the work he was doing before. Sylvia joined Scott in the family room and told Scott about their conversation.

"Funny he happened to forget telling us that part," Scott said.

"He could've forgotten," she said.

"You really think he'll make a list? Or that he wants to volunteer?"

"I think a list will give him trouble, but I think he'd try," she said. "And no, I don't think he wants to do anything. Mostly because he can't imagine where he'd fit in. But Dr. Nora will help him with this and encourage him."

"But where would he fit in? Hospitals freak him out. Schools wouldn't take him. Nursing homes, maybe?"

"Maybe. At least with the elderly, he'd be the young stud and feel better about himself," she said.

Scott laughed. "And he loves talking about the past, the good ol' days. Did you ask her about a recommendation for another psychiatrist?"

"No. I told her we didn't think much of his doctor. She's heard some negative things about her, too, but wasn't specific. She thought Steve

that they could spend about fifteen thousand on the house. They made a list: interior/exterior painting and replace carpeting, dishwasher, sink, kitchen counter, flooring, and wallpaper Steve's downstairs bedroom. Part of the house needed new roofing, but that could probably wait until next year. A few new light fixtures were needed and a new kitchen table and chairs. Steve also needed a new mattress—the coils were popping out on one side and he was ripping his pants and scratching his calves on them. Because he spent a large part of his day in bed, lying mainly toward the side by his nightstand, the mattress had become almost four inches lower on that side. They decided they could flip it and solve the problem for now, since the other side was against the wall.

"We need to get estimates to make sure our budget will be enough," Scott said.

"You mean I'll need to get them," Sylvia corrected. "You leave tomorrow."

"I know you can handle it," Scott gently squeezed her shoulder. "I trust you implicitly."

"Of course you do," she teased. "What choice do you have? I actually might have fun with this. Redoing our old homestead, giving it a facelift will feel good. I think I'd rather be here than at home right now anyway. I need to be occupied."

"When does Trevor get out of rehab?" Scott asked.

"Next week. Then he goes to sober living." Sober living for alcoholics and addicts was like a half-way house after in-residence treatment, a group way-station to help them gradually adjust to the responsibilities of normal living. After four rehabs and four relapses, Sylvia was somewhat less fearful but mostly numb. At least this time her son had jail hanging over his head if he didn't stay sober for eighteen months. For a lot of addicts, jail seemed to be the most effective incentive.

"When I saw him last, he sure looked good. I even suggested he get into modeling and took a few Polaroids of him to take back to my agency."

"Oh, great. Easy drugs." Sylvia rolled her eyes.

"Drugs are easy anywhere—even at law firms, brokerage firms—"

"Okay, okay. I get your point, but easy money isn't a deterrent either."

Trevor would never be cured and neither would Steve, but Trevor could lead a normal life—work, marry, raise a family. His addiction "could be arrested, but not cured," and his only hope was total abstinence. A choice. The only hope for Steve was that he choose to take his meds so that he might eat, sleep, take showers, and brush his teeth regularly, get haircuts and change his clothes when dirty, or be able to concentrate long enough to read the newspaper or watch a movie from beginning to end. To Sylvia, Steve's future was more grounded, almost manageable, which was much less scary than her son's, where she had no control and saw no tangible direction for him.

"Somehow I think he's going to make it this time—I'll keep in touch with him while you're away," Scott promised. He had visited Trevor in every rehab. "Maybe we should flip Steve's mattress now, so we don't forget to do it before I go."

But as they approached Steve's room, they heard loud snoring and laughed. "I guess we'll do it later," Sylvia said.

Just then, Nancy walked in the door from work and heard it, too. "Sometimes I wear earplugs so I can sleep!"

"Smart woman," Scott said. "I wish I'd thought of that years ago."

They grilled steaks for their last supper with Scott, who was flying back to LA the next day, then got ice cream cones at Stoddard's, a family-owned stand that had been making its own ice cream for fifty-plus years.

The neighbors across the street, whom the family had known for years, recommended a reliable, reasonable contractor they'd used to

Sylvia for two light fixtures and the kitchen set. He chose a light oak-topped, rectangular table with white-painted legs and chairs to match. He lasted for two hours before he said he was done. Sylvia thoroughly enjoyed involving Steve with shopping for their childhood home and saw how much he enjoyed it, too. She hoped it might help him feel that what he wanted mattered. They had lunch at Friendly's, where Steve introduced his sister all around. It heartened her to be included in his world, especially to see that the waitresses treated him with kindness and respect. They seemed genuinely happy to finally meet the sister he'd talked about so often.

Sylvia planned to return in November, when the house was scheduled to be finished, in order to avoid the remodeling mayhem. Nancy and Steve would have to endure the two-week upheaval of having a painter in the house all day, then the carpet layers with the furniture shuffled from room to room. The kitchen would be torn up for almost a week, which meant, Bill, the contractor, would begin work as soon as possible. As it turned out, he was attractive and in his sixties, the same age as Nancy. Although Sylvia spent the most time with him, finalizing details before her departure, she noticed that Nancy oozed charm, wit, and allure whenever he was around. The fact that he was married didn't seem a deterrent.

9

AUGUST 1999

Now that Sylvia was gone, Nancy had managed to adjust her work schedule so she could be home more during the day. Bill was to arrive at eight-thirty to begin the kitchen remodel, so she got up at seven to get coffee started, bacon frying, make-up on, hair styled, and dressed for work. She could pretend breakfast was part of her daily routine. Nothing like the smell of bacon frying to stir a man's appetite and maybe even his heart. She let Sammy out on his own to do his business, since he knew the neighborhood by now, then she searched through her closet for just the right outfit. Maybe she'd take her work clothes with her—the boring white blouse with her name stitched in red on the pocket and black cotton slacks—and change when she got to the store. She had to be there by eleven, so she didn't have that much time. Perfect—her pink cotton V-neck Polo. The emblem was classy, and the shirt showed off her large breasts without advertising the fact. Well, one large breast. She was lopsided from the mastectomy she'd had fifteen years earlier, which left a terrible scar, but the bras they made were a miracle. Bathing suits, too. It was impossible to tell she'd lost one when she was fully clothed. Lost one. Like she misplaced it and couldn't find it. Saint Anthony, the saint of lost things, sure couldn't help her with that one. She still cringed at the thought of the operation, imagining a scalpel slicing it right off like so much excess fat that needed trimming. The doorbell rang.

She rushed to the door. "Bill!" she exclaimed, opening it wide.

Bill furrowed his brow and looked startled. "You weren't expecting me?"

"Oh, yes. Just glad to see you."

"Uh, good. You sounded surprised." He glanced down at his shoes like he was embarrassed. "I should take them off."

". . . . . . , ... , ... whatever makes you comfort able. I could wipe 'em off if you like."

"No, no, that won't be necessary." He headed toward the kitchen in his socks. "The new sink and dishwasher should arrive in a few days. I'll remove the counter top today and tomorrow."

"Would you like some coffee?"

He smiled, "I'd love some."

Steve suddenly appeared, brushing past them, staring straight ahead. He opened the refrigerator, took out the gallon of milk and took a big swig. He put it back and on his way out, turned, looking at them as if noticing them for the first time.

"Good morning, Steve," Nancy said.

"Hi, Steve," Bill said.

"Hi. Good morning, whatever." His voice was flat, his expression deadpan. "It takes me a long time to wake up," he said, annoyed that he had to deal with them at all. "I'm going to have a smoke." As he stepped into the dining room, he stopped short. "Is that bacon I smell?"

"Sure is." Nancy hadn't counted on Steve showing up. He was usually out having his morning iced tea or zonked out in bed.

"Do you like bacon?" Bill asked Steve.

He seemed astonished by the question. "I love bacon. Don't you?"

"I do, but I don't eat it anymore." Bill tapped his chest. "Not good for the ol' ticker."

"Ticker?" Steve blinked. "Oh. You mean your heart." He stood there a moment, digesting it all. "Everything I love is bad for my cholesterol." He gestured dramatically toward the sizzling pan, "Like bacon." He shrugged his shoulders and rolled his eyes. "I'm not supposed to have hamburgers, French fries, even steak! My dad told me that when I started taking Lipitor." He smiled knowingly, like he'd outsmarted the system. "And it's working, so I just keep eating what I want."

"I guess that sort of makes sense," Nancy said. "Well, the bacon's here just for you."

"Really?" Steve's mood was lifting. "That's great, Nancy. Is it okay if I have a smoke first?"

"Take all the time you need. Do you want some scrambled eggs with that?"

"Sounds good." He went outside to the front patio.

"Bill? How about you?"

"Uh, no thanks. I already ate. My wife fixed me oatmeal this morning."

"Does she usually fix you breakfast?"

"She does. And always a healthy one." Bill took the cup of coffee Nancy offered. "Takes real good care of me."

"Aren't you a lucky man? Still, it's fun to mix things up on occasion," she said in a singsong voice. "And you don't look like you need to watch what you eat." Bill was shorter than Nancy, of slight stature, and he looked fit and muscular in his slim blue jeans and plaid work shirt.

Bill set his coffee down and dug into his tool box, his back turned to her. "Just being careful at my age—family history of heart problems."

Nancy was deflated. "Cancer runs in my family, and here I am still smoking." She figured her cancer chip was cashed. She'd licked it. "I'll just take my chances."

"I hear it's awfully hard to quit. Do you have any sweetener?"

"I think I've run out unless you want the real thing."

"That's okay," Bill said. "I'll drink it black."

She opened the cupboard and rooted around. "Here's some Equal."

"Perfect," he said.

Nothing was perfect as far as Nancy was concerned. "I'll let you get to work unless there's anything else I can do for you."

"Coffee's all I need, thanks." He looked out the kitchen window to the backyard. "Isn't that your dog?"

That I know.

When Steve came back, sure enough, Sammy grabbed the bacon and Nancy grabbed him. "You crazy dog."

Steve asked if the eggs were ready yet. Nancy said she forgot and they'd only take a few minutes, but Steve said he wanted to go to Friendly's now anyway. He ate the rest of the bacon on his way out, wiping his fingers on his wrinkled khakis.

Nancy changed into her work clothes, grabbed a can of Coke, and was headed for the garage, when the phone rang. Bill picked it up in the kitchen. Nancy waited to hear who was calling. Bill called to her—it was her son, Danny, and he sounded upset. Nancy went to her bedroom to pick up the extension phone. "What's the matter?" she asked, without saying hello.

"Becky wants me out," he said.

"What do you mean?" Nancy felt her blood start to boil just thinking about Becky and how she railroaded Danny into marrying her. He was a big basketball star in high school, and she'd had her sights on him since then. When he lost his leg in the accident, she appeared out of nowhere, visiting him every day, helping him walk again, driving him wherever he needed to go. She was like Clara Barton until she got pregnant and he married her. The last thing he needed was to be saddled with a wife and baby after what he'd been through.

"She's crazy and wants me to leave. I don't have anywhere to go, so

I was hoping I could stay with you and Steve for a few days. Just until she calms down."

"I never did like her attitude. What's got into her now?"

"I was asleep on the couch when she got home last night and started screaming at me that I was passed out drunk and not fit to be alone with the children. She said the baby was crying, that her diaper was soaking wet, and Luke was asleep in his clothes."

Nancy figured Becky didn't come home until after two in the morning, and she had the nerve to call Danny unfit? "She knows how much you love those kids, how good you are with them. Not many husbands would do what you're doing!"

Danny had lost his job and he was taking care of the kids—Mr. Mom—while his wife worked two jobs as a waitress. Nancy didn't know that he was fired because he'd missed a lot of work. According to Danny they were cutting back and, since he was disabled, he was the first to be let go. He decided it was more lucrative to stay home with the kids, collecting unemployment and disability, than to pay daycare and work a mundane job tracking inventory for a mold and die company that he hated.

"Where are you now?" she asked.

"I'm home, but she wants me out tonight. She says her sister will watch the kids. So can I stay with you? Steve won't mind, will he?"

"Maybe he'd enjoy a man around the house to talk sports with, since he's alone most of the time. I'll ask him. Don't you worry, we'll figure something out." Nancy hung up and was fuming. That bitch. Poor Danny was doing the best he could, just a lot of hard knocks. She wished his dad would help him somehow, but he was long gone, married to another bitch who didn't want anything to do with his kids. How did this day go so badly when it started out so well?

"Everything all right?" Bill asked.

"It'll work out. My thirty-two-year-old son is having marital problems."

"What does he do?"

"Right now, he's not working, but he has a job lined up at the bank in the Falls," she said, wishing it was true.

"That sounds good. My daughter just married an investment banker and they're doing very well in New York. They met in college."

Bully for them. Nancy barely had enough money to buy the essentials, much less afford to send her kids to college. Danny was never a student anyway, and the teachers sure never gave him a break. He

[text obscured] Maybe Steve would

pick him up. Maybe they could get lunch together, Danny's treat. One good thing about the day occurred to her: with Sylvia now back in Los Angeles, Nancy wouldn't have to ask permission for Danny to stay. He could be in and out of the house without Sylvia even knowing about it. Timing was everything. Sylvia probably would've refused—too disruptive for poor Steve. It irked her that they thought they knew what was best for him, when she was the one living with him. She saw him every day, cooked his meals, wrote him notes, reminded him to take his meds, shower, shave, get haircuts, and she was even cheerful about it. And wasn't it her idea to let him quit the job that was making him sick? Sylvia and Scott really didn't have a clue.

She entered Friendly's and spotted Steve at his table at the back in the smoking section. Shoulders rounded, chin thrust forward, he leaned to suck on the straw in the tall glass of iced tea that sat in front of him. Partially torn open pink packets of sweetener were strewn haphazardly in the middle of the table, their fine white contents dusting the surface. Cigarette butts filled the black plastic ashtray. Nancy approached as he lit another, his face scrunching with the inhale.

Steve sat up, startled. For her to be here was out of sync.

"Surprise!"

"Nancy, what are you doing here? I thought you were at work."

She hovered at the table before he gestured for her to have a seat in the one-person booth opposite him. "I'm on my way, but I wanted to ask you something first, sort of a favor."

"A favor?" He snubbed the butt out and said something under his breath. "Do you want something to drink? Are you hungry? I'll get Marge to bring you something if you want. Here she is." He flagged Marge over to the table. "This is Nancy. She's my . . . uh, sister-in-law? Are you my sister-in-law? No, well, I guess you're my . . . "

"We're roommates!" Nancy said heartily.

"My roommate. That's it." He shrugged, smiled half-heartedly, and poured another glass of tea from the pitcher.

Marge and Nancy smiled politely at each other in acknowledgement, like two nurses placating a geriatric patient.

"I'll just have a Coke," Nancy said.

"Comin' right up." Marge dashed off.

"So, what's the favor? You want me to cook dinner tonight?" He laughed. "That's a joke."

"Yeah, good one, Steve."

"What will we do about dinner with no kitchen?"

"I'll bring home chicken tonight, how's that? Actually, the favor is about Danny."

"Oh. Danny."

"He and Becky had a fight and—"

"They fight a lot, don't they? I've heard you on the phone before. I wonder what they fight about."

"Money mostly. She's never happy," Nancy said. "And she wants him out of the house, but he has no place to go—"

"How could she do that? He can barely get around." Steve's eyes widened. "She sounds mean." When he met her last Thanksgiving, she was so quiet and serious, shy even. And Danny seemed the opposite— always joking around, kind of loud. Steve couldn't imagine she'd have the gumption—his dad's word—to demand anything. "I feel sorry for him."

"Me, too. He has it so hard."

Steve sat quietly a moment. "I have an idea!" He seemed ecstatic with himself. "We have the whole upstairs. He could sleep there! Maybe he wouldn't want to, but for a few days it might be okay."

Nancy felt like she could cry. She was touched by Steve's sympathetic ear, his big heart. Who said schizophrenics aren't capable of empathy? Or feeling sorry for another's plight? Maybe Steve was the exception

... going to ask you if Danny could have dinner with us tonight, but you're a step ahead of me. He'll be staying with us anyway!"

"Tonight? Oh, right. He'll be staying upstairs."

Nancy pulled out a five-dollar bill and put it on the table.

"What's that for? I'll get this."

"Let's just say I appreciate your kindness and generosity with my son. Order yourself something to eat, on me." Nancy thought better than to ask Steve to pick Danny up. She left the restaurant and went straight to her son's house to tell him the good news.

Nancy forgot to ask Steve not to mention the new arrangement to his sister or brother. Bill, the contractor, might pose a problem too, since he and Sylvia kept in touch regularly on the progress of the kitchen remodel. If she said nothing at all, it might look like she just didn't want to bother them with her family's problems. If they found out about Danny, she could act innocent about it. *I'm sorry I didn't think to ask you. Probably because it was a temporary situation and I didn't want to burden you with my stuff. Blah, blah, blah. And I thought Steve might enjoy the company.* Besides, it's not like they'd throw her out. They really did need her.

She pulled onto Danny's street, Madison. Like so many neighborhoods, the streets were named after former presidents or maybe statesmen—from Ohio? She didn't know. Adams, Van Buren, Tyler, Hayes,

Monroe. The sixty-year-old homes were modest bungalows on small lots, but well maintained, the trees full-grown and plentiful. Danny's house was a two-story with wood floors and a separate garage. He and Becky had been so excited to be able to purchase a house two years ago. They'd worked hard to save the money for a down payment and were so happy with the location: school within walking distance, sidewalks, and lots of young families. Such big plans, and all gone to hell in a hand basket.

She parked the car at the curb and wished she'd thought to bring him an Egg McMuffin. She peered in the window from the front porch, but saw no one. She knocked hesitantly, waited, and then rang the doorbell. Danny was probably asleep. She might have to call him from work. She heard movement and slowly the door opened. Danny stood there bent over slightly, posing on his arm crutches, his robe open, in his underwear, his prosthetic leg exposed. It hurt her every time to look at it. She wondered if it would hurt less had he been wounded in a war instead of a car accident, but there was no war going on then. She went inside.

Toys were scattered throughout the living room, an infant swing sat in a corner, and a full baby bottle nearby on the floor. A pillow and blanket lay rumpled on the couch. Squeals of delight burst intermittently from the game show on TV. Danny's round face looked puffy, his eyes were a little bloodshot, and he needed a haircut, but he was still handsome as ever, over six feet tall when he stood up straight. "What are you doing here, Mom?"

That was the second time she was asked that this morning. She told him excitedly about Steve's invitation. "Pack a bag!" she said.

He hesitated, turned, and sat down on the couch, staring at the TV.

"You don't seem very happy about it," she said.

"I'm barely awake." He lit a cigarette. "Getting kicked out of my own home doesn't really make me happy, you know."

"You're right. I'm sorry. At least you have a place to stay for a while. Better than hanging at one of your friends, isn't it?" Nancy thought of his friend, Bud, who was such a bad influence. He meant well, asking

Danny to get out and have a little fun, hang with the guys to make him feel better, but he never held a job for long, and she knew Becky couldn't stand him. Nancy honestly couldn't blame her.

"Yeah, it's better. Bud offered to let me stay at his place, but yours is closer. Do you want me to go with you now?"

... can do. Can I

get you anything before I go?"

He grinned at her in his teasing way. "Scrambled eggs?"

She sighed and tilted her head at her son. He looked like he could use a good breakfast. Guess she'd be fixing eggs after all. "Oh, what the hell," she said. "How many times do I have the chance to look after you?" She set her purse down and went to the kitchen. She quickly called work and said she'd be a little late due to traffic problems. Dishes were piled in the sink, and plates with meal remnants sat on the table. She grabbed a dish towel to protect her blouse, warmed the slightly dirty frying pan still sitting on the stove, and took out half a dozen eggs. The bread wasn't securely tied, so it was stale. Perfect for toast. She popped in two slices. All was ready in only ten minutes. She checked for orange juice, but no luck. "Do you want coffee or something cold to drink?" she called out.

"Just grab me a cold beer."

She reluctantly took the can of Miller's out of the fridge and noticed the trash can in the corner, full of beer cans. She went back to the living room and handed him his breakfast. "You drink beer in the morning?"

"Shoot, Mom. That's about all I drink."

10

Steve chatted with Marge, the waitress, between her comings and goings with other customers, about the weather (August was always too hot), the upcoming election (he didn't vote but if he did he'd vote Republican, since his dad always told him to), his roommate (Nancy took good care of him and he liked her dog), and the house upheaval (the painter was coming soon to paint the whole inside). "Oh! And Nancy's son, Danny, will be staying for a few days." He tapped his cigarette to knock off the ash.

"Sounds like you have a lot goin' on," she said, setting the "Two of Everything" bargain breakfast in front of him. Two eggs scrambled, two slices of bacon, two sausage patties, two buttermilk pancakes, and two slices of white toast.

"Wow. This looks great," he said. "All this for three bucks!"

"We serve it every day from nine to eleven. Didn't you know that?"

Steve shook his head. He rarely ordered food here unless somebody else was paying, like his dad or mom or his case manager, and today—he had the five dollars Nancy left him. Fast food was always the best deal, but today he could splurge. He wanted to dig in, but he didn't want to eat in front of her. Not polite.

"You and your iced tea," she laughed and walked away.

Most of the waitresses were nice and talked to him like he was a regular guy. Sometimes he wondered if he had a chance with any of them, but the ones he found attractive were in college, probably too young, and they never stayed at the restaurant for very long anyway. He'd share stories about his college days, how he ran track and hated the grueling daily practice, how hard he studied and still couldn't get good grades, the riots on campus in the early seventies, the fraternity hell week when he got so worn down he had to drop out of school. Sometimes he said he'd been in and out of psych units for the past thirty years and took meds. If they got a serious look on their faces and became real quiet, he thought maybe he'd said too much. Dr. Nora had told him it might be...

...sometimes more than one), or ended up living with guys on drugs and weren't even married. He was surprised that lots of people had it even worse than him. Where he grew up, everybody he knew graduated from college, had a good job, married their college sweetheart, and had a family, like his own brother and sister. But come to think of it, his sister divorced her first husband and had to work. Still, she wasn't like the waitresses here.

Steve finished eating and pulled out his wallet, overstuffed with bank withdrawal slips, old and new appointment reminder cards from his doctors, prescriptions for his meds, his Social Security card, driver's license, pharmacy discount card, AAA, proofs of car insurance—expired and current—and a picture he and his dad had taken last year for the church directory. Going through his wallet made him feel important, like everyone else who had business to take care of. He hardly ever threw anything away, unless his wallet wouldn't fit in his back pocket, and he always carried everything with him, just in case. He liked to look through it all when he had nothing to do, check and double check that nothing was missing, or inspect the dates for his next appointments. As he looked through it now, he saw the reminder for his appointment with his psychiatrist, Dr. Pandi. He mumbled the date and time to himself, August 20, 1999, at 2:30 p.m. He repeated it several times. Today! He looked at his watch. It was only two hours away. He'd better not go home and take a nap or he might not wake up in time. He shoved his empty plate across the table, counted the number of smokes he had left, tallied his money—nine dollars—ordered another pitcher of iced tea, and sat and watched and smoked and sometimes mumbled to himself.

A baby in a highchair at the table next to his started crying. *Oh, brother. Just my luck.* The father, if it was the father, just smoked his cigarette. Steve shot him a glance and the man looked back at him angrily. *What did I do? Why would you bring a baby to a restaurant anyway?* The mother picked the baby up to calm it down, but it didn't stop crying.

"What did you say?" the man asked.

Steve realized he was asking him. "Nothing. I didn't say anything." *Or did I?*

"Yes, you did. Mind your own business."

I'm trying to, Steve wanted to say. *Asshole.* He got up without looking at the guy, grabbed his check, and hurried to pay the cashier. He checked his watch and saw that he was ten minutes late. By the time he got into his car, he was breaking out in a sweat, which only got worse. He couldn't figure out why the air-conditioning wasn't working. Hot air blew in his face when he turned on the fan. Then he noticed he only had a quarter of a tank of gas and wasn't sure it was enough. A least the doctor's office wasn't far. When he pulled into the parking lot, sweat was running down his face, and he wiped it with the back of his sleeve.

The receptionist sat behind a glass partition. He signed the clipboard and waited until she finally looked up to acknowledge him. "Hi, Steve. How're you doing?"

"I know I'm late."

"Not to worry. Dr. Pandi's running behind today. Have a seat."

He was alone in the waiting room. He sat on one of the cream-colored vinyl couches with chrome arms and legs. Posters on the walls and brochures in cardboard stands advertised the latest medications for mental or mood disorders—Zyprexa, Risperdal, Clozaril. "Prohibits hallucinations, promotes clear thinking, improves concentration, reduces negative symptoms such as lack of motivation or emotion," the advertisements promised. In fine print, a list of possible side effects—

weight gain, high cholesterol, restlessness, nausea, vomiting, constipation, diarrhea, sleeplessness, chronic fatigue, increased blood sugar, liver damage. Steve never read the advertisements. He was depressed enough that he even had to be here. He wondered if he'd ever "snap out of it" and be his old self again. Probably not. Not after twenty-some-

...ing his head. I mean, no. I'm not a criminal."

"Driver's license photos are not so flattering for anyone, Steve," the doctor reassured him.

He followed her plump frame down the hall, into her office. Dr. Pandi sat in the swivel chair near her desk, turning to face Steve. He sat in his usual armchair to her left. Immediately, he told her he never missed taking his meds. Twice a day. Once in the morning and once at night.

She rambled off a list of questions, barely waiting for his response. Was he still working at Clean Sweep? Sleeping too much? Unable to sleep? Hearing voices? How was he doing without his dad?

"I don't hear voices anymore," he lied, "but I guess I sleep too much. Sometimes all day. I miss my dad and mom, but Nancy is with me. It's okay I guess. She cooks for me." He didn't want to tell her he wasn't working anymore.

When she asked him what he did with his time, he told her he didn't do anything.

"What would you like to do?" she asked.

"I can't do anything. I wish I had a college degree, but—"

"Maybe you take one course and see how it goes?"

He wished he hadn't told her now. "Naw, it's too hard to concentrate. And I can't sit still very long. Maybe I'll be ready later."

"But you sit for long time at Friendly's, don't you?"

"But I don't do anything there. It's like being at home." Steve tried to change the subject, to talk about how glad he was that he didn't go to anymore psych units.

"There's a new medication that helps concentration and motivation. Maybe help you want to do something more with life? To feel productive?"

"Productive?" he laughed. "I was a bank messenger once, but I didn't like it. Too much driving. I don't want to work. You don't mean Clozaril, do you?" His parents had tried to talk him into trying it a few years ago, even though they were aware it could cause severe liver damage and possibly be fatal. His mom had figured he didn't have a life, so why not give him at least a few good years, a chance for a normal existence. Besides, if he took the required weekly blood test, any potential danger would be flagged before it became a serious problem. But Steve had refused adamantly.

"No, not Clozaril. I know you don't want that one. Resperadol has very few side effects. Many feel better. I give you prescription and you see me in a month. You call if you have a problem. What do you say?" She began writing out a prescription at her desk. "You gradually reduce the Prolixin that you now take while you introduce Resperadol," she explained, describing the decreases and increases in dosages.

Steve had trouble following her. He started twirling his hair. "Do I have to? I don't know. Do I need to take shots?" He hated needles.

"No, no. It's safer for your liver and no hand tremors."

"But I don't have hand tremors."

"You might if you take Prolixin for many years." She handed him the slip.

Steve left feeling confused. Maybe he should call his sister or talk to Dr. Nora, but he wouldn't see her for another week.

When he got home, he was relieved to find no one was there. Sammy trotted over to him, but receiving no pat on the head or words of welcome, he returned to his bed in Nancy's room. Steve reveled in the coolness of the air-conditioned house, flopped on top of his bed, and fell fast asleep.

—

Nancy picked up her son, Danny, at eight o'clock that evening. She had

When he reached the car, Nancy hustled around to open the back door for him. She saw his clothes stuffed in the bag. "No duffel bag to use?"

"I couldn't find it. Something smells good. I'm starved." He tossed his crutches on the floor in the back, along with the bag of clothes and spotted the bucket of chicken. He ripped off the top and grabbed a leg, eating it as Nancy helped him get settled in the front seat.

Nancy laughed, "We're only five minutes away!"

"Can't wait that long," he cracked. He reached back for the whole bucket, dropped the cleaned bone inside and grabbed another piece. He asked her to stop at the store for a six pack of beer, since it was on the way. "Any kind."

"Maybe tomorrow. Steve's probably waiting for his dinner. Besides, the way you're scarfing that down, it'll be gone by the time I get out of the store."

"Or you could go back after dinner," he said. "I'll buy you some cigs for your trouble." He reached his arm around her shoulder and gave her a little hug. "Cause you're such a good mom."

She smiled back at him. "It's a deal."

They heard the rattled snoring the moment they entered the house.

Danny shook his head. "I think the walls are shaking. How am I going to sleep with that? How do you sleep?"

"Ear plugs. But you'll be upstairs."

Sammy came tearing around the corner to greet them. Nancy scooped him into her arms and said she needed to take him outside. On her way out, she showed Danny the staircase leading to the upper bedroom.

"No way can I get up those," he said. "The steps are too steep and too small."

"Never thought of that," she said. "How about the hide-a-bed in the family room? And there's a TV in there."

"That'll work."

When Nancy came back in, she got paper plates and placed the food containers on the dining room table. Danny suggested they watch TV, so she filled two plates and joined her son in the family room.

By the time Steve woke up, it was dark outside and his stomach was rumbling. He slowly sat up in bed and saw that it was ten o'clock. He wondered if he'd missed dinner. He glanced toward Nancy's room, saw that she wasn't there, and headed to the kitchen. Walking past the half-empty bucket of chicken on the table, he caught a whiff of the unmistakable aroma. He turned on the light and, relieved, spooned what was left in each container onto a paper plate. Heading back to his room, he heard voices and the blare of the TV, so he circled back through the living room and in his best stealth move, peeked slowly around the corner to see who it was.

"Hey, big guy! I see you," Danny called out.

Oh, no. Danny's here, thought Steve. *I forgot.* "Hi, Danny."

"Why don't you grab some dinner and join us?" Nancy asked.

"I'll just eat in my room," Steve said as he walked away, words trailing behind him. "I just woke up. The TV's too loud. I don't like TV."

Danny drained his beer. "Who's he talking to?"

"Steve talks to himself a lot."

"Would you get me another one of these?" Danny held up the empty can.

"Comin' right up." Nancy took the plates and beer cans and went to the kitchen where she found Steve holding a gallon jug of milk. She reminded him to take his evening meds, and he showed her the handful of pills before he threw his head back, popped them in, chasing them down with a few gulps of milk. "You're way ahead of me," she said, as she took a beer out of the fridge.

"I'm sure it wasn't you. That's just what doctors do. Nancy almost suggested calling Sylvia but held her tongue. "When are you supposed to start with the new one?"

"I'm not sure. Probably after I'm finished with the old one. I have six left."

Danny should be gone by then, she thought. "Let's not worry about it now."

Steve went out for his final round of iced tea before Friendly's closed. He got back around eleven. From the garage, he had to pass through the family room where he found Danny asleep on the couch. The TV was still on, wasting electricity. *Just like his mom,* Steve thought. *He probably sleeps with it on all night.* Steve wanted to shut it off, but didn't want to make Danny mad. *Why isn't he sleeping upstairs anyway?*

The next day when Steve woke up and headed to the bathroom he found it occupied, so he went upstairs. When he came back down, Danny was looking through the refrigerator in his Jockey underwear. Steve recoiled at the sight of the metal leg and the naked man in his kitchen—well, almost naked. He couldn't imagine the nerve of Danny to parade around like that in his house.

"Hey, Steve. Can I get you some breakfast?"

"Not unless you get dressed first," Steve said, already in his bedroom by the time he finished the mumbled sentence.

"Or we could go out for breakfast," Danny called out. "My treat."

Steve sat on his bed, contemplating the offer. It sounded pretty good, but he hoped Danny wore long pants to cover his leg. But he couldn't ask him to—that wouldn't be nice. Free breakfast two days in a row. "It's a deal," he yelled back. "I'll drive."

Danny was in the hallway now, outside Steve's door. "You have to drive," he laughed.

They went to Bob Evans, famous for its pork sausage. To Steve's relief, Danny wore jeans and a T-shirt. He felt sorry for him with no leg, or half a leg, and felt lucky that it wasn't him. He couldn't fathom not being able to drive, and he offered to take Danny wherever he needed to go.

"Mighty nice of you, Steve. I don't want to put you out, though. You've done enough by letting me stay at your house."

"No problem."

They had breakfast, puffed away on cigarettes, talked about their athletic days, sports figures, and college football teams. Danny flirted with the waitress, who seemed to like it.

"She sure is a cute one, don't you think? Great knockers."

Steve looked down at his plate, laughing, but nodded in agreement. "I was trying not to stare."

"You can check 'em out without staring, you know. Anyway, lots of women think it's a compliment when you look 'em up and down."

"You mean the trashy ones," Steve said.

"Who cares? You're not going to marry them. I sure wish I hadn't."

"I'll never be married," Steve said. "I wouldn't know how to get to know a woman that way . . . I can't even . . ." Steve poured more iced tea in his glass and wondered how this subject ever started. How had he managed to open his big mouth?

"You mean you can't get it up?"

Steve shot Danny a glance. "Because of my meds. Can we talk about something else?"

"No problem. Let me just tell you that I couldn't either when I was taking a lot of medication for my leg. Or if I've had too much to drink. Have you tried to jack off?"

Steve suddenly felt like talking about this. He never had before, and Danny was so easy-going about it. "In the bathtub I used to, but nothing works anymore."

"I used to do that, too. While I looked at sexy magazines. Sometimes that helps."

house chaplain, and no one tried to thrust an uninvited sexual encounter on him again.

"But do you ever think about it? Having sex?" Danny seemed to be enjoying himself.

Steve wished he'd wipe the grin off his face. "Sure. I think about it."

"I have a few dirty magazines if you want to see them. We could stop by my house to get them."

"I don't know. Maybe. But not if they're really gross. Like porn flicks. The guys in college watched them, but I couldn't."

"I don't think you'll mind these," Danny said. "Let's go."

11

Huge breasts. Nipples. On hands and knees, their bare butts staring you in the face. Lace underwear that you can see through—even pubic hair—and their legs are spread open like they want sex. They're just whores. Steve was dumbstruck.

Danny just kept flipping the pages, pointing to the teasing girls, mouths open, tongues licking their lips, fingers spread on their privates. "Check this one. Now those are tits!"

Steve wanted to stop looking but he couldn't. He thought of his dad's ballpoint pen with the picture of a woman in a black one-piece bathing suit, one hand on her hip, like a beauty pageant contestant. When you turned it upside down, her bathing suit slowly disappeared, just drained right off of her. Steve kept it in his nightstand drawer and took it out every now and then, but it was nothing compared to these. "They're so beautiful. But why would they need to do this?"

"For the money."

"The love of money is the root of all evil. The Bible says so. Maybe I shouldn't look anymore."

"Why not? Don't you like them?" Danny picked up another magazine.

"I like to look, but they're bad . . . it's like devil worship. I might not be able to stop seeing them in my head."

Danny laughed out loud. "So what?"

"I might have bad thoughts."

"That's the whole idea!" Danny lit up a Marlboro and Steve took out a Newport.

With Danny narrating and talking dirty, Steve kept staring at the

pictures, at every thigh, breast, and "pussy"—Danny's word. He began
to sense a slight stirring in his loins, an unsatisfied craving, a feeling he
hadn't had for a long, long time. It frightened him a little, but he won-

to gain balance and finally got up on both legs. "Gotta take a leak." He
nodded at the magazines and smiled. "You can keep those if you want.
You know, give it the ol' college try."

"Maybe I will," Steve replied. Steve believed the devil was inside of
him and always had been, as it was in everyone, lurking, waiting for the
minute you let your guard down or hung out with the wrong people.
Was Danny the wrong people? Probably. Making him look at dirty
pictures and urging him to play with himself again—to masturbate—
proved it. He remembered when he was little and played "doctor" with
his sister, Sylvia, and the neighbor girl across the street. They'd hide in
the walk-in closet upstairs and check each other's "tinkers." He'd get
hard, and he liked it. The girls would laugh, and he would too. That
was before any of them knew about sexual intercourse or masturbation
or orgasm. Come to think of it, he didn't know how babies were made
until the fifth grade when they had sex education in school. A big, fat,
ugly nurse, in a dark blue uniform with a cap to match, drew a uterus
and a penis on the blackboard and a long line showing where the penis
went inside the vagina. He and his friend got kicked out of class because
they couldn't stop laughing. He never looked at his parents in the same
way after that. It seemed so gross to imagine them "doing it." He wished
he didn't want to have sex, but he did, and now more than ever.

Steve took the magazines and stole upstairs to his old room where
nobody would disturb him. He'd been spending more time in his old
room since Danny had moved in. He'd lay on his bed, on top of the

covers because the air conditioner hardly worked up here and it was so stifling hot. He smoked and talked to himself, or to the little boys whose innocent voices came and went, always asking the same thing: "Help us go home. We need to find our home." Steve felt so sorry for them and tried to console them, "It's going to be okay. I'll try to help you find home." But they never seemed to know where home was, so he didn't know how to help. When he didn't hear them for several days, he figured they'd found their way. He had no one else to talk to and found he missed them; they'd kept him company. And then, out of nowhere, they'd be back. He felt comforted and knew they felt it, too. They might giggle and sound happy for a while, but they always ended up asking him the same thing again, and it left him feeling sad.

He stretched out on the bed and undid his pants, reaching under his Jockeys. He held his soft, shriveled penis in his hand and stroked his scrotum with his fingers. With his free hand, he opened a magazine and imagined the beautiful, natural-looking blonde—mouth open slightly, tongue touching her lower lip, with dark, hard nipples—reclining next to him, her legs open, just asking for it. And he wanted to give it to her. He picked up speed, rubbing harder, hoping for some reaction, but it kept flopping from his hand. Even so, the arousal seemed to climb higher and higher and he kept going. Over and over, he retrieved the limp sausage, praying for an erection. Sweat poured off of him and he felt almost light-headed. "You want it, don't you? I'll give it to you," he gasped. The sudden burst from inside took him by such surprise that he cried out as if in anguish. His heart was racing and he thought he was having a heart attack. Semen squirted all over his khakis and dribbled into his palm, down his groin, matting his pubic hair. *My dick never got hard. How can this be?*

He lay there a moment, exhausted, trying to catch his breath. Then he worried that Danny might've heard him. He sat up to listen. Nothing. A wry smile crossed his lips. *I had an orgasm.* The sticky, milky ooze gave off a sweet, fungi smell like clotted cream, a smell he never noticed before. *Probably 'cause I was always in the bathtub.* He didn't like the smell. He looked down at his soiled Jockeys covered with his slime. *Looks like tapioca pudding. Yuk. I hate tapioca pudding.* He got up, letting his pants drop to his ankles and stepped out of them. He glanced back at the magazine with a look of disgust and quickly closed it.

Steve went to the half bathroom and washed his hands several times.

chute along with the Jockeys but realized he didn't want Nancy to find the evidence. *I'll have to wash them! I don't know how to do the laundry. Maybe I could just throw them away.* He decided to figure it all out later. He wadded them into a lump and stuffed them under his bed. He was so tired. He sat on the edge of the bed and lit a cigarette, thinking about what he'd done to himself. It was Danny's fault. He put out his cigarette and decided to throw the magazines away. But it felt so good. *God doesn't get mad as long as you don't hurt somebody else, does He?* He fell back on the bed, his legs dangling over the edge, and mouth open, hands placed gently across his bulky chest, he was out like a light, snoring louder than ever.

A loud rapping on the bedroom door at the base of the steps woke Steve up with a start. He bolted upright and looked around. The magazines were strewn across the bed. He quickly started stuffing them under the mattress.

"Hey, Steve," Danny called out. "You asleep up there?"

What does he want now? Steve grumbled back, "I was."

"Sorry, just wanted to tell you Mom called, and she'll be an hour late."

"So?"

"I just thought if you were going out again, maybe you could take me to get some cigs. I'm out."

He flopped backward on the bed. *Danny's wearing me out. How many more days will he be here?* "Be right down."

—

The next day, the kitchen remodel was finished: white counter tops, white porcelain sink, white tile-like linoleum flooring with small, dark blue squares adjoining each corner, and wallpaper with clusters of fruit and flowers on a white background adorning the walls against the maple wood cupboards. Steve thought the change was remarkable.

Since Steve usually resisted any change in his parent's home and wasn't involved in the remodeling plan, he was relieved when Bill, the contractor, had managed to save the fifty-year-old red-and-white Vitrolite tile that served as the backsplash. "It still feels like the same kitchen, but now it looks classy," he told Nancy. He was proud of the new table and chairs and the hanging light fixture he'd helped select.

"Let's celebrate tonight with my mean pot roast," Nancy said. "And we'll eat in the dining room on real plates!"

That evening, Steve joined Nancy and Danny for dinner, since they weren't eating in front of the TV. As they sat down, the phone rang. Sylvia's voice came over the answering machine, and Nancy hopped up to answer.

"Well, how are you?" Nancy sang.

Sylvia hadn't called the Ohio homestead for at least two weeks and now was a good time. She was feeling more at peace than she'd felt in a long while. Her son, Trevor, had been clean and sober for six months, a milestone for him. He was still in sober living, taking the bus (cars weren't permitted—too much temptation for an addict) to and from work as a waiter in a nice Italian restaurant. In short, he was thriving. Sylvia still hadn't told Nancy about him, however, but thought she would on her next visit in November, the year anniversary of their dad's death.

"Good enough, thanks."

"What's up?" Nancy asked.

"I haven't talked to you guys in a while, and I just wanted to check in." She was glad to hear the kitchen was finished on schedule, asked when the painter was to arrive, and finally how Steve was doing.

"Everything's just hunky dory here," Nancy said. "The kitchen looks

said.

"Doctors. They're all alike," Nancy said.

—

Sylvia never asked Nancy to be responsible about the particulars of his medication. The adjustment to living with Steve and establishing a friendly relationship seemed a tall enough order. She didn't want to overburden her with nursing-type duties and, frankly, wasn't sure she'd be willing or capable. Steve was touchy and easily offended about someone else overseeing what he determined was only his business. Even Sylvia had to approach him with kid gloves when she wanted to verify that he'd filled his pill tray properly. She couldn't blame him. He wasn't sure who to trust, since their parents had handled everything. They were all learning the how, what, who, and where of Steve's life. It was new territory. "I'll call Pandi tomorrow to find out what the med changes are about."

"Sounds like a good plan."

Sylvia asked to speak to her brother, but Nancy wanted to get off the phone before he had a chance to talk to his sister and possibly mention Danny. "He's eating dinner now, but I'll let him know you'll be checking with Dr. Pandi. Don't you worry about a thing."

"Thanks, Nancy. I'll call you when I have more information."

—

A week went by and Danny was still living there. Steve did his best to stay out of his way, but also thought he should stay home and track his movements, especially since Nancy was gone a good part of the day. Danny spent most of the time lying around on the hide-a-bed in the family room, which he never folded away. Maybe he couldn't do it by himself. The TV rumbled constantly in the background. He talked a lot on the phone to his friends or argued with his wife about the kids. Sometimes Steve listened from the living room and got an earful—joking, swearing, yelling—'lowlife talk' his dad would've called it. Back and forth, back and forth Danny went, crutches thumping, the metal leg creaking with each labored step through the narrow stairwell to the tiny kitchen, where he'd stand (too long) in front of the open refrigerator (the food wouldn't stay cold), rummaging around. Steve wondered who was paying for all the food Danny ate and his beer. He always had a beer in his hand. *Probably our money,* he thought.

When Steve did leave the house, he tried to slip away so Danny wouldn't ask to tag along. He had to go through the family room to get to the garage. On the way, he had to pay his respects to Danny, so sometimes he waited for the perfect getaway, like when Danny was in the bathroom. He'd make a beeline to his car. As he backed out the drive, relief would pour through him. *I made it.*

Not only had Danny set up camp in the family room, but the painter had been there for several days, too. Steve could barely stand it. He had hoped the mayhem and the smell would make Danny want to move back home, but no such luck. Danny and the painter seemed to enjoy each other. When Steve retreated upstairs, he could hear their muffled conversations, their laughing it up, and he wondered how the painter would ever get the job done in two weeks. Danny even offered food and beer or to help move some of the furniture, but the painter refused, which made Steve sometimes feel obliged to help. He wasn't a cripple. At least Nancy rearranged her schedule and was home most mornings to assist where needed. Steve wanted to ask Nancy about her son's plans, but he figured it wasn't really his business. And he didn't want her to feel bad—he was embarrassed enough as it was.

Dr. Nora was shocked. "Does your sister know he's living in your house?"

"I haven't told her. And I don't think Nancy has either," Steve answered.

"She needs to know right away. He has no right to live with you. Would you like me to call her?"

Steve brightened. "That'd be great," he said. "I wouldn't want Danny or Nancy to hear me."

—

Dr. Nora called Sylvia early the next morning.

"Steve's showing signs of agitation and muddled thinking due to Danny's constant presence. The situation is delicate for him because he doesn't want to offend Nancy or her son, so he's walking on eggshells, pretending he's fine, but feeling like an outsider in his own home." Dr. Nora explained that Steve's willingness to speak to her openly was a positive step, a cry for help if you will. "He stood up for himself by coming to me, so at some level he knows how to take care of himself. But Danny clearly has to move out, and the sooner, the better."

Sylvia was fuming. How could Nancy bring her drunken son to live with Steve? And leave them alone while she's working? "I'm struggling to understand how Nancy could do this, especially after Dr. Rita pointed out to Nancy that Steve can regress with too much stimula-tion—talking, noise, visitors!"

"She probably convinced herself that her son is 'guy company' for Steve, and her son's in trouble," Dr. Nora said. "Mothers can be in strong denial when it comes to saving their children, even when they're grown."

Sylvia began biting a fingernail. She knew too well the truth in that statement. She'd bailed her twenty-eight-year-old daughter out finan-cially a dozen times and almost had to be held down to leave her son alone. She and Dr. Nora concluded that Danny could stay two more nights, and Sylvia would need to call no later than the following day. She needed the rest of the day to calm down and collect her thoughts, to figure out how to be compassionate toward Nancy yet firm, without getting angry. Nancy was essential to the arrangement for Steve, and she couldn't risk upsetting her. She dreaded the conversation. That night, she told her husband about his sister's bold move, but Adam didn't understand the problem. He took a purely practical approach. "Well, there is enough room for him and Steve likes him. Danny might be good for Steve." His stance surprised her, but she chalked it up to 'blood runs thicker.'

The next morning, still filled with dread, she placed the call. Steve answered, groggy.

"Is Danny there now?" she asked.

"I don't know. He sleeps in the family room. I'm in my room. Did Dr. Nora call you? Oh, yeah. She must have. I didn't." He coughed and apologized for it. "Danny's probably here. He's always here. Do you want to talk to him?"

"No. I want to talk to Nancy."

"Are you mad? Don't be mad when you talk to Nancy. Danny's not so bad. He's her—"

"He shouldn't be there anymore," she said firmly.

"You sound mad, Sylvia. I told Nancy it was okay. He didn't have anywhere to go."

"I understand you wanted to help out, which was very kind of you.

You're a good guy, Steve, but Nancy should've checked with me, too. She stepped over the line."

"What line? Mom used to hang the clothes on the line, remember? But there isn't one anymore. There's a phone line."

"It's okay, Steve. I'll be nice. Will you get Nancy for me?"

"I'll see if she's up."

Sylvia heard the phone drop, rustling, and Steve's faint voice call out to Nancy. She waited, rehearsing how to begin.

Nancy got on the phone. "Hi there. Have you got some good news about Pandi?"

"No news on Pandi. I haven't reached her yet, or rather, she hasn't called me back." She sighed deeply. "I'm actually calling about Danny."

Nancy didn't expect this so soon. She put on her best nonchalant air. "Is there a problem?"

"Well, yes, there is. Dr. Nora called me and was concerned about Steve's welfare. He's not equipped to handle the added stress of someone around him all day and he has become unhappy with Danny living there, so . . . "

"Steve and Danny get along great, and Danny is so easy. I didn't think he'd be a problem for such a short stay," Nancy said quickly, as if grasping for balance as a rug was being yanked out from underneath her.

Sylvia had dropped Dr. Nora's name into to the conversation, so Nancy would see that Steve obviously wasn't as comfortable with the arrangement as she wanted to believe. Sylvia sensed that Nancy was dodging the real issue. "I wish that you'd talked to me about it first, though."

"I didn't want to bother you with my family problems when you have enough to worry about, living so far away. Since it was only for a few days, I didn't see any harm. Just 'til he and his wife sort things out," Nancy said.

"Believe me, I know how hard it is when your kids are struggling and you want to be there for them," she reassured her. She almost mentioned Trevor's problems but didn't want to get off track. "But Dr. Nora was pretty adamant, and it's my job to put my brother's well-being first. Maybe Danny can stay with a friend for a while."

"Of course. I'll see if he can find another place to stay, but I don't know how soon . . . "

Sylvia's patience was tried. "Dr. Rita explained when we all met with her last year how stressful it is for Steve to have too much stimulation, which Danny is. And his drinking sounds excessive. It's a bad combination and not good for Steve."

"Danny may drink a bit, but it's only beer. I'm sorry I didn't ask you. I'd been meaning to talk to you, but what with all that's going on here at the house, it just never came up. I'll talk to him right away. Is another night okay, though?" Nancy asked.

"One more night is fine. Thank you for being so understanding, Nancy, and I hope he can work things out with Becky." Sylvia hesitated, then offered, "It's not really my business, but have you ever talked to him about AA meetings?"

"He'd never go since it's only beer, and he doesn't drive. At least it's not drugs."

"That would be worse," Sylvia agreed. She'd come to realize, whether out of fear of facing the truth or delusional hope the problem would just go away, the mother was the last to know. If Danny was using drugs, she didn't want confirmation while he was living with Steve. And now she wouldn't have to worry—Danny would be gone after tomorrow.

12

For Sylvia's son, in high school, pot smoking had become the problem, not beer. Two years after high school, when she'd found pieces of aluminum foil with black burn streaks in Trevor's bedroom, she knew something was very wrong. She would wake up in the middle of the night, tearful and afraid. She had asked her husband if he knew what they might be. He didn't know, but he suggested she get the foil pieces analyzed at the pharmacy, get Trevor in for a physical, get out of denial, and ask him what he was doing. So she did.

Trevor didn't skip a beat. He said they were hashish marks. "Don't worry, Mom," he tried to assure her. "It's just a stronger form of pot."

Sylvia detected a strategic ploy—if confronted, provide plausible information with an air of nonchalance. So she plunged on, "You're so thin. You look ill, and you sleep till two in the afternoon. I'm taking you to the doctor."

Once she'd made the appointment, she waited anxiously for her older daughter's return from France. Trevor and Alice were five years apart but quite close. Sylvia had hoped he might open up with his sister, and she counted on Alice to help them. When Alice arrived home and saw her brother, she was astounded by his condition.

Sylvia hugged her hard and started to weep. "I'm so glad you're home to help me find out what's going on."

"It's okay, Mom, I'll find out right now," Alice said. She walked down the hall to Trevor's room at the far end of the house. Sylvia heard his door shut and their muffled voices, then abruptly turned and walked quickly back to her bedroom. She flopped down on her king-size bed and hit the remote.

An hour later, Alice entered her mom's room. Sylvia shut off the TV. "I'm afraid to know. But I need to know," Sylvia said.

Alice sat down on the bed by her mom. She pursed her lips and cleared her throat. "I've given him twenty-four hours to tell you, or I will. I pretty much guessed from looking at him. It's not good, but he'll be all right."

That evening, Trevor came to Sylvia. His hair was straggly and he had dark circles under his eyes. He was so thin, he looked skeletal. "I need to tell you something," he said. "Let's go to my bedroom."

He sat on his futon bed and hung his head. "I don't need to go to that doctor appointment. I have to go to rehab."

"I thought maybe," she said. "But I'm relieved and glad you're willing to go." She sat down next to him and held him close. "I love you, honey."

He held her tight and started to cry. "I love you, too, Mom. I'm sorry." He told her he knew about a place that his dealer went to. She said she'd make the call.

Sylvia found out the following day that Trevor needed to be evaluated first. An out-patient facility was nearby in West LA. That afternoon at the facility, Sylvia sat next to her son as he filled out the evaluation forms. She still didn't know his 'drug of choice,' but she assumed it was marijuana or hashish. She glanced down at the form. In the box headed "Substance," she read heroin. Slowly, mechanically, she rose from the chair, excused herself, and, once in the hallway, ran to the restroom and vomited.

Trevor spent his twenty-first birthday in detox. On the second night, he jumped the fence. The treatment center had his wallet, his clothes, and his acoustic guitar in its safe. Within two hours, Trevor returned. He would stay clean for sixty days, then he'd relapse.

His counselor told Sylvia that relapse was part of recovery. "He's an addict. He's one of us. At least he's still here."

Overwhelmed with despair from his relapse, Sylvia lost her focus for daily tasks: unpaid bills piled up; hair, nail, and dental appointments were made and missed; keys appeared in the linen closet and milk ended up in the pantry; she couldn't concentrate enough to read the newspaper. Even her neighborhood looked unfamiliar. Every Sunday and Tuesday evening Sylvia attended 'family day' and parent support meetings at the treatment center, a two-hour drive round trip. Entire mornings passed on the telephone with either the insurance company or other mothers of addicts, or at Al-Anon support meetings for friends and families of alcoholics or addicts.

Trevor had spent three months in residential treatment and another twenty days in a sober living house near the treatment center when he called home to say, "They kicked me out because they thought I used."

"Why did they think that?" Sylvia asked.

Trevor told her it was a long story and asked if she'd come and get him. He had no place to go, he claimed. It would only be for one night then he'd find another sober living house, he promised. So Sylvia agreed. She called his drug counselor, who told her not to let him come home. Instead he'd arrange for Trevor to stay in a homeless shelter. Sylvia ignored his advice. *Maybe he's wrong. Maybe he didn't relapse. They've only known him a few months.*

Trevor was home for four days before he finally admitted he'd used. The only boundary Sylvia was clear about was that he couldn't live at home if he was using drugs. She called sober living houses, but he had to test negative to get in. He tested positive, but he refused to go back to any residential treatment. Sylvia knew what she had to do. She took his house key and his car keys, and she said, "I love you with all my heart, but you can't stay here. Call me when you want treatment again." He left on foot, with only his backpack and no money.

Sylvia's husband, her daughter, and the few friends she'd confided in told her it wasn't her fault, that she'd done all the right things and had always been there for him. *Walk in my shoes,* she thought. She was numb and vacant and guilt-ridden from the years of her haphazard choices that tumbled and tripped over each other: her affair then her divorce from her children's father; her out-of-state move with her children to marry her lover, Anthony, who turned physically abusive (at least they never married); the abrupt move back to Oregon then, ten years later, another move to Los Angeles after marrying Adam only a month after her ex-husband, Tom, was killed in a car accident, when Trevor was sixteen. Wasn't it the mother who was usually to blame for the wayward child? It was payback to her. The "if onlys" of yesterday ricocheted in her mind like ping pong balls in a Keno machine.

The counselor's advice had been clear: "Stop being a mommy or he'll die." But she didn't know how to unlearn her mothering instincts. She'd tried to follow the rules:

Don't give him food.

She did.

Don't give him cash.

She didn't.

Don't let him in the house.

She did.

Change your locks.

She didn't.

Hide your jewelry and your wallets.

She did.

Box up his belongings and put them in storage.

She didn't.

Don't believe anything he says; he's lying.

She did.

Tell him you love him.

She did.

Don't give up.

She didn't.

She was told that he had to "hit bottom," but she had to reach hers before he could reach his. The bottom kept lowering.

Trevor would show up at the front door, and she'd prepare his favorite foods: hamburger pie, boneless, skinless chicken breasts, eggs sunny-side up, or crepes. Sometimes, she'd let him sleep in his own bed. His handsome face was gaunt. He was six-feet tall and weighed 128 pounds. When Sylvia looked into his eyes, she couldn't find him.

He was never angry or belligerent, just vacant. When he'd leave, she'd follow him out the door, watch him walk away, his shoulders hunched, backpack on his emaciated frame, head down, ashamed. Then, as if he knew she was watching him, he'd turn and wave his wave. Just like when he was ten and the pitcher in Little League. Before the game began, he'd look for her in the bleachers, call out to her, and wave.

He'd gone from preppy, athletic kid to a hippie teenager after their move to Los Angeles. But the change seemed to occur slowly. Maybe she'd been too close to see. By the time he was a senior, he'd let his hair grow and had worn it in a ponytail. He worshipped Jimi Hendrix, attended Grateful Dead concerts, and extolled the virtues of hemp. When he moved away to college in Arizona, Sylvia had lost track.

"I only smoke pot. It's just a phase. I'll never use hard drugs. It's stupid," he'd said.

Yet.

"I only smoke heroin. I'll never use needles. I'm afraid of needles."

Yet.

"I'll never pawn my guitars."

Yet.

"I'll never steal."

Yet.

The past two years had been a series of yets. He'd stolen tips from restaurant tables and been arrested three times for possession. Four times, he'd said he couldn't go on anymore and requested treatment. She'd taken him to the hospital for the usual three- to seven-day detox, or the methadone clinic for his daily dose.

Some things she learned quickly. While he'd been in hospital detox, she double checked his backpack for drug paraphernalia the staff might have missed: a dirty spoon, a box of baking soda, a yawning paper clip with carboned tips, an empty Bic pen, cotton balls, or sugar packets. Sometimes she educated the staff.

She brought him oatmeal raisin cookies and iced mochas. Sometimes he was too drugged to feed himself, and she spoon-fed him his meal. Or he'd have wet his pants staggering to the bathroom, and she'd take his clothes home to wash. She often waited by his bedside, watching him drift off to sleep, curled in a ball, shaking, methodically stroking his childhood blankie that rested under his cheek. When he was twelve years old, he'd laughingly said that when he grew up and carried a briefcase to work, he'd be the only one to open it and have his blankie inside. The hospital detox staff loved him. His high school buddies had long disappeared.

Somewhere in between, under the guidance of an addiction medicine specialist and armed with a bag full of prescription medications, she'd tried to detox Trevor at home, all by herself. It was the worst nightmare she'd ever had.

That harrowing experience—witnessing drug withdrawal firsthand—had brought the reality of the disease home, literally. The initial ten hours had been somewhat smooth, and she never let him out of her sight. Trevor went along with her efforts to keep him occupied: they played cards, watched their favorite movies (*Lost In America*, *A Sure Thing*), cooked or ordered take-out, tracked the medication schedule, and oddly enough, actually had a pretty good time together. But when the grip of physical withdrawal became increasingly intense, and he couldn't sit still, she knew she had to get him out of the house. Sylvia drove him around town then to the beach for a long walk. Trudging in the sand in a gray afternoon drizzle, he quietly, apologetically admitted that he didn't want to be sober after all, that he didn't think he could ever be sober. Of course, she tried to convince him otherwise.

When they returned home, he said he needed to call his dealer, and the insanity took hold. Sylvia ran through the house grabbing all the phone receivers, hiding them in drawers, cupboards, and closets, with Trevor close on her tail. He finally locked himself in the bathroom. While she banged on the door pleading and crying, he was shooting up—somehow under her watch he'd managed either to score heroin or to access a hidden stash. What she'd heard so many times before had now come true for her—they get high and we get crazy. Trevor went back to living on the streets.

Maybe she'd finally hit her bottom and accepted that there was nothing she could do but get out of his way. She was powerless to cure her son. Slowly, she learned to embrace the mantra, "Relapse is part of recovery."

The last time he'd been arrested, he ended up in jail and had called her in the middle of the night. When she asked him what happened, he said he was arrested for having only one headlight. She didn't believe him and told him so. She had reminded herself to never talk logic with an addict. She thought of the Sepulveda joke she'd heard in a treatment center, where the cop pulls over a normal person driving under the influence on Sepulveda Boulevard in Los Angeles. When he goes before the judge, who admonishes him that he could've killed someone, the normal person is very apologetic, saying he'd never do it again and is ashamed of himself. When the cop pulls over the addict or alcoholic driving under the influence, and he goes before the judge who admonishes his behavior, the addict thinks, *I should never have taken Sepulveda.* Trevor had finally fessed up to Sylvia, "They searched me and found marijuana and some wrappers."

She pictured the empty, once mysterious, crinkled wrappers she used to find strewn in his bathroom drawers, his pants pockets, and backpack. Later she learned that the two-by-two inch opaque plastic held white powder (cocaine) or black tar-like balls (heroin). *Which wrappers had the cops found this time?* she wanted to ask.

He'd begged Sylvia to bail him out of jail. She refused. She told herself she had made progress. She used to rescue him, but she'd learned to put one foot in front of the other, to take it one day at a time, and to live her day. She had graduated from a fetal position to upright, though catatonic. She still looked away when passing young mothers with bright-eyed, toe-headed toddlers in their arms, chubby hands clutching tight. She learned what to avoid in order to stay upright: old photo albums, depressing movies, parents of his friends, his closet where his robe hung next to his golf shirts and his old soccer shoes still caked with dirt. She no longer avoided the UCLA pool where she swam laps surrounded by healthy, vibrant students so close to her son's age.

Trevor finally wanted to go back to residential treatment. Even though he'd stayed clean for six months, she'd lived with so much pain and crushing disappointment that she tried to block out any thoughts of the future, a nowhere place filled with dashed expectations. But she still had hope for Trevor, and she chose not to suffer. She played golf again, took voice lessons, went on trips with her husband, reached out to her daughter, and enrolled in creative writing classes, which she loved. Writing became the only place she could get lost in time, unaware of the passing hours.

Because Steve's situation had been thrust upon her when her son's addiction appeared most hopeless, she decided it wasn't a coincidence. What, at first, seemed to demand more from Sylvia than she thought she could handle had surprisingly turned into an essential distraction from her son (essential for both their sakes). Sylvia's ongoing involvement was vital to Steve's growth toward some degree of independence, whereas her son's survival was more assured without it.

13

Pills lay strewn haphazardly at one end of the dining room table next to the half-filled pill tray. Amber-colored vials, lids off, scattered at random, stretched across the table's width, and Steve sat hunched over the disarray, trying to make sense of the recent changes Dr. Pandi had made to his dosages. Sorting and counting, counting and sorting. *From ten milligrams of Prolixin to five? One pill instead of two? Thirty milligrams Resperadahl instead of five Prolixin? Can't be. That's too much. Three hundred milligrams Lithium. No change. But there aren't enough pills to fill the tray! And there should be, I think. Start over.* He tried different combinations to make it work. Nothing made sense, and now the whole morning had gone by. He was sweating so heavily that droplets fell into the open slots of the tray, and he started trembling. He tried to control it, to steady himself, but the more he tried the worse it got, and the small pile of pills sitting in his open hand sprinkled onto the floor. He stooped down, scrunching his face to see where they'd landed—too far out of reach—he had to get on his hands and knees to retrieve them. Breathing hard, he grunted and struggled and grabbed a few, and then spotted several more wedged between the carpet and the heat register. As he reached, his glasses slid off of his nose, dropping onto the carpet.

"Shit! Goddammit!" He flung the pills in his hand against the wall and flipped onto his back staring up at the underside of the table. He closed his eyes. He lay there a long time trying to calm down, maybe even dozed off while he thought about calling the pharmacy, his sister, Dr. Pandi, or Nancy. But what could they do? If they tried to explain it to him, he wouldn't get it anyway. Pandi would want him to come to her office. No way. *What's the use? I give up. This is too hard.* He didn't feel right, something was off. He heard noises and wondered if someone was in the house. He thought someone was trying to tell him something, but he couldn't quite make out the words or recognize the voice.

"Nancy? Danny?" But no one answered. "Oh, right. Danny's gone. Unless he came back. Danny? Is anybody there?" Nothing. Maybe it was Sammy, but the dog was in Nancy's room and the door was closed. *Sammy's too quiet. What if he's dead?* His stomach rumbled. His mouth was parched. *I'm dying of thirst. I need iced tea. And a hamburger. I need to get out of here.* Glasses in hand, he scooted out from under the table and went to his room to find his wallet. He glanced in the mirror on his way in. *When did I get so fat? My neck, my neck, I don't even have one. And this gut!* He knew the medication made him gain weight. Maybe he could get thin again if he didn't take it, and get an erection. *No woman will ever want me if I can't get it up.* He combed his unwashed hair and tucked his tight-fitting navy blue polo shirt—which only emphasized his protruding belly—into his wrinkled, pocket-torn khakis, the cuffs hitting just at the ankles. He cinched his belt tighter to make himself look a little thinner, but now his belly hung over the belt, so he loosened it a notch.

More confidant now that he had purpose and a place to go, like most people, he was ready to head to his favorite hangout, where he knew he fit in, where they paid attention to what he had to say when he felt like talking, where he felt good when he remembered to tip the waitresses or had enough money to, which reminded him. *Where's my wallet?* And the search began.

It wasn't on the nightstand or the chest of drawers or under the bed. He wandered from room to room, trying to retrace his steps, but he couldn't remember where he was last. *What if I left it at Friendly's? Maybe I should call.* He went through coat pockets and the car—the floor, under the seats—and back through the house two more times. Defeated, he tromped into the living room and, slumping into his favorite chair, felt the uncomfortable, unmistakable bulge in his back pocket. He jumped up, dug his hand in his pocket, and pulled out his wallet. "I had it all the time. I'm such a dumb shit!" He shouted. He checked to make sure no money was gone, as if it had been missing or stolen and returned—ten dollars. More than enough. Off he went to Friendly's.

—

When Nancy got home and saw the dining room table, she was worried. She wondered if Sylvia ever spoke to Dr. Pandi and decided to give her a call. She left a vague message saying all was well, but Steve's pills looked a little disorganized. Then she waited for Steve to come home, or for Sylvia to call her back. She thought about dinner—*Sloppy joes. They're easy, and Steve loves them.* There were buns in the freezer. Potato chips. She grabbed the instant packaged sauce from the cupboard to add to the ground beef. While it was browning, she took care of Sammy.

The new carpeting was to be installed the next day, which meant the house would be in an uproar again, with furniture moved from room to room, so she'd have to move some of Steve's things back upstairs. He'd been up there a lot lately, she noticed. Maybe a habit that started with Danny around, but she hadn't checked the upstairs for who knows how long and wasn't thrilled with the idea. Who knew what she'd find up there?

She stirred the sloppy joe mixture then headed to Steve's bedroom now on the main floor. Dirty clothes everywhere. Socks, Jockey underwear (which she didn't want to touch), shirts with dark rings at the neck, shorts, all either dropped on the floor or draped across the chair and bed. *Oh brother. He just doesn't get the need to wash. His clothes or his body.* She bundled all of it, carried it to the laundry chute in the kitchen, and tossed two or three items at a time into the small opening. *And I'll have to do his laundry, again. He never did learn how to do his own.* She'd tried to show him, to keep it as simple as possible; he'd made a few attempts without any problem, but not often enough to become routine. Every time she pointed to the designated washday on the calendar (Sylvia's idea), he just moaned and said he was too tired and "Let's do it later," but later never came. Even the twice weekly shower days were avoided. As if scheduling tasks on a calendar would get Steve in the habit of taking care of himself. *What a joke!* Sylvia was clueless. Did she really think Steve might suddenly take an interest in doing housework? Like making his bed, taking out the trash, or getting his car washed? (Washing anything seemed out of the question.)

Nancy grabbed some of his clothes from the drawers and closet, then some toilet articles from the bathroom, and headed upstairs. The temperature seemed twenty degrees hotter in the attic bedroom, stifling. She turned on the floor fan and put the clothes in a chest of drawers. The twin beds on either side of the center windows were rumpled, the covers askew, pillows balled up. She set the toilet articles on one of the beds and wiped a finger across the nightstand, looking disgustedly at the thick, gray smudge of dust it picked up. Hands on hips, she stared at the work to be done, wondering where to begin, how she'd ever get out of this living arrangement, and when she'd meet the man to whisk her away. She noticed a funny smell and saw what looked like khakis sticking out from under the bed. She reached under and pulled out the wadded up pants and underwear. "Ew!" The stains and smell were unmistakable. Steve was masturbating? Holding the soiled clothes at arm's length, she strode to the bathroom, turned on the light, and shoved them down the laundry shoot. Another stronger odor caught her off guard and she lifted the toilet lid. She reared back, covered her nose, and reached quickly to flush it down. *Christ, I need some fresh air.* She took off down the stairs, called Sammy, and they dashed outside to the backyard.

By the time she went back inside, the sloppy joes were burned, but Steve was sitting in the living room hunched over a paper plate gobbling down the first of two overflowing hamburger buns.

"Hey, big guy. I see you found dinner."

He barely looked up, with a scowl, grunted, sloppy joe plopping off the sides of his bun, and mumbled something about he liked to be left alone while he's eating. She watched as the sandwich droppings dribbled off his plate onto the carpet. She held her tongue. *New carpeting tomorrow anyways.* "Sorry I burned the dinner," she said.

"Tastes good."

She started toward her bedroom and glanced down at the pill mess on the dining room table. She wanted to ask him if he was confused but decided to wait until he was finished eating. "Can I get you anything else? Potato chips? A glass of milk?"

"I can get it myself."

⸺

Sylvia hadn't heard back from Steve after leaving him a message a few days ago, so she decided to try him again.

As luck would have it, he answered on the first ring. "Steve! I'm glad I caught you. I left a message the other day."

"I wasn't here. I didn't see it," he said in a deadpan voice.

She tried to engage him in idle talk before the business at hand, but he wasn't in the mood. "I spoke to Dr. Pandi, and she explained your medication changes to me." Sylvia didn't tell him how frustrated she was after speaking to his psychiatrist, that Pandi wouldn't talk to her at first, saying how important it was for Steve to manage his medication on his own. Pandi talked out of both sides of her mouth. Hadn't she told Sylvia and Scott that Steve would never be independent? And now she's suggesting he needed to learn just that? She'd called Dr. Nora, who gave her a recommendation for another psychiatrist, but a change couldn't take place until Sylvia was back in Ohio, which wasn't until November. "Can we go over this together?" Sylvia asked.

"Now?" he responded.

"I think we'd better. Do you have a piece of paper to write it down? And maybe we should get Nancy on the phone, too. She can make sure—"

"You're going too fast. Nancy isn't my doctor."

"Of course not, but—"

"She doesn't know anything about my meds."

"That's why I wanted her to help—"

"I don't need any help. I don't need meds either. Too confusing. Doctors are all alike. Nancy said so."

Was he disassociating or whatever the shrinks called it? Losing track? Off his meds? She wondered if he was hearing voices again. "Steve?"

"What?"

"You're right. Doctors are all alike. Remember what the nurse told you in the hospital a long time ago?"

"You'll stay out of the hospital if you take your meds," he spoke in a singsong, I-don't-buy-it-anymore tone.

"Hasn't that been true?"

"Hasn't what been true?" he asked.

Shit, he's not following anything. "That you've been taking your meds regularly and you haven't had to go back to the hospital."

Moments passed. "Yes," Steve relented. "I guess so."

She let out a quiet sigh of relief. "So, let's write down exactly what Pandi told me. Okay?"

"Okay."

Sylvia decided not to press the issue of Nancy. She'd tell Nancy afterward. Steve said each word out loud as he wrote it down. At least he was taking the time with her to understand each dosage reduction and corresponding increase of the new medication, and he asked to read it all back to her to be sure he'd gotten it right.

When Nancy got on the phone, Sylvia asked her to write it down, too, and to check the pill tray regularly. "I never anticipated you having to do this, but it's too important to let him flounder on his own, sorting out the change."

"You're so right. No problem," Nancy said. "I'll do my darnedest." She told Sylvia about the new carpet being installed the next day and that, within a few days, all would be spic and span. "Maybe it'll even lift Steve's spirits."

"Has he been down, lately?"

"A little out of sorts is all," Nancy said. "I think he's been unsettled about the meds."

"I really appreciate your help with this. Will you call me in a day or so to let me know if he's on track again?"

"I sure will," Nancy said.

—

After they hung up, Nancy went to the dining room where Steve sat with his vials and the large scrawl of his scribbled notes stretching at a diagonal across the page of the legal pad. She suddenly felt sorry for him, his struggle to get through the day, sort through the mixed up, crowded thoughts that must overwhelm him constantly. "How about if I write down the med changes on an index card, Steve? Then you can look at it every time you fill your tray."

His forlorn, troubled expression seemed to relax. "Thanks, Nancy."

Nancy found several four-by-six index cards in the desk in the family room then she pulled out a chair and sat next to Steve.

"You're crowding me," he said.

She scooted farther down and started to copy her notes. "Let's compare what you wrote down with what I have. I want to make sure I didn't make a mistake."

He turned the pad so she could look. He named each medication, the dosage, and when to take them—morning or evening or both. He told her what they were for. "The Resperdahl keeps the voices away, same as the Prolixin, but that's what Pandi is changing. Lithium keeps my moods stable." He painstakingly dropped each pill into the slots as he spoke.

"You sure know all about it!" she said.

"I guess I do."

"Thanks for teaching me," Nancy said.

Steve gave her a closed mouth smile. "You're welcome."

After he'd finished, Nancy asked, "How about a brownie? I brought some home from the store."

He beamed. "Great!"

"We deserve a reward for our hard work, don't you think?"

"I like rewards," Steve smiled.

14

Steve's moods were spiraling downward. He avoided eye contact and spent more and more time in his room with his door closed, only coming out to eat and sometimes not even then. Some days, he didn't leave the house at all. Nancy heard him talking to himself at all hours of the night. *He's like an infant. His days and nights are turned around,* she thought. At Sylvia's request, she'd been checking his med tray every day and leaving him the usual reminder note, to no avail. He missed his morning dose for three days straight and two evening doses still sat in the tray—the flaps were down. Finally, she called Sylvia with a full report.

"How long has this been going on?"

"About a week. It's hard to know exactly," Nancy said. "He says he doesn't feel good on his new medication. Maybe that's why he's not taking it."

Sylvia felt a knot in her stomach—a week? She knew it took at least two weeks to a month for a medication change to be effective. Each person reacted differently, and finding the cocktail brew that worked was hit and miss. Had it been two weeks yet? She chastised herself for not keeping track of the dates, and she was angry that Dr. Pandi wasn't monitoring him closely. It was the job of his doctor to schedule frequent appointments to check his reaction to the new antipsychotic, or at least to verify that Steve understood how to slowly introduce the new one. He was doing fine before, and he didn't have hand tremors, which was the reason Pandi said she took him off of Prolixin. Even though Sylvia didn't trust Pandi to do right by Steve, Dr. Pandi was all they had at the moment.

"I think he needs to see his psychiatrist right away. I'll call her office, but I may need you to take him, if you can."

"Well, sure," Nancy agreed, sounding rattled. "Do you think he'll let me?"

"I don't know. Maybe call Dr. Nora as a backup." Sylvia wondered why Nancy hadn't called Dr. Nora when Steve was obviously going downhill then realized it was Dr. Rita whom Nancy had met when she first moved in, not Dr. Nora. It was Dr. Rita who'd told Nancy to call for any situation that might arise. She couldn't expect Nancy to know what to do when even she had a hard time deciding whether to call the psychiatrist or the psychologist. Christ, she was floundering herself. Maybe she should fly to Ohio before November. Or maybe Scott could go. "I'd better talk to Steve first. Would you get him?"

"He's not here—he went to Friendly's," Nancy said. "Maybe that's a good sign. First time in a few days."

Sylvia said she'd call Dr. Nora rather than have Nancy call her, because she wanted to discuss her recommendation for the new psychiatrist and arrange an appointment. If not right away, in the near future. But first, she'd contact Dr. Pandi.

"Just let me know what you want me to do," Nancy said, relief easing her voice. "I'll stay right by the phone until I hear back from you."

—

Hanging up the phone, Sylvia just wanted to crawl into bed and burrow under the covers, or watch movie after movie and not think anymore. How much could a person take before they really gave up? But she wouldn't—she couldn't. Instead, she went into overdrive. She wondered what her parents had done or would have. This wasn't the first time Steve was off meds, but in past episodes her parents had skimmed over the details. "He won't get out of bed," was all she'd gotten from them. What prompted them to commit Steve to a psych ward? How did they know it was time? The only volatile episode she'd witnessed was during a visit with her kids, when he knocked the pill tray out of her dad's hand and ended up yelling in the driveway at no one in particular. The police came, and Steve went willingly to the local institution to be stabilized. Other than that, she really had no idea what to expect. How paranoid could he get? She wondered if it was true that the most dramatic symptoms taper off with age. Was that just hearsay? Her hunch was that nobody really knew what to expect. Not even the experts, who straddled the fence with, "Each case is unique to the individual." Sylvia started making the necessary phone calls.

Dr. Pandi was out of town. Another psychiatrist was on call, and Sylvia left a message. Then she left a message for Dr. Nora. And then she waited. She called Nancy to tell her she was waiting to hear back, and then she waited some more. She tried not to exaggerate the situation. Steve wasn't ranting and raving in the streets. He wasn't threatening anyone. He was just reclusive. Sylvia still felt shaky. He couldn't be off his meds much longer, or he might lose all sense of reality.

She heard back from Dr. Nora first, who said she'd immediately call another psychiatrist she collaborated with regularly. Dr. Nora was sure the psychiatrist she knew would see Steve, if not that afternoon, then no later than the next day. She said she'd go to Friendly's or to his home to find him. As long as Steve knew that Sylvia was behind the decision, Dr. Nora said she was certain he'd cooperate. If need be, she'd rearrange her schedule to accompany Steve to the appointment. Sylvia was astounded. To have a professional she could trust, who cared enough to act on Steve's behalf, seemed to lift her burden physically.

"Dr. Nora, you're a godsend to me," Sylvia said.

"I can only imagine the emotional load you're carrying, being so far away," she responded. "And your father hasn't been gone even a year yet. You can take a breath, Sylvia. You're allowed."

With Dr. Nora's heartfelt words, Sylvia's wall came tumbling down. She cried in relief—to be given permission to breathe, to receive expert advice she trusted. When had she started expecting herself to have all the answers, make all the decisions, fix every problem? When did she start feeling that as soon as one shoe dropped, she had to be ready for the other one? It seemed like forever. Why was she always in charge?

The more she took on (or had dumped on her), the more tightly she seemed to hold on, unable to let go. Maybe Steve was the lucky one. He'd probably outlive them all.

—

Steve was sitting in his usual spot, hunkered down in the red vinyl booth at Friendly's. He didn't need to order his iced tea. The waitresses knew to bring a pitcher and a glass when he walked through the door. He puffed on one cigarette after another, staring down at the table. The restaurant was crowded, and at the table next to him sat a noisy four-some of twentysomethings with a fussy toddler. Steve scowled and mumbled and gave sidelong, dirty looks. *A bunch of rowdies, lowlifes. I hate kids. Crying, whining, shrieking. Who brings kids to a restaurant? There oughta be a law.*

One of the men, a burly tattooed guy with a moustache and an atti-tude, snarled in Steve's direction. "Who do you think you're talking to?" The other three snickered.

"Just wanna drink my iced tea in peace," Steve said, sure they were talking about him, making fun of him. He thought he heard the woman call him a loser. Then a retard or a looney. They were laughing at him now.

"Then shut the fuck up!" the guy said.

"Fuck you," Steve said under his breath.

"What'd you say?"

"Nothin'," Steve said, focused on pouring more tea into his glass.

The guy stood up and hovered over Steve. "What's your problem?"

A waitress scuttled away and flagged Woody, the manager.

"You're the one with a problem," Steve said, launching into rambling incoherence about jerks with tattoos jerks with kids jerks allowed in family restaurants jerks who wore T-shirts in public. The whole restau-rant seemed to freeze into a wide-eyed hush.

Woody rushed to the table and, turning his back on Steve, asked the guy to sit down. He spoke quietly, making a circle with his index finger to his head, saying that Steve was, "you know," and didn't mean any harm, just ignore him. Grumbling that crazies shouldn't be allowed to harass people, the guy eased back into the booth.

Woody turned to Steve and gently placed a hand on his shoulder, but Steve shrugged it off without looking up. "Why don't you go home and come back later?" Woody suggested.

"I haven't finished my iced tea," Steve said.

Although Steve had been coming in daily for over fifteen years, and the ice cream restaurant sat on a busy road near the freeway entrance, most of the customers—and even some of the staff—didn't know Steve or his family. None of them lived in his Silver Lake neighborhood. Steve had never caused any trouble, he always paid his bill, and he left a tip for the waitress, but his odd behavior made Woody leery of him. The days when Steve was downright surly, snapping at the waitress, scowling and mumbling under his breath, unshaven, hair greasy, shirt torn, were the days Woody kept a watchful eye from the back of the restaurant, by the dirty dish bin, where he could appear to be busy. That's when he steered clear of Steve, just hoping he'd leave. Woody felt sorry for Steve, but worried that he was a loose cannon. Woody wished he knew someone to contact, like the sister Steve talked about, or the woman who was staying with him now that his parents were gone. Shoot, he didn't even have Steve's home phone number. "Maybe you've had too much iced tea, Steve," he said hesitantly.

"Fuck you, Woody."

Woody had never seen Steve so obstinate and angry, and he couldn't risk an altercation in his ice cream parlor. "I think you'd better leave."

Steve glared at him. "I told you. I'm not ready to leave."

Woody, a scrawny, freckled redhead over the age of fifty, tried to put on a stern posture. "You have to leave or I'm calling the police."

Steve scoffed, mocking him, "No way will you call the police. You're such a joke." He remained in his seat, sipping from his straw. The people at the adjacent table watched and listened. Humiliated, Woody left the table to make the call. Then he returned to Steve's table. Shoulders back with an effort to stand tall, he sternly warned Steve, "The police will be here in ten minutes, since you won't leave willingly. Don't come back for six months."

"What?" Steve was shocked. "What did I do?"

"Just leave now, Steve. The police are on their way."

Steve scooted out of his booth, stuffed his cigarettes in his jacket, and, head down, walked outside. Once on the front sidewalk, he realized he left without paying. *What if they think I'm trying to skip on my bill?* He went back inside. All eyes were on him. Woody stood behind the cash register with his arms across his chest, about to speak, when Steve held out a few dollars, stammering that he forgot to pay. Woody waved him off saying it was on the house. He almost apologized, but Steve hurried back out the double glass doors. He felt for his keys, then worried he'd left them inside. When they jingled in his pocket, he kept moving. As he stepped into the parking lot, the police cruiser pulled up. Steve shuddered and hoped he could get away before they tried to make him go with them. Two policemen quickly got out, greeting Steve politely by name—the police knew Steve no matter where they were from—asking if the problem was taken care of. Steve took a deep breath and forced a meek smile. "All taken care of, officers. No problem. I'm leaving."

Steve was unlocking his car when he heard a woman calling his name. He turned and sighed in relief. "Dr. Nora! What are you doing here?"

15

Dr. Nora decided not to tell Steve the real reason she was there. It was better to engage him gradually, or he might dig in his heels. "I thought I'd grab some lunch. Would you like to join me?"

"Woody kicked me out!" Steve blurted. "He even called the police!"

She'd seen him talking briefly to the police as she pulled into the lot, but she'd assumed he was just being polite and deferential, out of his underlying paranoia that they might be after him. She was taken completely by surprise. "What happened?"

Steve looked off beyond the parking lot, his eyes frozen in a stare of sullen disbelief behind his thick-lensed glasses. "This guy—rough, tattoos on his arms—was laughing at me." Suddenly animated, he thrust his arms outward in innocence, as if pleading, and looked directly at Dr. Nora. "Then he got mad. I didn't do anything!"

Dr. Nora felt a familiar anger rise inside at the pervasive ignorance and injustice toward the mentally ill. She would bet money that Steve wasn't at fault, even if his meds were a little out of whack. To her, his behavior was more civil than most 'normal' people and often under more trying circumstances than one could imagine. Day after day, the mentally unbalanced struggled to put one cohesive thought in front of another just to perform a basic task, to live like other people and strive to appear normal to the rest of the world. Very few people had understanding or empathy for a disability that wasn't physical, one they couldn't see, even though the physical evidence was widely visible in every city. Homelessness, drug addiction, and violent crime often stemmed from the untreated population—and the prisons were filled with them. *Would people ever wake up?* she wondered. She couldn't deny that biographies like *Beautiful Mind* helped increase awareness of schizophrenia, but in truth, the genius, "beautiful" mind of John Nash—who won a Nobel in Economics and remained for the most part accepted and cloistered in academia—was a rare example. She was frustrated that mental illness still carried a stigma and still seemed to come last on the list for government monies or fundraisers. She'd tried in her small way to help, spearheading programs for the local AMI chapter then running a halfway house until it lost funding. Weary of the futile struggle with the bigger picture, she decided to work one on one, as an advocate for the individual, with the various "Steves" in her own little corner.

"Do you want me to go in and talk to the manager?" she asked.

Steve shook his head. "I can't come here again, and I don't want to." A short silence ensued then he pursed his lips and raised his eyebrows. "We could go to Pizza Hut—it's right next door. Their iced tea isn't as good, but I love their pizza. Maybe you don't like pizza."

Dr. Nora smiled and said that sounded fine. She loved pizza, too. She had to marvel at his ability to adjust so quickly, though she was not ruling out her arrival time as a factor either. Somehow Steve had what it took to adapt, if even in an innocent, Magoo-like way. Perhaps it was due to his overall willingness and desire to "do the right thing," which he probably learned early on from his parents and the tight-knit community he grew up in. Come to think of it, not unlike John Nash, Steve was accepted—or maybe tolerated—and cloistered, too, in a unique way. His situation was also a rarity. Whatever set him apart from other severe schizophrenics, she had hope that, in the long term and along with his siblings' support, he might eventually be able to live by himself. At the moment though, she had to convince him, cautiously, to go with her to meet a new psychiatrist. The appointment was in an hour, and they needed to stop by his house first to bring all of his medication.

They drove their respective cars the two hundred feet next door. Dr. Nora took her moment alone to call Sylvia and let her know she'd found Steve and had set up an appointment. She'd call her back when she had more information. Sylvia suggested that if Steve wanted encouragement from her or just a stamp of approval, she'd be available to talk to him.

—

Sylvia then called Nancy but there was no answer. She left a message. An hour passed and Nancy called her back. After Sylvia filled her in, she asked Nancy if she wouldn't mind being on standby until after Steve's appointment, even though Sylvia couldn't think of a particular reason why.

"Um, okay," Nancy said. There was a pregnant pause. "It's my day off and I have a few errands, like take Sammy to the groomers and later I was going to meet a few girlfriends to have a drink, but I can wait on that."

"I'd really appreciate it, Nancy," Sylvia said.

"I'm sure surprised that Dr. Nora is so devoted."

"I am, too, but I have no idea what's above and beyond the call of duty for a therapist."

"Believe me, this is way above," Nancy said. "When Danny lost his leg in the car accident, he needed all kinds of therapy, and I had to push for his rights for proper care through the whole mess. There was no one like Dr. Nora."

Sylvia doubted the circumstances were similar enough to make the comparison but got her point.

"I think I hear Steve coming in—yep, and Dr. Nora. I'd better go," Nancy said.

After they hung up, Sylvia tried to pin down what she felt, but her thoughts were all over the map. Relief that Dr. Nora had jumped in and taken charge. Anger with Dr. Pandi, who never called her back and left Steve to fend for himself. Helplessness living so far away and unable to attend the session with the new psychiatrist. Mostly she felt unsettled about the future. Then she thought of Scott. She needed him now—his calm voice of reason to settle her down, his innate ability to prioritize, much like her dad always seemed able to do. Sylvia could count on Scott to be there for her whenever she asked. So used to handling everything herself, being in charge and taking control, sometimes she simply forgot to ask him. She picked up the phone.

—

Helping Steve recognize that his thinking was confused, that his perception was distorted, and that he needed immediate help was a tricky endeavor, even for Dr. Nora, akin to helping a functioning alcoholic recognize his drinking was out of control. But Steve couldn't get "sober" and reflect on his own behavior. Without the proper balance of meds, his reasoning ability would worsen, until all sense of reality and time were blurred. Increasing paranoia usually set in, heightening his distrust of others and his fear they were conspiring against him. Dr. Nora knew it was critical that Steve's medication be adjusted as soon as possible.

With Sammy in tow, dancing around her feet, Nancy greeted them as they entered the house, introducing herself to Dr. Nora. "You sure are a lifesaver, I'll tell you that."

"What do you mean?" Steve asked. "Lifesaver? She's not a lifeguard, you know."

Dr. Nora chuckled at Steve's misinterpretation and looked warmly at Nancy, who was obviously doing her utmost to be positive. "We're just taking it one step at a time. If you'll excuse us, Steve and I need to take a look at his meds."

"Of course you do. I'll just duck into my bedroom, get back to my video game. Holler if you need anything," Nancy said scuttling off, Sammy on her heels.

Steve guided Dr. Nora to the dining room where his med vials lay scattered across the table. She gazed at the disarray, wondering how he could ever make sense of them.

"Steve, I have an idea. You know I don't prescribe medication. I'm not qualified for that."

"Because you're not a psychiatrist, right?" He stared over her head at the old sorority photo of his sister. "Sylvia doesn't look like that at all anymore. When did she get so old?"

Dr. Nora chuckled. "We all get old, Steve. But you're right, I'm not."

"You're not what?" he asked.

"I'm not a psychiatrist, so I can't prescribe meds."

He rolled his eyes and sounded indignant. "I know you're not. That's why I have to see Dr. Pandi."

"Exactly right. Since your meds are a little mixed up, and Dr. Pandi is out of town, I thought we might visit a psychiatrist I know who could help us sort them out."

"You mean right now?"

"The sooner the better, don't you think?"

"Not much, I don't," Steve chuckled, thinking he'd made a joke, but she wasn't laughing. "It's kind of sudden. I don't know."

"Do you agree that the changes in your meds have become confusing?" she asked.

He looked down at the floor, as if disappointed in himself. "Yeah. I don't know what to take."

"And you know how important it is for you to take them, don't you?"

"Yes, so I can stay out of the psych unit," he said.

She didn't want to make him nervous by explaining that psychiatric hospital stays needn't be threatening. While some mentally ill people learn to identify their symptoms themselves and actually inform their doctors when they feel they need a few days in the hospital, Steve was still far from that mindset.

"Mostly, your meds help you lead a more normal life. That's been your goal. Why don't you get a plastic grocery bag to put these in so you can show them to my psychiatrist friend."

"Friend?" Steve stood a moment trying to sort it out, as if wondering who would want a psychiatrist for a friend. "Are you going with me?"

"Of course. I'll drive and stay right by your side, Steve."

"I guess it's okay, then."

He turned toward the kitchen when Nancy suddenly appeared. "Let me get the grocery bag for you. I'm not sure you know where I keep them, Steve."

Steve scowled, bothered by Nancy's sudden appearance. "They're in the drawer under the stove where mom always kept them."

"You do know!" She rushed past them to the kitchen. When she grabbed a bag from the overstuffed metal drawer, ten more came spilling out. She just let them lie and handed Steve the grocery bag. "Do you need anything else?"

Dr. Nora said they didn't and started dropping the vials into the bag while Steve held it. Relieved, she watched in awe that Steve was so consistently cooperative with her. But in her heart she sensed that he could trust her. And that's all that counted.

"I'll have dinner for you when you get back," Nancy said. She just stood there, acting as if she didn't quite know what to do with herself. Sammy came bursting into the room and she scooped him into her arms. Dr. Nora smiled at her then, saying they were all set. And they left.

—

The psychiatrist sat behind an ornate, imposing wood desk that seemed to fill half of the room. Sitting opposite him, Steve figured the desk must make him feel important. The doctor stared at Steve, drilling him with questions. Avoiding eye contact, he stumbled through the questions, trying to remember the doctor's name. Was he able to sleep? How many hours a night? (Does during the day count?) Did he have any friends? (Only in high school. I'm too old for friends anyway.) Did he hear voices? (I can't tell him about the little boys.) Had he ever been violent? (I don't think so. I don't remember.) The doctor was talking too fast. Steve couldn't keep up. His brain was too tired. Then Dr. Nora was talking about what happened at Friendly's today. The police. *I thought she was on my side!* The doctor kept going. Did he imagine other people were talking about him or watching him? *They are!* Steve was on the hot seat, scared he wasn't giving the right answers. When the doctor asked what medication he was taking, Steve mixed it all up. Dr. Nora handed the doctor the bag of pill containers.

He poured at least twenty vials onto his desk and looked at Steve in surprise. "Why do you keep the empty ones?" he asked. "Most of these are expired."

The doctor had a deep voice and straight black hair, shiny as coal, that kept flopping across his forehead. Steve thought of Hitler. He was glad the doctor didn't have a moustache. He was wiry—maybe a runner? And he wore a dark blue and yellow striped bow tie—Michigan's colors—that moved with his Adam's apple when he talked. His tortoise-shell glasses made him look intellectual.

"I can't throw them out!" Steve retorted.

"Why not?" the doctor asked lightheartedly.

This doctor must be stupid, Steve thought. "How will I know what I'm supposed to take?" Steve was exasperated and got up and paced the room. "I can't sit anymore. What am I doing here? I never had a man doctor before."

"Does it make you uncomfortable that I'm a man?"

Now what am I supposed to say? Steve looked at Dr. Nora for an answer. She just nodded at him as if it was okay to tell the truth. He felt the sweat rolling down his face. His hands were shaking. *When did that start?* He wondered if he could smoke in here. *Probably not.* He studied his hands and shoved them in his pockets and stared at his shoes. *I should've worn my tassel loafers. Tennis shoes look stupid, like I'm trying to look like an athlete. Not anymore. Not with this gut.*

"Steve?"

"What?"

"Would you like me to help you with your meds?" the doctor asked.

"But you're not my doctor."

"That's true. I know your doctor is Dr. Pandi, and she's out of town. I should've explained this to you earlier, but before you arrived today, I got in touch with Dr. Pandi and explained the situation. She agreed for me to act as your doctor for now."

Steve narrowed his eyes in suspicion. *Situation?* "Sometimes I can't understand Dr. Pandi."

"Can you understand me?" the doctor asked.

"Yes, but you go too fast." Steve sat back down next to Dr. Nora. His eyes narrowed, and he looked at her suspiciously.

"Then I'll slow down," he said. "With your permission, I'd like to help you get back on track with your meds. You'd only be in the hospital four or five days. What do you say?"

Steve stared at the doctor, trying to decide if he was joking about the "permission" part and noticed he was very thin, maybe a runner, and wore a bow tie that moved up and down with his Adam's apple when he talked. It was funny. Steve had to look down to stifle a laugh. "I always take my meds." He stood up again and turned to Dr. Nora. "Do you think I should?"

"Yes," Dr. Nora said. "Dr. Varga and I often worked together with patients. I trust his opinion."

Dr. Varga. Dr. Varga. Dr. Varga.

"I think Dr. Varga is an excellent doctor. He can help you," she said.

It was going all wrong. Dr. Nora was agreeing with this guy that thought a few days in the hospital was a good idea! "Another psych unit? What did I do wrong?" Steve asked in disbelief.

"You did nothing wrong, Steve," Dr. Varga said. "It's so we can adjust your medication to stabilize you again."

Steve started to laugh, mumbling to himself. *That's funny. I've never been stable. I'm not even a man. How could I be? I never graduated from college, got married, or had children. I hate children. I don't even have a job. I'm a male, but not a man.* He tried to stop laughing but couldn't. It was all such a joke. Why were they so serious?

"Steve?" Dr. Nora asked.

Both doctors stared up at him like a couple of frogs. Blinking at him. Just waiting to jump. Dr. Nora's eyes were bugging out of her head. She started talking. A frog that talks. He never heard of such a thing. He laughed even harder.

"You'll feel better after a few days, and then you can go home," Dr. Nora said.

"I want to call Sylvia," Steve demanded. "I want to talk to my sister."

"Of course. Let's call her right now," Dr. Nora said.

Steve spoke to Sylvia first. Then Dr. Nora spoke to her. Then Dr. Varga. Then Steve spoke to her again. She promised she'd fly out right away. Scott was coming, too, but a few days later. She said she'd visit him every day in the hospital. The psych unit. And she promised she'd bring him back to his home herself. He stared at the floor. "Okay, I'll go," he said despondently. "I need a cigarette." He got up, hiked up his pants, and, without a glance back, left the room.

16

It was day. It was night. Breakfast, lunch, and dinner came on trays to his room. He ate. He slept. The days blurred, and he couldn't keep track. Nurses came and went with pills in tiny paper cups. Steve didn't know what they were, but he had to take them while the nurse waited or he'd be in trouble. But wasn't he already in trouble? Why else would he be locked in here? Doctor's orders. Dr. Pandi? Dr. Varga? Dr. Nora? *Who is my doctor?* He tried to remember the nurses' names, but it was never the same person. Someone was using his bathroom. The toilet flushed. Water was running. A strange man came out and without a word crawled into the bed next to Steve's. *I'm sharing a room?* No one was familiar.

"How long have I been here?" he asked out loud. Silence echoed back, and he asked again. A grunt came from under the covers of the neighboring bed. Steve eased himself upright and glanced at the window. The heavy curtains were pulled shut, but it wasn't dark inside the room. He couldn't make out the clock on the far wall. He noticed his glasses on the nightstand and put them on. He looked at the clock again—seven o'clock. Morning or evening? He slowly stood, looking down at himself, not remembering when he got dressed. His feet were bare and cold. He shuffled to the window, pulling the curtain back just enough to peek outside. *No way to tell if it's morning or evening. What difference does it make anyway?* He found his soiled socks in the corner. He was putting them on when he heard clattering from the hall. The door opened, and a black man with a food tray walked in.

"Nice to see you up, Steve. Maybe you'd like to eat your breakfast in the cafeteria today?"

So it's morning. Kinda rude—he could at least introduce himself. "What's your name?" Steve asked. "Have you been here before?"

The guy smiled big. "I'm Terry. I've been bringing your breakfast every day."

"How long have I been here?"

"Two days now. Why don't you put your shoes on, and we'll go down to the cafeteria to join the others."

"Others? You mean patients?"

"Sure. C'mon with me, I'll show you."

"I don't know if I can be ready in time. I have to put on my shoes and . . " Steve felt his tongue thickening as he spoke, making it hard to form the words. *I can't tell him I have to go to the bathroom, and bad!* "My food will get cold."

"No problem. You won't need this tray of food. You can go through the line and order what you want."

Steve thought that sounded pretty good. "Like pancakes?"

"I think they are serving pancakes today, as a matter of fact. I'll leave this tray here for Brian in case he wants to eat."

"Brian?" Steve asked.

"Your roommate. He just got here yesterday. Take your time to get ready while I deliver a few more trays. I'll be right back."

Steve moved toward the bathroom, waiting for Terry to leave the room, then he rushed to the toilet. He had diarrhea.

Terry returned, and they walked down the hall together. A few nurses they passed greeted Steve directly, saying how nice it was to see that he was feeling better. He didn't recognize them, but he nodded and smiled back, just to be polite. There was a low hum of conversation as they entered the cafeteria where men and women sat at tables either alone or in small groups of three or four. Windows extended across two walls and a glass door led to a small patio, where some people were smoking.

"Am I allowed to smoke?"

"Anytime you want, but only outside on the patio," Terry said.

Steve couldn't decide what he wanted more, a cigarette or breakfast, but he didn't know where his cigarettes were. Maybe in his room. He hoped nobody had stolen them.

Terry steered him to the food line, grabbed a tray, and told him to order what he wanted. Steve's hunger took over: hashed browns, sausage and bacon, scrambled eggs, and pancakes with syrup. Not coffee, iced tea. Terry was guiding Steve toward a table where two guys were eating, but Steve cut him off at the pass, saying he wanted to eat by himself. Terry left, and Steve huddled over his food, gobbling it down without looking up. When he was done, he surveyed the room to see what he was supposed to do with his tray. He waited until someone else got up with a tray and turned to watch where he was going. On the wall by the food area, he spotted a sign marked TRASH. A red arrow pointed down to a large black bin with trays and plates stacked on top. Steve followed, deposited his dirty dishes, then wandered out to the patio.

Buildings in the distance, on the other side of a highway bridge, looked familiar. It was downtown Akron, not far from home. From this vantage point, Steve realized he must be in St. Thomas Hospital, not some mental institution in the middle of nowhere. He didn't know what that meant for him exactly, probably a shorter stay, which made him feel much more at ease. A clean-cut looking man dressed in pale blue, loose-fitting shirt and pants sat smoking right in front of him. *Maybe an orderly. Nurse? Not a doctor. Doctors don't smoke.* He nodded to Steve and held out his Marlboros. "I'm Jim. Wanna smoke?"

"Don't mind if I do," he said, pulling a cigarette out of the pack. "Thanks, I'm Steve."

Jim lit his cigarette, and Steve took a seat in the plastic chair next to him. The sky was blue, the sun felt good on his face, and, like waking up from a bad dream, he relaxed. Maybe he wasn't in trouble after all.

17

her a tangible sense of the passing of time. Seventy- to eighty-degree
temperatures and clear blue skies throughout most of the year made it
seem like time stood still. Without the seasonal calendar, November
and December came as a surprise—Thanksgiving turkeys and Christmas trees didn't belong.

Had she been able to come in November, the original plan, cold
weather would've been a sure thing, with the possibility of snow. *Can't
forget to cancel that flight,* Sylvia thought—yet another thing to add
to her list. The thousands of minor, practical details she had to track
cluttered her mind to distraction. She had a whole notebook tabbed by
category for Steve's life: doctors, community services, mental health
support groups, car and health insurance, bank/stock accounts, and
home maintenance.

With Trevor recently clean and sober and working as a waiter, she
had set his notebook aside some months back. Her son was on his
way to managing his own life, which had opened a space for Sylvia to
breathe again. Until Steve's hospital admission. The emotional toll of
her son's tenuous struggle with sobriety and her brother's helplessness
wrapped around her like a blanket of heavy fog that wouldn't lift. Even

with brief moments of reprieve, she kept groping to find her way, praying for a path to clear so she could enjoy life again.

To arrive in Ohio and not to be greeted by her dad or mom was still disconcerting. Missing them wasn't getting easier; she thought about them more with each passing month. In Los Angeles, she had seen a man in a grocery store, who resembled her dad so much she burst into tears and dashed down an empty aisle. In her dreams, she'd be with her mom and vividly hear her voice, only to wake up and face the harsh reality that she was gone. Sylvia hated that nothing ever stayed the same in life. Nancy living in their parent's bedroom didn't feel right either, and Sylvia scolded herself for finding the change so hard to accept, when she should feel fortunate that Nancy was willing to live with Steve. If Sylvia was still adjusting, she could only imagine how hard it must be for Steve.

The outside lights weren't on when Sylvia pulled in the drive, and with no streetlights on their block, the minute she turned off the car, blackness enveloped her. She got out of the car to unload her bags, but she was barely able to see where she was going, so she went back to turn the headlights on. Since Nancy was at work, she'd left the sliding glass door unlocked for Sylvia. There were no keys to the house and never had been, at least Sylvia never had one, never had seen one used by anyone in the family—another plus to living in this community. When the house was locked, the garage door opener was the only access inside. If there was a power outage or the garage door was broken, Steve and Nancy wouldn't be able to get in. She'd better add keys to the house maintenance list.

Lumbering her way to the front patio, crunch-crunching on the gravel with each slow step, she maneuvered around the overgrown hemlock bush that practically blocked the walkway—add gardener to the house maintenance list—then finally slid the door open and stepped inside.

Except for a dim stove light in the kitchen, the house was dark and eerily silent. She set down her luggage in the family room and immediately began turning on lights. She'd forgotten about the remodel and suddenly noticed how much brighter and prettier the room looked. The pale, lime green, wall-to-wall carpeting that Nancy had chosen was perfect. Sylvia loved it and decided to tell Nancy how pleased she was. In a rush of enthusiasm, she took off to check the rest of the house. The cheery kitchen was transformed, brand new. She was anxious to see the new wallpaper she'd chosen for Steve's room but once in the hallway, she heard yapping, then scratching coming from Nancy's room—Sammy. Sylvia let him out of the bedroom and grudgingly

sheets were in a ball, pillowcases grimy, and the mattress sagged at the edge of one side, as if Steve slept where he dropped. Upon closer inspection, it got worse. A thick layer of dust caked every surface, cobwebs clustered in the ceiling corners and under the bed, and the new carpet had several dark stains that looked like Coke. It even smelled dirty, like stale cigarettes, deep-fried food, unwashed body, and clothes worn every day for a week. Sure enough, Sylvia found two oxford shirts, with major rings around the collars and cuffs, lying on top of the over-stuffed hamper.

Regular household cleaning might not be Nancy's strong suit, but in addition to meal preparation, housekeeping was part of the deal, especially Steve's room. No agreement had been formally drawn up—after all, Nancy was family, her husband's older sister—and Sylvia had thought she could trust her to do what was expected. This last minute visit turned out to be the best way to see what was really going on. Steve's mental state may have been sliding for longer than they knew. Come to think of it, maybe he wouldn't let Nancy in his room at all. If he wasn't cooperating, her hands were tied.

Sylvia decided she should give Nancy the benefit of the doubt.

Looking after Steve was complicated. She had to believe that Nancy would never have let it get this bad if she could help it, especially before Sylvia and Scott's arrival. She turned out the light, closed the door, and dragged her luggage upstairs to Steve's old room, almost afraid to see what she'd find. The half bath was clean and the twin beds were tidily made, and at that point, that's all she needed to see. She decided to forget unpacking for the moment and just sit outside and breathe in the autumn air, contented to have some time alone.

On her way outside, she couldn't resist going to the basement to check the laundry situation. In the stairwell, she brushed her hand along the exotic bird mural her daughter had painted when she was thirteen, admiring the colorful jungle landscape that covered every inch of wall space, including the birds in flight along the sloping ceiling. Sylvia was still in awe of her mother's loving, free spirit, encouraging her granddaughter to paint the walls with abandon. She reached the bottom step, entered the laundry room and found, on the floor, a three-foot-high heap of Steve's dirty clothes and sheets. Sylvia begrudgingly threw a load in the wash, trudged outside, and lit a cigarette, wondering how she could broach these issues with Nancy without losing her temper.

She didn't have to wonder for long. Nancy brought it up soon after she returned from work. "I know Steve's room is a disaster, but he didn't leave it long enough for me to do anything." Sylvia wanted to say that she could've tackled it when Steve went into the hospital two days ago, but she didn't want to broadcast her disappointment. When Nancy heard the washing machine running, she sort of apologized. "Try as I may, Steve just doesn't want any part of doing laundry, even with the new machine."

"He's probably afraid he'll screw it up," Sylvia said, "but it needs to be done. Maybe while I'm here, we can work with him on this together, like set a specific day of the week for laundry, and start him off gradually until he feels more comfortable. I could also write on a calendar . . . "

"Follow me," Nancy laughed. "I want to show you something."

Sylvia followed her into the garage where Nancy pulled a torn poster board from the trash bin and held it up for Sylvia to see. It was a chart of daily and weekly tasks—get mail, take out trash, do laundry, put dishes in the dishwasher, brush teeth, shower—with a few gold stars affixed to the corresponding chore. "I hung this on his bedroom door in hopes a gold star would inspire him to do his chores."

"I'm impressed," Sylvia said. "So what happened?"

"He went along for a while but then last week he blew up at me. 'You treat me like a child! I'm not a child!' He ripped it off the door and threw it in the trash."

[illegible]

[illegible]

[illegible]

when he gets home. Maybe there were too many tasks? One thing a week instead of five might work better?"

"I bet our favorite psychologist would know," Nancy said.

"Of course. Maybe you and I could see Dr. Nora. And if you'd be willing, you and Steve could go together, sort of on a regular basis."

Nancy said she was willing, but Sylvia sensed reluctance. Who could blame her? Steve wasn't *her* brother. Nancy and Sylvia retreated to the house for well-deserved glasses of wine, commiserating about how little influence they had over Steve and how hard it was to make him do anything he didn't want to do.

The next day, Sylvia and Nancy visited Steve at the hospital and found him lying in bed. He refused to join them outside on the patio or to even leave his room. By the fourth day of his stay, they were amazed to find him outside engaging with others, friendly even, as he introduced them to some of the patients and nurses. He seemed to know everyone's name and, playing host, he even offered his sister and roommate something to drink. "There's coffee and tea, even iced tea for me," he smiled. "Or, Nancy, maybe you want a Coke?"

Apparently getting him stabilized in the hospital was working. After the stresses of so much change, after trying to manage his own life, this break, this time of rest and relaxation was exactly what he needed.

By the time Scott arrived, Steve had been in the hospital five days, and Dr. Varga determined that he was ready to be released. After seeing Steve interact so well with others in the hospital, Sylvia wondered if he'd be better off in a group home, where he could socialize more. Maybe he'd sleep less and participate in daily activities? When she brought it up with Scott, he handily dismissed the idea.

"You know that was tried before and he never stayed. He only wants to be home. Who can blame him? Maybe it makes him feel more normal."

Sylvia conceded that Steve needed his comfort zone. The medication setback didn't mean living at home wouldn't ultimately work out. In fact, with a new psychiatrist and routine sessions with Dr. Nora and Nancy, Steve might improve. Most things got worse before they got better. The arrangement with Nancy needed more time—by Thanksgiving, it would be a year.

—

The afternoon they brought Steve home from the hospital, light conversation in the car became more and more uncomfortable. Scott drove with Steve next to him in the passenger seat. Sylvia sat alone in the back.

"Car runs good. And the heater seems to be working fine. It's not really cold out though," Scott chuckled. "I'm hot, aren't you?" He looked over at Steve, who sat staring straight ahead. "I bet you're anxious to get back home," he offered.

"I'm not anxious," Steve said firmly.

Scott immediately wished he hadn't used that word. When speaking to Steve, he tried to choose his words carefully. Steve took most things literally and was easily offended by turns of phrase, especially words like "crazy" or "out of his mind." Steve didn't want to hear them, and he told you so. "Ready" would've been a better word than "anxious." On the other hand, Steve expressed himself in superlatives— "the best meal I ever ate," "the meanest coach I ever had," "the scariest movie I ever saw"—and inflammatory words like horrible, terrible, always, and never. "Running track was a horrible experience," he'd say. Or "I was never happy as a child." Or "Nancy's always in her room," he'd complain, punctuating his declarations with exaggerated facial [illegible, faded text] If only he thought of it as R&R rather than a prison sentence. Scott and Sylvia exchanged a glance in the rearview mirror. She raised her eyebrows at him like *I said the wrong thing.* She knew better than to try to coax Steve into agreeing with her positive spin. It was like tricking him into agreement, and he could detect it. Why should he agree just to make them feel better? Their mother often traveled innocently down that dead-end road. Instead, Sylvia could've asked him why it was terrible or what was terrible, which would've shown more of an interest in his feelings, leaving hers out of it.

Scott suggested they stop for lunch, "How about Friendly's?" But his light-hearted sarcasm was lost on Steve, who began to recount the details of Woody forcing him off the premises. "I was kidding," Scott said. "Where do you like to go now?"

"Pizza Hut is good. The waitresses are nice there," he said flatly. "Maybe later. I'm too tired." When they got home, Steve went straight to his room and closed the door. Nancy and Sylvia had thoroughly cleaned his room and together they'd finished the laundry, just before Scott arrived. "I almost wish you could've seen it," she said.

"I saw plenty when I lived with it," Scott replied. "That's partly why

I stayed away as much as possible. I practically lived at my girlfriend's house."

"I keep forgetting that," Sylvia said. In recent years, Scott had shared with Sylvia the painful details he'd kept hidden under his joke about their transition from the Cleaver family to the Addams family. Unless Steve was in a hospital, Scott never had friends over for fear of what Steve might do. Like when he'd gone through his "I'm a rock star" phase and sang off key in the basement all day long. Or when he went through the "God speaks to me" phase and had mumbled incessantly, reciting phrases out loud from the Bible. Scott just wanted his normal life back, with available, untroubled parents. He longed for time to pass quickly so he could graduate from high school and leave for good. With their parents now gone, he had no desire to return home unless Sylvia was there. He'd done enough penance.

Scott said he'd sleep in the hide-a-bed in the family room and put his duffel bag out of sight in the far corner of the L-shaped room. He could only stay four days because he had to fly to London for a modeling job.

The two of them met with Dr. Nora to discuss how better to oversee Steve's status from week to week. With the approval of his new psychiatrist, Dr. Varga, he'd be taking his medication once a day instead of twice, which would be much easier for him to track.

"One of you should keep in regular contact with him, say once a week. As long as he knows he can rely consistently on one of you, he'll feel more emotionally stable."

"Obviously, that would be me," Sylvia said.

"We both like our big sister best," Scott said. "But I'll keep in touch with him, too, of course."

They explored ideas about volunteer work for Steve. "He must find something where he feels he's contributing," Dr. Nora suggested. Nursing home or hospital environments were of no interest to him. She said she tried to talk to him about it a few months back.

"Our dad thought he might enjoy working in a library," Scott said.

"And the local one is five minutes from the house," Sylvia said. "That would be perfect for him, I think. Quiet. Respectable. No hard labor."

"Unless they want him to vacuum," Scott said.

"Ha. Ha."

Sylvia said she'd contact Steve's case manager, who should be involved with setting it up. "I think he came to visit Steve in the hospital," Sylvia recalled. "Steve likes him."

As they wrapped up the conversation with Dr. Nora, Sylvia and Scott felt like they'd accomplished something constructive. Since the weather was like a warm summer day, they decided to barbecue steaks on the grill. They stopped at the store for T-Bones, baked potatoes, green beans—the only green vegetable, other than peas, that Steve liked—and a bottle of red wine for themselves. Nancy was spending the evening with her son, Danny, whose wife still wouldn't allow him back in the house. He'd been staying with various friends.

When they returned from the store, they found a note on the kitchen table from Steve. "Going to Pizza Hut for iced tea! (Real exciting!!) Then, also to fill up the car with gas!!! Make yourselves at home!! But it *is your home!!*" With his loopy scrawl on a slant up the page, exclamation points in abundance, and his usual touch at sarcastic humor, they knew Steve had rebounded once again.

18

Sylvia spoke to Steve's case manager, Ted, about the possibility of volunteer work at the local library, assuming they had a program.

"I'll call right away," he said. "I'd like to arrange this for Steve before I move out of state."

"Then you really are leaving?" Sylvia said. "I'd hoped Steve was wrong about that." Ted was reliable, patient, and seemed genuinely to enjoy Steve's company. He was also the only man in Steve's life, unless he stayed with Dr. Varga. Steve had no friends or acquaintances, no one like Ted, who occasionally watched a sporting event with him on television. Steve could really talk sports, his only true interest—or the only one in which he felt confidently knowledgeable. Whether basketball, track, football, Olympic games, or sometimes baseball, he could recall players' names and field positions. He could quote game statistics, runners' times and records broken from as far back as the sixties to the present. And now Ted was leaving? "You've worked with him a long time," she said.

"I think almost nine years. I'll be sure to *choose* my replacement. Steve is rare, one of the easier clients because he's cooperative and tries hard to get along with others. *And* he's one of the fortunate few who has a close, supportive family. I really admired your parents." Sylvia remembered that Ted had attended both their funerals. "I'm leaving social work," Ted explained, "and opening an art gallery in Florida with my wife." After twenty years, he was burned out and needed a complete change. Sylvia could understand burn out.

"That sounds wonderful for you," she said. "We'll miss you, but Steve most of all." She could hear Steve now, rejecting the need for another case manager, just like he resisted finding another psychologist after Dr. Rita died. Another change, another new person to adjust to, another round of trying to convince him that it was necessary. The truth was, however, that Ted hadn't been involved with Steve's medication, doctors, insurance, Social Security disability, or Medicaid benefits. Their parents had always managed all of that, so it actually made sense that Steve would question the need to find someone else. But with their parents gone, it was critical that Steve had a competent case manager. Or was it social worker? Living specialist? The titles seemed always to be changing, which made no sense to her. As long as they worked in the same capacity, what did the title matter? Most likely, Steve would ask for a woman case manager, once he accepted that he couldn't wriggle out of it.

"Steve will adjust fine," Ted assured her. "Work in a library would suit him perfectly. Being around 'normal' people might lessen the stigma he carries and make him feel better about himself. Let's get on this. Would you like to be on the call?"

"I think I would," Sylvia said. "Since I leave in four days, I hope we can put it together before then. I need to speak to Steve about it, too, of course, but let's find out first if the people in charge at the library will even consider the option."

That afternoon, Ted arranged a conference call with the director who was unexpectedly encouraging and spoke highly of the volunteer program at the Stow-Munroe Falls Library. They arranged an interview for Monday afternoon, the day before Sylvia's departure. Now all she had to do was tell Steve.

When she spoke to him that evening, he sounded excited, at first.

"Really? I could volunteer at the library? Dad used to tell me I might like working in a library. What would I do?"

"We'll find out on Monday when we meet with the director," she said.

"Like an interview? I can't do an interview. What if he finds out I'm a mental case?"

Sylvia had to admit she'd questioned that herself—would Steve be considered capable in the director's eyes? She assumed the director would know he had a disability, since Steve's case manager arranged it. It was probably politically incorrect, actually illegal, for the director to ask. "Having a mental disability doesn't mean you can't do volunteer work. And it's not *really* an interview, just a meeting so he can explain what you might do there." Essentially, though, it was an interview, a term that threw many people into nervous prostration because their livelihood depended on getting the job. Even without such pressure, Steve regarded the prospect just as seriously. He still had to look presentable, engage coherently, and give the impression that he wanted to work. In other words, he had to be on his game.

Steve thought for a minute. "What's the director's name?"

"John Morenti."

"Sounds Italian. He probably has a temper. Are you coming? Is Ted?"

"Ted will be there, and I'll come if you want me to."

"I have to think about this," he muttered, shifting on his feet. "Can I leave now? I want to go to Pizza Hut."

As the weekend wore on, Steve became increasingly anxious. Sylvia wondered if she told him too soon—too many days for him to dwell on it. Then again, he usually needed time to make a decision. He never liked something sprung on him at the last minute. The proverbial rock and a hard place. And she needed to let him process, without coaxing, without encouraging, without mentioning it at all. She thought she might need duct tape to cover her mouth. *Just sit tight.*

Saturday night, he told her he was sorry but he didn't want to go.

"It's up to you," she said calmly.

"Are you mad?"

"No, I'm not mad." *Why does he always ask me that?* she wondered. "You don't have to decide right now."

Sunday afternoon, he woke up at three in the afternoon and went to Pizza Hut. At dinner that evening he said he might go.

"The waitresses said I should. They made me feel better about it. How many hours would I have to work?"

"Probably as many as you want. Remember, it's volunteer work—you don't get paid," she said.

"Oh, right." He looked down at his shoes. "I'll need to polish my shoes before I go. What should I wear? Do I need to wear a tie?"

Sylvia had to laugh. "No, no need for a tie. Let's go look in your closet and pick out a nice shirt and slacks."

Steve meticulously laid out his olive green cords, a pale, sage green Polo shirt, socks to match, and his leather dress belt. She complimented his choices, but unable to avoid making suggestions, she mentioned the khaki raincoat he should wear. He had a habit of pulling out old, worn jackets that were too small. She wanted to hide them or give them to Goodwill, but he loved them and she didn't have the heart.

"I never wear that coat," he said.

"It's supposed to rain tomorrow and it looks clean cut, sort of professional," she said.

He scoffed. "I'm not a *professional!* I'll never fool anybody."

Sylvia backed off. What difference did the raincoat make? Tomorrow he could change his mind again about even going.

But he didn't. He polished his shoes, showered, shaved, and ended up wearing the raincoat. (It was raining.) Handing Sylvia the car keys, he asked her to drive the short distance to the small neighborhood library. Ted was waiting for them when they arrived, just inside the front doors. Steve seemed almost relaxed and happy to see him. The spacious entryway opened to a reading room on the left and the checkout counter on the right. They walked further inside toward the circular information desk. About ten bookshelves stretched to the back along both walls of the main floor. There was an air of hushed activity, much busier than Sylvia had expected, but she imagined Steve could feel at home here. The librarian at the information desk pointed them toward the offices at the very back of the room, and John, the director, greeted them halfway.

His open, warm demeanor put Steve visibly at ease, along with the fact, perhaps, that they were both "big and tall" guys who looked the same age. John ushered them into his office and pulled three chairs near his desk, while Steve battered him with questions and side commentary, barely giving John a chance to respond: "How long have you worked here? What a beautiful office you have. Are you really the director of the whole library? Where did you go to college? Where are you from originally? I ran track there once." With genuine interest, John pursued the history of Steve's track days. The two bantered back and forth, as if they were seated at the counter of a coffee shop, sharing customary small talk.

Steve chuckled, "But that was a long, long time ago."

John smiled patiently and took advantage of the lull to redirect the conversation to the business at hand. "Maybe you'd like to hear a little about our volunteer program, Steve."

"I always talk too much," Steve said.

"Not at all. I like to talk a lot, too," John said. He took out a letter-size notepad and pen, then he explained that they have ten volunteers and could always use more. "The duties range from returning books to the shelves in alphabetical order by author, organizing videos by title, cleaning CDs, entering information in the computer . . . "

"I don't know anything about computers," Steve said.

"That's no problem, many people don't. Do you think putting books back on the shelves would be something you'd like to do?"

"I'm not sure."

"As long as you know the alphabet . . . "

Steve looked perplexed, "I don't really know the alphabet that well."

Sylvia rolled her eyes and laughed, "Steve, you do so know the alphabet."

Ted gave him a teasing nudge on the arm, "C'mon, Steve."

Looking at Ted, Steve started to explain himself. Ted interrupted him. "Why don't you and I step out for a few minutes to look at the way the books are arranged, so you can see if it's something you might like to do."

Ted raised his eyebrows, looking at John for agreement.

"That's a good idea," John said. "You two go ahead."

"Oh, you mean the Dewey Decimal System?" Steve shook his head and said he never understood it, but he'd go look anyway. He and Ted got up and left the office.

John turned to Sylvia, seated to his right, and mentioned that his wife, who was in her forties, was recently diagnosed with bipolar disorder. He had a lot of compassion for her struggle and would help Steve in any way he could. "He's a really good guy. Working here would do wonders for him, I think."

Sylvia was startled to hear about John's wife. "How fortunate for us to find you," she said. "Someone who has empathy for mental illness."

"There really are no coincidences, right?" he said.

She nodded. "Right."

"Do you think he'll want to volunteer here?" he asked.

"I do. He'll be a bit anxious at first, but one thing Steve has going for him is he wants to belong where he's among 'normal' people." She told him a little about Steve's work history, cleaning the courthouse, and how he hated going. "This would be a real boon to his self-esteem, I'm sure."

"I can understand that," John nodded. "I'll be sure to make him as comfortable as I can."

Sylvia was elated, finally someone else who would be in Steve's court.

When Ted and Steve came back, they were laughing.

"I don't think I'd want to put the books back on the shelves," Steve said. "Is there something else I could do?"

"You can do whatever you feel comfortable doing. How about cleaning CDs to start? Robin, the head of the volunteers would show you what to do. She's very helpful and will answer any questions you might have. Or, you can always come to me."

"Thank you very much, sir. I could maybe clean CDs," Steve said.

Pen in hand, John began to take notes. "How many hours would you like to work a week?"

"Um, I guess one hour a week," Steve smiled with a glint in his eye, as if he knew an hour was the tiniest of commitments.

John sat back, smiling, and set his pen down. "One hour?"

Without hesitation Steve chuckled and pointed to John's notepad, mocking his own response. "Be sure to write that down."

They all burst out laughing.

"Good one, Steve," John said. "Maybe you'll want to jump to *two* hours a week in the future?"

"Maybe," Steve said, still smiling at his own resistance. Just showing up once a week would be enough for now.

To Sylvia, Steve's self-recognition—to take it slowly without embarrassment, to be honest with what he felt able to do—was a milestone. He didn't cower to what might "look good," unlike herself.

Steve chose to work Fridays from eleven to noon. John took them on a quick tour of the library. The children's section was on the second floor—good news, since Steve became unnerved around little kids. He would be working behind the check-out desk, in a room closed to the public areas.

Steve smiled, thanking John, then he shook his hand. Ted led the way out of his office with Steve close behind. John reiterated to Sylvia that she could check with him anytime or he'd get in touch if need be. In the parking lot, Ted told her that he'd be sure and introduce her and Steve to his replacement before he left.

How all the moving parts had fallen into place left Sylvia stunned. On the drive home, her relief was so palpable that she was overcome with fatigue and could barely keep her eyes open. She could now look forward to relaxing on the long flight back to Los Angeles.

19

Over the past few years, Nancy had become friends with Andrew, who photographed children with Santa and the Easter Bunny at the grocery store. She offered to act as Santa's Helper or pass out Easter candy in brightly colored plastic eggs, and she dressed accordingly: green, faux-velvet elf outfit and pointed hat for Santa; white, puffy-sleeved blouse and gingham apron for a homespun, countrified Easter effect.

Since Andrew had his own photography studio and worked at the grocery store only during the holidays, Nancy didn't see him that often. It was pure happenstance that Andrew and his father, Martin, who was visiting from England for the summer, came to the store the day Nancy was working in the bakery. Andrew introduced them, and though Nancy and Martin bantered for only forty-five minutes, it seemed they'd known each other forever. Martin was jovial and engaging, trim and good-looking in an outdoorsy sort of way, and Nancy's heart was aflutter just listening to his sophisticated British accent. In those brief moments, Martin told her a lot about himself: he was retired and pushing seventy (nine years older than Nancy), he volunteered, driving a shuttle for the mentally deficient, and he was an avid fisherman.

"Andrew tells me you've dressed as Santa's Elf when he's taking the children's photos."

"Oh my," Nancy laughed, "he told you that?"

"It's a bit incredulous actually, because I dress as Santa Claus for the disabled."

"No! What a coincidence," Nancy said, picturing herself by his side as Mrs. Claus, dressed and ready for the part.

But the icing on the cake—Martin was a widower with four grown children. Nancy had four children, too. There was only one hitch: he was leaving the next day. Home to Manchester, England. He wouldn't return until the following summer, a whole year away. How could she possibly get a relationship off the ground?

When Nancy later learned from Andrew that Martin would receive an award as Volunteer of the Year in his hometown, she asked for his address so she could send a card to congratulate him. The correspondence began.

Within two months, they were writing each other weekly letters. Martin wooed Nancy with his poems, sent pictures of his family in England, and by late spring hinted about plans to be together. Letters might have been considered an old-fashioned, seemingly distant way to get to know someone, but Nancy found they brought an intimacy to each of their innermost thoughts and feelings, without the distraction of planning dates, facing each other at dinner in restaurants, waiting for a good night kiss (or more), and deciding when to meet each other's families. Nancy came to the conclusion that letters were an even better way to court. She didn't know how or when or where, but she was giddy in love and ready to jump in with both feet. The long-distance whirl-wind romance from across the pond was the answer to her prayers for the man she'd been yearning to find.

—

MAY 2002

Steve overheard some of Nancy's phone conversations with her friends or her daughter, Lisa, and started to worry that Nancy might be planning to leave. *Did I do something wrong?* he wondered. *Am I too grumpy to live with?* He'd noticed the unusual thin-papered air-mail envelopes in the mailbox with the return address from England.

How would she know anybody there? Who's Martin Graham? He considered searching for the letters when she wasn't home, but decided it wasn't right to read her mail. He also noticed some changes in Nancy: she was happier, lots thinner, and more forgetful than usual, like when she didn't leave him notes about her schedule or reminders to take his meds or call to tell him she wouldn't be home for dinner. He thought about calling Sylvia to ask her if she knew what was going on, but he didn't.

—

JUNE 2002

When Martin arrived, Steve was certain that Nancy was planning to leave. Nancy and this guy seemed crazy about each other. She always had her arms around him, looking at him like he was some hunk (which he wasn't). He couldn't believe it. Martin was hanging around the house a lot. He was a nice guy, but Steve started to feel like an intruder in his own home. He didn't want to walk through the family room where they sat close together, giggling, joking, and watching TV into the late hours. Sometimes Martin stayed for dinner, and Steve retreated to his room even more than he usually did. He sometimes stood out of sight to listen to them, but he couldn't follow their conversations well enough. He even saw them kiss! It was disgusting. They were too old.

Steve finally decided to call his sister. She was coming to Ohio in July, and her husband, Adam, was coming later for their high school reunion.

"I know Nancy's been falling for a British man she met," Sylvia said. "I didn't know he was there yet."

"He's here all the time!"

"Does he ever stay overnight?"

"No, he just hangs around a lot."

"At least he hasn't stayed overnight! Do you like him?"

"He's okay. He's nice and talks to me and laughs a lot, like Nancy. They're always laughing and joking around. Is he going to move in here?"

"Oh, no. Don't worry about that." But Sylvia wondered what Nancy might be thinking. If Nancy was serious about him, he might relocate to the states. She might be hoping he could live there.

"I'm glad to hear you say that," Steve said.

"Are you uncomfortable when he's there?" Sylvia asked.

"It's just cause they act lovey-dovey sometimes, and I don't really know him."

"That'd make me uncomfortable, too." *Another sticky situation*, Sylvia thought. *First, her son, Danny and now a boyfriend?*

"So, you're still coming in July?"

"Yes, I'll see you soon."

"Do you have your ticket?" Steve asked.

"Yes, I'm all set."

"Okay, great. I just wanted to be sure."

A week before Sylvia's visits, as usual, Steve called her every other day until her departure date, "Just to be sure."

—

JULY 2002

Sylvia met Martin several days after her arrival. Jolly, with a ruddy complexion, somewhat flustered gaze, and an easy smile, Martin shuffled his feet slightly before extending his firm hand. "Awfully nice to meet you," he said. "And what a lovely home you have here."

"And you, as well, Martin. Thank you. We're fortunate to have our childhood home, especially for Steve's sake."

"Lucky lad, that. Pretty rare to stay in the home where you grew up."

"Very true," Sylvia agreed. "It's only been possible with Nancy's help, of course."

"It's been a good situation for me, too," Nancy said. "And he's much more independent than when I arrived."

Past tense? Sylvia thought. *It's* been *a good situation?* Was Nancy leaving?

With everyone on their best behavior, they made small talk for the next half hour, while the elephant sat in the living room. They invited Sylvia to join them for lunch at the restaurant where Nancy's daughter ... the cheery chatter

ing in love ...

well its hold over rational thinking. So what? Nancy was ..., ing a small piece of the sun, no matter how things turned out. Anyway, Adam would be there soon, and he'd get to the bottom of the situation.

Sylvia and Adam returned from their reunion about midnight. When they entered the family room, Nancy and Martin were waiting for them arm in arm. Beaming, Nancy announced they were engaged.

Adam looked nonplussed (rare for him) but managed to offer effusive congratulations.

Sylvia smiled tightly while offering hers.

"So, when's the big day?" Adam asked.

"We're planning a September wedding," Nancy said.

Martin just stood there, his face flushed, like he didn't know what hit him. "At our age, you can't wait too long. You never know how long you've got!" He sounded a bit too enthusiastic, like he was trying to convince himself.

"Well, you sure haven't waited," Adam laughed.

Steve joined them. "What's going on?"

When they told him, he acted cordial, extending his hand with congratulations. "So what happens now?" When no one answered, he retreated to the garage for a smoke, or three.

Sylvia wondered the same thing. *Yes, now what?*

Adam suggested a drink in celebration. "Too bad we don't have champagne!"

"No problem for me," Martin said. "I don't drink alcohol."

"And I'd rather have my vodka on the rocks!" Nancy took orders and headed to the kitchen. Martin, a glass of apple cranberry juice. Sylvia, a chardonnay. Adam, a glass of red.

With raised glass, Adam made a toast—his standard—to the happy couple. "May the best days of your past, be the worst days of your future."

Nancy hugged Adam. "What a terrific brother I have."

"Now that's a toast. Have to remember that," Martin nodded to Adam. "I thank you, kind sir."

"So, have you made any plans?" Adam asked.

"I'm moving to England!" Nancy said. "Hopefully in September, but there's a lot to figure out."

"Like what?" Adam asked.

"I have to get a visa, which might take at least two months. We have the summer to figure it all out," Nancy said.

"In case you haven't noticed, there's not much left of the summer," Adam said.

Nancy pretended to give him a kick in the shins. "Okay, about two months."

"And if it doesn't come in time? What then?"

"I put a rush on it," Nancy said. "It has to. "

"So should I start looking for someone to live with Steve?" Sylvia asked.

"Probably a good idea," Nancy said.

"Nothing like the last minute, Nance," Adam said.

"I know how unexpected this is, but I just found out myself!"

Martin looked down at his shuffling feet.

The next day, when Sylvia and Adam had time alone with Steve, she explained that Nancy would be leaving to move to England once she and Martin were married.

"She must be out of her mind. She ought to have her head examined!" Steve said.

"There's wisdom in that," Adam said.

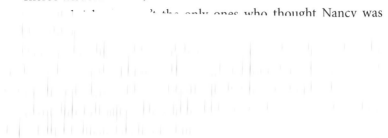

't the only ones who thought Nancy was

But Sylvia had bigger concerns. How to find someone not only trustworthy and compassionate, but also competent and even-tempered enough to live with Steve. The wife of the director at the library where Steve volunteered ran a local caregiver agency that placed home helpers. Sylvia contacted her, and they arranged to have lunch. After Sylvia explained the situation to her, she told Sylvia she thought she could find many people who would love the situation with Steve. Sylvia couldn't believe her luck.

And then it all changed.

20

Nancy sounded despondent and disoriented when she told Sylvia about the change of plans. She said everything was falling apart. Her visa would take longer than two months. Martin had to return to England by the end of September, before his visa was up. Nancy didn't know what to do about her job. And the final blow, Martin suggested they wait until December to marry. She asked Sylvia to call off the search for someone to take her place, so Sylvia did. But Nancy's biggest worry: What if he left her behind and changed his mind?

Sylvia told Steve that Nancy might not be leaving after all. At least, not right away.

"What? Why can't she make up her mind?" He sounded exasperated. The uncertainty of Nancy's situation, the on-again, off-again of her plans seemed to be taking a toll on Steve.

And then it changed again.

Nancy told Sylvia that they would get married September 12th. She could stay in England for four months after they were married, but would have to return after that until her visa came through. So the search for a caregiver could resume. She asked if she should tell Steve, or did Sylvia want to?

Now the changes were taking a toll on Sylvia. "I need to think about that." Should Steve know now? Or should she wait until after her trip to Canada with Adam at the end of August? Sylvia polled everyone: Adam said he should know now; Scott said he should know now; and

Steve's case manager agreed. Dr. Nora said Steve needed to know, but she'd tell him when he had an appointment with her the weekend of Sylvia and Adam's return from their trip.

21

More than ever, Sylvia needed to get away, to have a break after being yanked in so many directions for so long. She'd been juggling the bills for their entire marriage—child support, private schools for his kids, and attorneys from his ex-wife's constant demands for more. Then there was her son's drug addiction, which had drained her close to a breaking point. And now Nancy's yo-yoing.

To celebrate their tenth wedding anniversary, Adam had arranged a five-day getaway to Jubilee Island on the French River in Canada. His family used to own the island, and he'd spent every summer there as a child. After twenty-some years, he wanted to see it again. A family friend now owned the island, since Adam and his sisters either couldn't afford to keep it or didn't find it feasible to travel there. Sylvia had been asking Adam to travel somewhere that didn't require dressing up or make-up, where they didn't have to make plans, where they could pass five leisurely days swimming, boating, and fishing. Jubilee Island seemed perfect. And it was free.

The isolated island was all Sylvia hoped it would be. The pristine, crystal clear French River flowed around the island. Clusters of pine trees sat between large boulders that dropped into the river, and an expansive porch surrounded the three-bedroom cabin. There was even a flagpole with the Canadian and American flags furling in the breeze. Sylvia and Adam fished and fried their catch. They swam naked. They made love. And on the third day, Steve called.

"I didn't want to bother you, but I couldn't reach Dr. Nora or my case manager." He rattled on without a breath. "I found a letter Nancy wrote to her work. It was just sitting on the desk in the family room, so I read it. She was asking for a leave of absence. In September! I don't know *what's* going on!"

Sylvia was furious. How could Nancy be so careless? She explained to him that Nancy was getting married after all, in September. Nancy had asked Sylvia if she should tell him or did Sylvia want to, and finally Dr. Nora had said she'd tell Steve when she saw him this weekend.

A moment passed. Steve sighed, "Nancy does care about me. She asked you what to do." He sounded relieved.

Sylvia choked up. "Yes, Steve, she does care."

"Should I spill the beans and tell Nancy I read the letter?" he asked. "Maybe I'll ask Dr. Nora."

"That's probably a good idea."

"Did you find somebody to live with me? I want it to be a woman. Maybe a Playboy Bunny!" he laughed, then he took it back. It seemed he was already moving on.

Sylvia laughed, too. "Not yet, but I'll work on it when I get back."

"Do I have to go to the wedding?" Steve asked. "I don't want to."

"Neither do I," Sylvia said.

Sylvia told Steve he didn't have to go to the wedding, and before she hung up, she reminded him that she'd be back in two days. Then she stood by the phone, thinking Steve was accepting it better than she was. But he wasn't in charge. She had to be.

Adam came into the living room. "Everything okay?"

"No. Your sister! I'm tired of picking up the pieces. So done with her messes." She told him about the letter and Steve's frustration. "How can she be so thoughtless?" Sylvia asked, pacing back and forth across the room. "She doesn't care about anyone but herself! Running off to England with a man she hardly knows? And jerking us around through it all!"

"I know it's been a rough few months for you," Adam empathized. "I'm as skeptical as you are about what Nancy's doing. For your own sanity, try to focus on how much she helped out by living with Steve when you needed someone right away. How she jumped in and made the best of a trying situation. You know Steve's not easy to live with. You and Scott would've been stuck without her."

"You mean *I* would've been stuck," Sylvia spat, turning to look at her husband. "Don't forget she needed a place to live! And she hasn't had to spend a dime. She's been living there for free for three and a half years. She couldn't have asked for a better deal!"

"Fine! You're right. So you both got what you needed. Sounds like it's run its course, but it was good while it lasted."

"I don't know if I'd say 'good,' more like trying . . . "

"Good enough!" Now Adam was angry. "Now it's changing, and you're all moving on. Nancy won't be there much longer, so don't add more drama to these final days." Softening, he took Sylvia's hands and looked into her eyes. "There's nothing more to say about this. It is what it is. Let's try to enjoy our last two days together here. We need it, and you most of all."

Sylvia wrapped her arms around him. "Okay," she agreed. "I will. I guess I needed to get it all out."

"That's what I'm here for," Adam said. He took her hand and led her outside where they sat on a boulder overlooking the pristine, flowing river.

21

After Sylvia and Adam returned from their trip, he had to go back to Los Angeles for work. He said he'd return for the wedding, of course. Sylvia had to change her flight plans as well. She'd need more time to start searching for a new caregiver, to train that person, and to attend the wedding. And then she was faced with a new twist.

Nancy asked if she and Martin could live with Steve after they were married. "It would only be for two weeks and then we'd leave for England."

Sylvia thought it was a gutsy, inconsiderate request. Uncomfortable with the idea after so many changes to their plans, she didn't trust that it would be only two weeks, which was still too long for Steve. She figured the adjustment simply would be too much for him, and he'd worry again that they might stay for good. "I would like to accommodate you," Sylvia said, "but I think I should consult with Dr. Nora on that."

Sylvia met with Dr. Nora the next day.

"Steve's welfare is your first priority," she told Sylvia. "The constant changes in Nancy's plans have caused him more anxiety than he should have to handle. And you, I might add. Steve's never invited them both into his home. Martin just showed up," Dr. Nora said.

Sylvia never thought of it that way—that it was a matter of common courtesy for Nancy to ask Steve if Martin could hang around like he had been. "I guess after living with Steve for three and a half years, I've felt it was Nancy's home, too," Sylvia said.

"It's a sticky situation for sure," Dr. Nora affirmed, "but it *is* Steve's home. He has to be assured that it will stay that way and he will not feel like an intruder."

"Before I arrived, Steve did mention that he was worried Martin might want to live there," Sylvia recalled. "And I don't trust that it would be for two weeks."

"You can't. As his advocate, you must act in his best interest. That's your role. Nancy needs to move out as soon as possible," Dr. Nora advised.

Even though Sylvia knew Dr. Nora was right and understood what she had to do, she was squirming inside. She looked down and absent-mindedly started biting a nail. "So I need to tell Nancy right away."

"Yes," Dr. Nora confirmed.

—

Sylvia didn't expect that she'd have to face both Nancy and Martin. They had returned from dinner at Martin's son's home, beaming, and seemed to glide into the family room. After some idle chitchat, Sylvia hesitatingly broached the subject. She tried to act assured and confident, but it didn't feel convincing, because she wasn't convinced—she was evicting a reliable, supportive tenant and caregiver, and a sister-in-law for god's sake. Somehow it didn't feel right, but she had to press on.

"Nancy, you know I was going to meet with Dr. Nora to discuss your request for both of you to live with Steve for a while after your marriage," Sylvia began. "Well, she strongly opposed the idea. She said the adjustment would be too anxiety-ridden for him."

Martin reared up like an angry dog. "What? How would she know what's best for Steve? Nancy's the one who lives with him every day!"

Sylvia's insides crashed, but her hackles reared. This outburst from Martin took her by such surprise she almost shut down. But she didn't. "I don't think Steve's welfare has anything to do with you, Martin."

"I know how these people are!" Martin retorted. "I deal with them every day, shuttling them around. Steve could never live by himself, you know. And you wouldn't know better than Nancy what's best for Steve, since you're hardly ever here!"

Sylvia lashed out. "What are you implying? I wasn't planning on

Steve living alone! I'm closer to Steve and know him better than anyone. I'm his only advocate! You have no right . . . "

Nancy sat on the couch twisting her hands. "Please, let's not argue. What do you want me to do?"

Sylvia turned to Nancy. "This is difficult for me, and I'm sorry to tell you, but it appears that the best thing for Steve is that you move out as soon as possible. The adjustment would be too difficult for Steve to have you both living here. It would be better for him if you took care of this now." Trying to catch her breath, Sylvia left the room, thankful that Steve was still at Pizza Hut.

Sylvia ran upstairs, grabbed her cell phone, and called her husband. Shaky and weepy, she spilled the whole story. She didn't expect Adam to be sympathetic with the unexpected news. He hadn't understood why Danny living there was a problem.

"It must've come as a shock," Adam said. "But Martin was out of line. He had no business interfering and yelling at you."

"I'm still rattled. My stomach's in knots," Sylvia said.

"I can imagine." Adam was silent a moment. "Would them living there after the wedding really be such a problem?"

"Yes! You know two weeks could end up being two months! Or longer! The uncertainty is terrible for Steve. Not to mention Martin hanging around all the time."

Adam backed off. "You'd know better than I would. If it's for the best, then you did the right thing."

"And I sure don't look forward to seeing her tomorrow. I feel like I've betrayed her. Or that she'll think that."

"Nancy won't want to make things worse," Adam said. "I can promise you that. She's been through a lot, and she'll handle this setback. It's not the worst she's been through."

Sylvia knew more about Nancy's upheavals than Adam did, because Nancy had told her—as in homeless, living in a car with her four kids, because her alcoholic husband couldn't provide. She'd lost everything and had climbed back. Without knowing this, Adam was still right. "Still," Sylvia said, "I dread having to see her."

"But how was Nancy?" Adam asked.

"She seemed upset, but mostly about Martin's reaction. She simply asked what she needed to do, and then I told her."

"See? Nancy will adjust. It makes me wonder why it mattered so much to Martin. A hidden motive? Like he'd hoped to live there? I still don't know what his financial situation is . . . "

Adam's comments reminded her of an inkling she'd had earlier. "Come to think of it, the two of them love the area, even looked at houses on the market here, but Nancy told me they could never afford it. Maybe Martin figured they could live here. And Steve was often worried about that."

"There you go," Adam said. "I only hope she's not leaping again."

"It does seem a leap," Sylvia concurred, "but what can you do? She's going to make this work come hell or high water."

"I know," Adam sighed.

"I still don't look forward to seeing her," Sylvia said.

"Don't worry. She probably won't even want to talk about it. And I'd suggest you do the same."

"So I avoid the elephant in the room *again?*" she asked.

Adam chuckled. "Exactly. Now get a good night's sleep. You'll feel calmer in the morning."

"My knots are gone already," Sylvia said. "Glad you were home to talk to me."

"I'm glad, too. And I'll be there before you know it." Adam would be back for the wedding. "I miss you, honey."

Sylvia climbed into bed, relaxing in Adam's assurance about his sister. Maybe her moving out would prove to be a good thing for all of them. And Sylvia could put her focus where it mattered—finding someone to live with Steve. She didn't look forward to the interviewing process, yet she found some relief in handling what was required, without all the unnecessary drama, with no one else in the house but the two of them, just Sylvia and her brother.

22

ancy was stunned by the news that she'd have to move out right away. It never occurred to her as a possibility. But Martin's outburst with Sylvia really shook her up. She'd never seen him react like that to anyone. After Sylvia left the room, Martin paced back and forth, rambling on about how selfish Sylvia was, how ungrateful, how cheeky, how unreasonable. Nancy urged him to sit down beside her, worried that Sylvia would hear him.

"I'm just as surprised by it as you are," her voice shook. "*And* by how mad you got."

He looked into her eyes and softened. "I didn't mean to upset you, love." Then he pulled her close and wrapped his arms around her.

Her head against his chest, she tried to relax in his arms, but her breathing felt shallow, irregular. "I can't catch my breath."

He gently rubbed her back, saying over and over how sorry he was. "It's just so unfair to you. I always fight for the underdog. We get taken advantage of you know."

Nancy didn't think of herself as an underdog, just someone with a lot of hard luck. *Who are the underdogs? Poor people mostly. People with too many mouths to feed. No family or too much family? People without homes, with no influence or connections.* Well, in that case, she probably fit the bill. At least now she didn't have too many mouths to feed. Just her own. But that was going to change for the better with Martin. Then Steve came into her mind. "Steve's more of the underdog, you know."

"He is that. But a damn lucky one. And you haven't and wouldn't take advantage of him."

He had a point, she thought. "But Sylvia has to fight for him. She's all he's got."

Martin sighed. "Okay. I'll give her that." He hugged her close. "You sound like you feel better. Can we try to put this behind us and move forward? We need to decide what to do next."

"But not tonight," Nancy said. "I need to get some sleep."

"Me, too," Martin agreed. "Let's dream about our future nights, lying together, side by side."

Nancy mustered a smile. "After all, tomorrow is another day."

Martin chuckled. "That's my girl. Already bouncing back." Martin thought it best not to come over to the house again; he didn't want to run into Sylvia.

Nancy agreed. "But I won't be living here much longer anyway," she offered. "Come to think of it, where is Steve?"

Martin had a twinkle in his eye. "Not your concern anymore, is it?"

"I guess not," Nancy shrugged.

They sat in silence, holding each other a while, then Martin slowly got up, and Nancy walked him to the door. They exchanged a few quick kisses, and he left.

Nancy scurried to the kitchen and poured herself another vodka on the rocks. She heard Sammy whimpering and, drink in hand, she went to her room. She picked him up then curled next to him on the bed. "And what am I going to do about you? I can't take you to England with us due to the quarantine there. Oh, Sammy, what a mess." Now *she* was whimpering. And thinking.

Seeing the darker side of Martin made Nancy wonder if he'd behave like that with her. It worried her a little. But her doubt was brief. *We're all capable of angry outbursts,* she decided. *We all have a dark side. He was standing up for me!* No man had ever stood up for her. Martin leaped to her side in outrage that she was being treated unfairly, and that's what she chose to focus on. Her future depended on it. She turned on the TV, which always helped her fall asleep, and sipped her vodka until it was drained, then chewed on the ice cubes.

23

While the drama was unfolding with Sylvia, Nancy, and Martin, Steve was on his way home from Pizza Hut. He drove past the house when he saw Martin's car in the driveway. He didn't want to walk in on them, never knowing if he and Nancy would be making out on the couch, or even just snuggling. Now that they were getting married, at least that's the last he'd heard, he figured they'd be even more likely to do whatever they felt like. He didn't want to picture any clothes off, some naked part of their gross bodies exposed. Besides, if he interrupted them *doing* something, he'd be embarrassed and have to apologize for being in the way. He just didn't want to confront that, or even to feel like he had to chat with them if they were only watching TV. They were always watching TV.

So Steve drove around the block twice, then saw he was low on gas and decided to pull into the far side of the driveway, which was split by a large bush at the entrance. There was enough space to let Martin out when he left. *What if he starts staying overnight now?* The thought creeped him out. Steve cut the engine, turned off the headlights, got out, and quietly closed the driver's door. He'd just walk around the village until Martin was gone. Steve liked to walk when it got dark because no one was around. The Silver Lake Police cruised the village all the time, so it felt safe. He didn't know what time it was, but he knew it was late. The clock in his car wasn't set right—he forgot how to do it, and his watch battery had died. *Better ask Sylvia to go to that store she found where they sell clocks and batteries. What's the name of it? Oh yeah, The Time Zone.*

Steve went with her once. He liked the small, old-fashioned store and the owner, an old man who fixed all kinds of clocks, even grand-father clocks. He pictured all of them lined up against every wall throughout the store, kind of like soldiers at attention. Smaller ones, like cuckoo clocks, hung on the walls. He liked the constant ticking all around him, it was soothing, and he liked how they chimed. The store wasn't far away. Maybe he'd go with Sylvia, if he felt like it.

The street was quiet and no cars passed. Most of the houses were dark with only a few lights in windows. The streetlights illuminated the sidewalks, but Steve liked to walk in the street, like in the old days when he ran track, except he did that in the daytime then. "I hated track, and I hate running now," he said. He raised his arms, gesturing with his hands. "I don't even jog." He rambled on, chastising himself for being so slow and lazy. He tried to pick up the pace, but when he started to break out in a sweat he figured he'd better slow down. *Not good for my heart, especially since I'm fat and on meds.* He went around the block and right past his house. Martin's car was still there.

He didn't know how long he'd been walking, but he was getting so tired, and he needed to pee. He wouldn't want to chance it and go in a bush. *What if the police saw me? They might arrest me!* He knew he looked suspicious. The police usually slowed down whenever he was out walking at night, which made him nervous even though they often knew who he was. He thought about what Dr. Nora told him: Don't look down at the ground. Just look straight ahead. He tried to do that, but he wondered how he was supposed to see where he was stepping? *What if I stumble? And fall!* Sometimes police officers stopped and said, "Hello, Steve. Out for a walk?" He was less nervous when they knew his name and sounded friendly. Still, he didn't want to see any of them now.

The wind started to blow, and the tree branches' moving shadows, cast by the streetlights, made the neighborhood look eerie. Even the streetlights looked scary. *They look the same as the ones in the movie* Dr. Jekyll and Mr. Hyde. *I might have bad dreams. I better head home.* Rain-drops started to fall, and Steve looked up at the sky—no more stars. His glasses were blurry. It rained harder, turning into a downpour. His hair was matted and his clothes were soaked through, so he ran.

He finally reached the house and jumped into his car, breathing heavily. Martin's car was still there. He didn't want to go inside. He decided he probably had enough gas to drive to the station. *I can relieve myself there.* He checked his wallet to see how much money he had for gas. "Ten dollars—that's enough."

Steve started the car, turned on the lights, and slowly backed out of the drive. The windshield was fogging up, his glasses were still blurred, and he fumbled with the dials trying to find the defrost. He couldn't see the road very well and, exasperated, kept turning dials non-stop. "How does it work? I'm such a dumb shit. Maybe it's broken." He weaved into the opposite lane and quickly overcorrected, almost bumping the curb. He rolled down his window, hoping that would help clear the windshield. Bright car lights glared in his rearview mirror. He squinted and could tell it was a Silver Lake police cruiser, right on his tail. He slowly kept going. When he pulled out of Silver Lake and onto the main road, the cruiser was still on him. "What are you following me for?" Steve slowed down well below the speed limit. The gas station was just ahead.

Suddenly the cruiser's lights were flashing then the siren wailed. He had to pull over. He gripped the steering wheel hard. "What'd I do? I wasn't speeding!" The cruiser pulled over a ways behind him. The siren was off but the lights were still flashing. Steve waited for what seemed a long time. And then he waited some more. He looked in the rearview, raised his hands and hunched his shoulders. "Well? Are you coming or not?" He waited a bit more. *Maybe he's not after me.* He inched back onto the road and went about twenty yards when the siren blared again. Now Steve was so nervous he barely managed to guide the car over. Other cars seemed to slow down, checking him out as they passed. "What are you looking at?" he yelled. The siren cut off. Lights still flashed. He sat. And waited. "You're taking too long. I have to pee so bad. I can't wait." Steve pulled out again onto the road to get to the gas station while checking his rearview. Sure enough, the cruiser was right behind. "Shit! I passed the gas station! Now I have to turn around!" The green arrow at the traffic light came on as he approached the main intersection. *Better not make a U-turn. I might get a ticket.* He made a cautious left. He wasn't in the Silver Lake district anymore, but the neighboring town of Cuyahoga Falls that touched its border.

Steve was about to pull over when two more cruisers raced toward him and jerked to a stop right in front of him. He slammed on the brakes. They sat sideways blocking the road. "The Falls police!" They always scared him, but now he was terrified—they were much tougher than in Silver Lake. The Silver Lake cruiser flew in on his left. "I'm surrounded!" Five cops jumped out of their cars. Sirens and flashing lights on all sides. "It's too loud! Too bright!" He slammed his forehead on the steering wheel, squeezed his eyes shut and covered his ears. A loud voice blasted over a megaphone. "Get out of the vehicle with your hands up!" The sirens stopped and he glanced up. They were all walking toward him.

Steve reached around the overhang of his belly to get the seatbelt unfastened but his hand shook as he fumbled to find it. So he opened the driver's door, still struggling to undo the belt. "I'm getting out! I'm getting out!" He yelled. He finally released it and turned to get out of the car, his whole body trembling. He raised his arms and two cops seized him, threw him down on the wet street, pulled his arms hard behind his back and handcuffed him. His glasses flew off.

Another cop beamed a flashlight in his face. "Where's your wallet? You got a driver's license?"

"Yes. I'm . . . I . . . I . . . my jacket, I think." Steve's voice was gravelly, and he felt like he was choking. He started coughing and peed his pants.

One of them roughly dug into his back pants pockets, then rolled him over and searched his jacket. He took out the wallet and walked to where the others were standing.

Steve ached all over. His forehead was stinging. His knees felt scraped. His arms felt like they were being yanked out of the sockets.

The Silver Lake cop joined the men.

One of them was studying Steve's driver's license. "He matches the description. And drives the same car, beige Taurus."

"Description of who?" the Silver Lake cop asked.

"Of the rapist we've been after for some time."

Steve overheard him. Panic roiled in his gut. "It's not me! It's a mistake!"

"Let me see his license," the Silver Lake cop asked. One of them handed it to him. He walked over to Steve and looked down at him, then rushed back over. "I know who he is. He's not your guy. He's locally well-known, mentally ill."

"So what? He could still be our guy."

"I bet the license plate doesn't match up though," the Silver Lake cop said.

They hadn't checked that yet. When one of them went to look, he came back shaking his head. "No, it's not the same plate. So why'd you call in backup?"

"He pulled over then drove off. Twice," the Silver Lake cop answered. "We'd better get an ambulance here. He needs a psych ward."

One of them got on his radio to call the ambulance.

Steve shouted. "No! Please, no psych ward. I just want to go home." He blubbered and sobbed. "I didn't do anything wrong."

"Uncuff him."

Someone uncuffed him. Steve's pants were soaked from pee and rain. He was mortified. And freaked out. *How could this be happening to me?*

"Call off the ambulance. I'll take care of this," the Silver Lake cop said. He helped Steve to his feet. The others got in their cruisers and drove off.

"You can drive home now, Steve. It was all a mistake."

"I don't think I can drive," Steve stammered. "I need my glasses. Where's my glasses? Are they broken?"

The cop found the glasses. "They're fine." He wiped them and handed them to Steve along with his wallet. "I'll drive you home, then."

"I can't leave my car here."

"I'll drive your car and take you home."

"Oh. Well, okay."

"I have to move my car first," the cop said. He parked it to the side of the road and turned off the flashers then cut the engine while Steve slowly walked over to his car. It was still running, the headlights on and wiper blades going. Steve tried to open the passenger door, but it was locked. When the cop got in the driver's seat, he reached over and unlocked the door. Steve hesitated. *What if he isn't really taking me home?* But he had no choice. He was at the mercy of a cop he didn't recognize. Steve got in and started to give him the address.

"I know where you live," he said.

The unmistakable smell of urine seemed to envelop the car's interior, so Steve lowered his window. Then the cop did. The rain had stopped, and the cop turned off the wipers. He pulled onto the dimly lit street, made a U-turn, and headed back toward Silver Lake. "My name is Paul, by the way."

Steve looked at him. "Um, I haven't seen you before."

"I've only been with the Silver Lake force a few months."

Steve didn't feel like talking to him, even though Paul was trying to be nice. He should be polite, he thought, especially to the police, but he couldn't think of anything to say or ask. He was still too rattled.

"Do you know why I stopped you?"

Steve stared straight ahead. "No."

"You were weaving all over the road."

"I, I couldn't see—the windshield was fogged up, and I couldn't find the defrost button."

"So you weren't drunk."

"I don't drink alcohol because I'm on meds."

"Right. That's good, Steve." Paul cleared his throat. "But after I pulled you over, why did you drive off?"

Steve was embarrassed to tell him, but he had to explain the reason. Paul probably smelled it anyway, so it didn't matter now. "Cause I had to relieve myself. I was on my way to the gas station, and figured I could go there." He looked at the dash and saw the fuel light was on.

Paul then looked at it, too. "We'd better get gas," he said. The Speedway was still open, and he drove in. When he got to the pump, Steve took out the ten-dollar bill and handed it to him.

"No, no I'll get this," Paul said.

Steve started to insist then decided against it. "You don't have to do that," he said, "but thanks."

"I want to." Paul got out of the car.

While he was pumping gas, Steve put the ten back and scanned through his wallet to make sure nothing was missing.

Paul got back in and drove Steve home. Martin's car was gone. Good news for a change. Steve hoped Nancy and Sylvia were asleep by now, so he wouldn't have to tell them what happened. Maybe he'd tell Sylvia tomorrow.

After they pulled into the driveway, Paul switched on the overhead light. "Would you like me to show you how to work the defrost button, Steve?"

"Uh, sure." Steve sat up straighter and looked at the dashboard, hoping he could concentrate. He noticed that Paul had filled the gas tank, something Steve rarely did. His car was a gas hog, a V-8 engine, and he never had enough money on him.

Paul took Steve through the process step by step: the defroster, the fan, and the back window defrost button. Then he asked Steve to do it. They went over it twice. "Do you want to go over it again?"

"No, I think I'll remember," Steve said, hoping he was right.

"When it's raining and foggy, it'd be a good idea to make sure you turn it on *before* you drive."

"*Before* I drive," Steve nodded.

"I see your clock's not right. I'll set it."

Steve watched him set the clock and was taken aback. One in the morning!

Paul hit the garage door remote and slowly drove in. He got out of the car and walked around the back end to the passenger side. Steve was gingerly getting out of the car, and Paul extended a hand. Steve groaned as he took hold of Paul's hand, slowly coming to a stand. He towered over Paul. *He's a shrimp!*

"Are you hurt?" Paul asked.

Steve looked at him and saw him more clearly in the overhead garage light. Paul had red hair and a face covered in freckles. *Kinda wimpy-looking and so young, like a high school kid*. But his kind eyes, the soft tone of voice, and the way he treated Steve gave him the feeling that Paul was a caring person. "Naw, just sore and stiff," he said.

"Please call if you need any help with anything, Steve. And get some rest."

"Thanks for filling the tank and showing me how to work the defrost," Steve said. "I've never had a policeman be that nice to me before."

"The least I could do," Paul smiled. "Be sure and call if you need to go over it again. Or for anything else."

"Okay. I will," Steve replied, but he couldn't imagine ever calling the police for anything.

After they said good night, Steve watched Paul walk down the driveway into the darkness. *He's so skinny his uniform looks too big. He'll never make it as a cop.* He heard Paul talking on his radio. Probably asking for a ride to his car.

Steve was dying for a smoke and went to sit where he always sat, in the garage, at his favorite small, white, round iron table, now rusting, that used to be on the patio when his mom and dad were alive. He grabbed the chair's arms to ease down into the seat. He reached for a can of Brisk iced tea from the twelve pack sitting on the garage floor and gulped it down. Through the open garage door, Steve watched a cruiser arrive to pick up Paul. He smoked four cigarettes in a row, had another can of tea, then looked down and saw the urine stain on his pants that wasn't quite dry. They still smelled. He eased out of the chair, hit the garage door button, and went inside. All was quiet and dark, save the light over the stove that served as a night light. He went to his room, stripped off his pants and underwear, left them in a heap and fell into bed.

24

The bright morning sunshine beamed through her lace curtains and stirred Nancy into making a mental list: call Lisa, get ready for work and resign soon (her heart thrilled at the thought), start packing, and talk to Sylvia. *Not looking forward to that.* She scooted out of bed in her turquoise floral nightgown, stuck her feet into her rabbit slippers and went to the kitchen to grab a Coke. "C'mon, Sammy, time to do your duty." He ran outside ahead of her. The backyard was bathed in green, the sunlight filtering through the branches of the giant pin oak trees, and the locusts were buzzing, a sure sign of summer's ending. Not a breath of a breeze, humid as hell.

"Sammy, I have to find you a new place to live because I'm moving to England! I know, I can't believe it either. I bet Marjorie will take you." *Add to the list: call Marjorie.* "You like Marjorie. And she adores you." Sammy tilted his head, as if listening to her every word. "Yeah, I know. You'll miss it here." For a minute, she thought she might miss the place, too. But only for a minute. New and exciting horizons awaited. Good riddance to this old life. She skipped cleaning up his doo-doo and went back inside, humming a tune. While she got ready for work she began singing one of her favorites, Karen Carpenter's, "I Won't Last a Day Without You":

I can take all the madness the world has to give
But I won't last a day without you.

Nancy called Lisa and explained what Sylvia had told them, leaving out Martin's reaction. She tried to come across upbeat and chipper, yet her resolve weakened in the telling, and Lisa picked up on it right away.

"How could Sylvia do this to you?" Now Lisa sounded angry. "Does Adam know yet?"

Nancy gathered herself. "Not yet, and I'm not going to call him. Sylvia can tell him."

"I think you should talk to him," Lisa suggested. "Maybe he can change her mind."

"What's done is done. I need to know if Martin and I can live with you guys after the wedding, 'til we leave for England."

Lisa offered her mother the basement bedroom, for as long as they needed.

"Have you thought about postponing the wedding?" Lisa asked. "To give yourself more time?"

"No way," Nancy said. "I'm moving on with my life. This is only a momentary setback."

"What about Danny? Do you know where he is?" Lisa asked.

"No. Have you heard from him?"

"I think he's living in his car. I let him stay here a few days, but I had to kick him out. I can't have him around my kids."

"Did he do something to them?" Nancy asked.

"No, Mom. He's a drug addict, alcoholic, whatever." Lisa sounded fed up.

Nancy couldn't talk about this now. It was too much. Her heart had been heavy for some time, knowing she'd be leaving him behind, living so far away. She'd been his advocate during his hospital stays after he lost his leg, then she'd arranged government health insurance, disability benefits, and physical therapy appointments. Then she'd supported him during his bad marriage. She'd been by his side through it all. Nancy had sought Sylvia's advice about Danny once it became clearer that he was probably an addict. So Nancy had suggested a homeless shelter or rehab to Danny, but he would have none of it. What more could she do? Not being there for him might be the best solution. She only hoped he'd find his way without her.

—

Lisa and Nancy planned the move for the upcoming weekend. Lisa's husband and Nancy's younger son, Kyle, would help her move out. When Nancy heard Sylvia coming down the stairs, she told Lisa, "I have to get to work," and hung up.

Nancy took a deep breath, put a smile on her face, and decided not to rehash the night before or apologize for Martin. She didn't want any awkward conversation or argument between them, but to simply stick to the business at hand. She met Sylvia in the dining room. "Good morning," Nancy said brightly. "Get a good night's sleep?"

Sylvia stood there in her blue pin-stripe nightshirt, looking hesitant. "Um, yes, I sure did. I'm still waking up." She wasn't about to tell Nancy about her phone call with Adam the night before. She mustered a smile. "I thought you'd be at work by now."

"I have another fifteen minutes," Nancy said.

"I hope you slept okay, you know, after last night." Sylvia found herself compelled to say the opposite of what Adam suggested. "Really. I am sorry for such abrupt notice but . ."

Nancy shook her head, "Nothing to be sorry about. You just did what you were told for Steve's best interest." Nancy had no problem being pleasant and understanding. She didn't want the current circumstances—her doing, she had to admit—to change the relationship they'd had. Sylvia was family. They'd shared many personal details of their upheavals in life. Though Nancy had thought Sylvia had led a charmed life, she had learned that they experienced some of the same problems: divorce, financial struggles, and her son's drug addiction.

"Oh, Nancy," Sylvia said. "You're sure making this easier for me."

"No need to make things more difficult. In fact, I spoke to Lisa this morning, so it's all set—we can stay with her family. I'll be moved out by this weekend."

"I can't thank you enough for getting right to it."

"You gotta do what you gotta do," Nancy said firmly. "It'll all work out."

Sylvia went toward the kitchen to make coffee. "If you need any help packing or moving or anything else, please ask me."

"I will, but for now, I think I have all the help I'll need." Sammy ran in. "I bet you want your morning treat, you little bugger!" Nancy gave him a biscuit. "I've got to get to work. We can talk later."

"Sure. By the way, did you see Steve come in last night?" Sylvia asked.

"No. I wondered where he was. Martin left around midnight, but Steve wasn't home yet."

"That's odd." Sylvia took her coffee and turned to check Steve's room. She heard Nancy call from the garage, "His car's here."

Sylvia glanced at Steve's pill tray on her way to Steve's room. Flaps down for yesterday. He didn't take his meds. She stuck her head into his room and saw him sprawled on his back, mouth open, snoring, the sheet barely covering his nakedness. Not attractive. But Steve never slept in the nude. Then she detected a pungent urine smell coming from his pants on the floor. *Did he pee his pants? Or wet the bed?* He wasn't old enough to have this problem, was he? She thought about grabbing the pants to wash them. *Later.* She closed the door and went outside to have a cigarette, sip her coffee, and breathe.

What a relief Nancy was taking it so well, and without an attitude. Not that Martin was, but who cared what he thought? The last thing Sylvia needed to deal with was a pissed sister-in-law, especially while living under the same roof. Her energy tank was on empty at the moment after last night's round with Martin. Thank god Nancy just rolled with it. Adam was right about her. Still, tricky stuff. Families— always something. Right now, interviewing had to be her first priority. Assessing if the person was a match for the situation would be a challenge. Maybe she should get Dr. Nora involved? And Steve's case manager?

Sylvia decided she needed to swim the lake, something she'd enjoyed since she was first able to cross the three-eighths mile width, when she was eight. All three of them swam the lake when they were young, and it felt like a great accomplishment, a rite of passage. Now it was a meditation. To return to Silver Lake as a woman in her fifties and enjoy the same childhood pursuit, residing in the home where she grew up—she had her parents to thank for that. They never left, like so many others had, to Florida or god forbid, Arizona, or wherever retired, elderly people went. On second thought, Steve was most likely the reason they'd never left here, so maybe she had him to thank. Even though the circumstances were demanding of her time and energy, returning to her childhood home brought her much solace and comfort. On that note, she got up to put her swimsuit on and walk to the lake.

Steve practically bumped into her on his way to the kitchen. He looked at her like he didn't know what she was doing there then he rolled his eyes. "I'm trying to get some milk. Do you mind?" He kept going, turning his shoulder to avoid touching her.

"What happened to you?"

He was surly and gruff. "Whaddya mean?"

"Your forehead! It's all scraped."

"I don't wanna talk about it."

"Well, you forgot to take your meds yesterday."

"That's what I was going to do now!" he snapped. He got his pills and, grabbing the milk carton, tossed them down his throat and took a few swigs. Then he went back to his room.

Sylvia stood there with her mouth hanging open. *What the hell?* So much for solace and comfort on the home front. She changed into her swimsuit and headed to the lake.

25

On the way back to his bedroom, Steve glanced at himself in the hallway mirror. He winced at his scraped forehead. The trauma of the night before replayed all over again—the cops, flashing lights, wailing sirens, his body thrown to the ground. Steve didn't want to remember. He had hoped it was a nightmare, just a bad dream from watching old horror movies. But his forehead wouldn't let him forget. *If I don't look in the mirror . . . but then how can I shave?* When he walked into his room, the strong urine smell was overwhelming. *Oh yeah, I peed my pants!* He grabbed his pants from the floor and threw them down the laundry chute in the kitchen then headed to the front patio for a cigarette.

Steve heard tires crunching on the gravel driveway and stood to look over the brick wall. *Nancy and Martin! And Lisa and her husband in their pickup truck. What are they doing here?* Steve sat back down, wondering how he could avoid them. Too late.

"Hi, Steve. My gang is here to help me move out," Nancy said. "Wow, what happened to you?"

"What?" Steve asked.

"Your forehead! Did you get in another fight?" Nancy joked.

"I don't get in fights." Disgusted, Steve got up and went back to his room mumbling to himself. "A fight? Why would she say that? How can I even go to Pizza Hut? They'll ask me, too." He flopped onto his bed and stared at the ceiling, talking to himself. "I fell. That's what I'll say. I tripped on the curb last night in the dark." He got up again.

Martin was standing in the doorway of Nancy's bedroom, or what used to be her bedroom. He greeted Steve, but he didn't say anything about his forehead. Apparently, he'd been warned.

Steve needed to get away from all the hubbub. He grabbed his car keys and went to the garage. The driveway was blocked by the pickup. Lisa and her husband were coming up the driveway. "Did you want to leave, Steve?" Lisa asked. "I can move the truck. Jesus, what happened to you?"

"I fell," Steve replied, shaking his head and pursing his lips like he was embarrassed at his clumsiness, almost believing his own story. "Yeah, thanks. I am leaving."

—

Returning from her swim, Sylvia sauntered across the neighbor's front lawn toward the house. She saw Nancy's car, a pickup truck, and then she stopped, stunned. Martin was carrying a bunch of trash bags of Nancy's belongings that had sat in the basement for three plus years. She'd hoped she wouldn't have to see him again until the wedding.

Martin looked up at her and flushed as if embarrassed. "I had to help out because Kyle couldn't come. Might be here awhile."

"I see. Well, carry on." Sylvia walked past him toward the house. She'd definitely be hiding out upstairs.

"Steve just left," Martin called out.

Lisa emerged from the house, carrying more trash bags. Sylvia mustered a cordial greeting, but Lisa, stone-faced, barely nodded. "Does Adam know that you kicked my mother out?"

"Adam knows everything," Sylvia answered coldly.

"It just isn't right."

"How would you know what's right for Steve?" Sylvia asked. "It's really none of your business."

"Oh yeah? I'm here aren't I? It sure *is* my business!" Lisa was getting worked up.

Martin hung back, watching from behind the pickup.

Sylvia wanted to run away.

Then Nancy rushed over. "Lisa, please! Let's just get this over with."

Burdened with trash bags, Lisa turned around in a huff. "Whatever you say, Mom."

Sylvia went into the house, Nancy following.

"Kids," Nancy said. "Can't keep their mouths shut."

"And it's usually the parents who can't."

Nancy laughed.

"At least your daughter is there for you," Sylvia said.

"That she is." Nancy changed the subject to the matters at hand. "I was thinking I'd leave the washer and dryer." She gestured to the bookcase that held the family room TV. "And the bookcase. And the Crock Pot. I can't take any of it with me anyway."

"That's great, Nancy. I'll pay you for them."

"You don't have to . . . "

Sylvia didn't skip a beat, offering her five-hundred dollars. Nancy didn't refuse.

They went in different directions—Nancy to her bedroom and Sylvia to the kitchen to find something to eat. She grabbed an apple and went upstairs to her high school bedroom. It hadn't changed much, same robin's egg blue walls, her maple vanity and bench, bookshelves still lined with her old paperbacks and textbooks, family photos. She paused to look at the photo of her and Steve at her college sorority dance—firing squad pose, both of them standing, smiling, looking straight head, ready for the shot. Steve sure was handsome. Many of his track trophies were scattered throughout the house. *Sure never thought he'd end up like this.* She sighed and laid down on one of the twin beds. She could overhear the cheerful chatter of the "movers" downstairs. She picked up the nonfiction book she was reading, *Seabiscuit* by Laura Hillenbrand. Sylvia usually read fiction, but the horse story appealed to her since her daughter, Alice, was an accomplished equestrian, although anti-horse racing due to mistreatment of the horses. Still, the book was engaging. She became engrossed but soon dozed off.

The creak of footsteps across the wood floor woke her up. Then Steve's voice.

"Sylvia? You up here?"

"I must've fallen asleep."

"Oh, sorry." He stood at the foot of the bed. "Mind if I stay up here?"

"Not at all. Too much commotion downstairs for me, too."

"I can't stand it," he said. "They never stop talking!" He laid down on the other bed.

Silence. Sylvia wanted to ask him again about his forehead and his smelly pants, but she decided to wait it out.

"Are you hungry?" he asked.

"I am. How about burgers at Swenson's?" Swenson's was an Akron landmark, a famous, local drive-in chain that had been around since the forties. Even their parents had gone there when they were dating. The carhops, known for their friendly manners, were college-age guys dressed in white shirts and black pants, who literally ran back and forth to the cars. Service was tops, and the hamburgers scrumptious, a secret recipe held in confidence for decades. Going to Swenson's was first on the agenda of anyone returning home for a visit.

Steve lit up. "Yeah! Can we go now?"

"Right now," Sylvia said.

Together, they snuck out of the house. They turned it into a game, quietly descending the stairs, listening. Sylvia heard voices coming from the basement and the pickup start up. Out the window she saw the truck back out the driveway.

"Coast is clear," she whispered. They rushed to Steve's car parked on their side of the street and took off.

On their way to Swenson's, Sylvia asked Steve if he wanted to take their food to the lake and eat. "It's more pleasant than sitting in the parking lot."

"Maybe, but I'm so hungry I don't know if I can wait," Steve chuckled.

The moment they pulled into the drive-in, a souped-up Camaro drove in beside them, windows down, music blaring.

"Okay, let's go to the lake," Steve said.

On cue, the carhop ran to the driver's window. Sylvia looked up. *A girl?* "Nice to see young women at this job," she said.

"It's about time, right? We've always been waitresses, so, hellooo? What can I get you?"

Sylvia laughed. "We'll have two burgers, ketchup only, one fries, a double cheeseburger, ketchup and mustard, and two Cokes to go," Sylvia said.

"Coming right up." The carhop took off in a flash.

Waiting for their food, Steve said he was ready to talk about what happened to him the night before. Did the prospect of food put him in a calmer, more agreeable mood to talk about it? No matter. He told her the whole story: his fogged windows, how he couldn't find the defrost, and being pulled over by a Silver Lake cop for weaving on the road in the village, the Falls police surrounding him and throwing him on the ground. "That's why my forehead is scraped. And my knees, too."

Sylvia could never have imagined that happening to him. Anger at the police, their incompetence, their insensitivity made her blood boil. A crusade against gratuitous harassment of the mentally ill surged inside her, and pity for her brother broke her heart. "But why? Why did they come after you?"

"They thought I was somebody else. A criminal. Rapist! I'm not sure. They even called an ambulance to take me to a psych ward!"

"My god, how frightening. I'm going to get to the bottom of this," Sylvia insisted.

"Naw, it turned out okay," Steve said. "I was freaked out and couldn't drive home, so the Silver Lake cop . . . um . . . Paul, that's it, drove me home in my car. He's new here. And he showed me how to work the defrost."

Guilt, she thought. *Just trying to make up for his mistake.* "Are you sure you're not hurt?"

"Just a little sore and scraped up is all."

"Something isn't right. It's police brutality, plain and simple."

Their food came, but Sylvia was too upset to be hungry. She drove to the lake, and they found a picnic table. Steve downed both his burgers. Slowly, Sylvia managed to eat hers.

He passed her the fries, "Here, have some." She took a few.

"Oh. I peed my pants when they threw me down. I put them in the chute."

Another mystery solved. Good thing he's not incontinent, yet. "Do you want to see Dr. Nora and talk about this?"

"No, I just want to forget it happened," he said.

"But didn't the Silver Lake cop recognize you?"

"Not at first. But when he looked at my license, he told the Falls police that I wasn't their guy."

"So he finally did know who you were," Sylvia said.

"Yeah, I guess."

The whole village "knew" who Steve was, just not the nature of his problem. Their parents had never divulged his diagnosis to any of their friends—the stigma too shameful to mention, the guilt too great. Somehow their parents, especially their mother, felt to blame, as if they'd caused it, even when the psychiatrist told them otherwise. No one knew what caused schizophrenia.

Sylvia had to think it through—what to do first, or next. Call the Silver Lake police department, she decided. Get a police report. Get the facts. Possible lawsuit? She didn't want to jump too far ahead of herself, and she'd have to wait until Nancy was out of the house.

When they got home, Nancy was there but apparently no one else. Steve asked if he could go to Pizza Hut, and Sylvia asked if he wanted her to go with him.

"Not really. I'd rather be alone," he replied.

Not the answer she wanted.

Sylvia found Nancy in the kitchen, fixing a vodka tonic. "It's five o'clock somewhere!" she said.

"How's it going?" Sylvia asked.

"Quicker than I thought! They'll be back for another load, and then we should be done. They took my bed. We'll be sleeping at Lisa's tonight, so we'll be out of your hair." Her voice had an edge.

"Take all the time you need," Sylvia said.

"I wanna make it quick, since there's so much else to organize."

"I know," Sylvia said.

"No, you probably don't. This sudden move has added a lot of stress to what I've been going through," Nancy said.

Uh oh, Sylvia thought. *Lisa must've gotten to her today.* "I'm sure it has."

"I've always thought of Steve, you know. What he needed, making sure he had food, letting him know my schedule, leaving him notes . . . "

Wasn't that part of the deal? Sylvia thought. "Well, I know you've tried, but it's not easy to put his needs above your own. The past few months have made that pretty clear."

"You have no idea how difficult it is to live with him!" Nancy insisted.

"I think I do!" Sylvia retorted.

"How could you? You've never lived with him."

Martin-speak, Sylvia thought. She wanted to diffuse the fruitless conversation, but she couldn't stop herself. "I've tried to stay as involved as I can from far away. Of course, it's difficult. I see that. And you've made a big difference for him. I do appreciate that."

"I'm not sure you do," Nancy spat.

"I've tried to accommodate your changing plans. That's been stressful for me, you know," Sylvia paused. "Since Martin."

"Martin is the first man that cared about me enough to stand up!" Nancy said. "To put me first."

"And I'm glad you found him. But that doesn't change what's been happening here. And that's what I have to focus on." Sylvia wanted to mention Danny staying there. The piles of laundry she'd find when she arrived. And not only had Nancy lived there for free, but she'd received money for groceries. But Sylvia held her tongue. No need to add to the heat, revisiting all the problems under Nancy's watch.

Nancy was quiet. Sylvia was quiet. Nancy turned her back to face the window, looking out at the backyard. Sylvia opened the fridge and grabbed the open bottle of La Crema Chardonnay. She poured a glass. "I think I'll join you."

Nancy turned around and clinked her glass to Sylvia's. "We're all moving on."

Sylvia nodded, "Yes, we are. And that's life isn't it? Nothing stays the same."

"Thank god," Nancy said.

26

After Nancy left, the house felt more peaceful than ever. Somehow it was easier, just Sylvia and Steve. Their parents' old bed and dresser were back in their bedroom—her bedroom now. She could think more clearly without accommodating anyone's needs, aside from Steve's. Hiring a stranger to live with Steve might be better—their relationship would be strictly a matter of business, with no family dynamics in the way. Sylvia could only hope. The interviews would begin the next day. Right now, she had to address Steve's altercation with the police. She called the Silver Lake Police Department.

Perhaps predictably, what Sylvia discovered differed greatly from Steve's story. Trauma distorted truth, and Steve wasn't that reliable. He'd failed to mention that he'd been pulled over twice and had driven off. She didn't know why, and she might never know. The police had no option but to stop him from "running," and his running had implied guilt. No wonder he was mistreated. She'd have to talk to him, to warn him *never* to drive away from the police. She'd have to wait for the right moment to explain that. But not yet.

First, Sylvia needed to prepare for tomorrow's interviews. She made up a list—ten basic duties:

1) Clean three main areas: Steve's bedroom, bath, and kitchen.

2) Laundry: his clothes, bed linens

3) Clean his eating area in dining room (food on floor)

4) Check that his med tray is filled and remind him to take them

5) Grocery shop

6) Prepare meals

7) Dump ashtrays in garage & patio areas

8) Clean fridge and check for spoiled food

9) Set out trash for Friday pick up

10) Extra time: vacuum, dust (cobwebs) living room, family room, upstairs, & basement

Sylvia decided to meet the candidates at a local restaurant, Bob Evans.

—

An obese, silver-haired woman waddled from her beater car—rusted doors, windows smudged with grime, dented front end—across the parking lot to the entrance of the restaurant where Sylvia was waiting.

"Dolores?" Sylvia asked.

"That's me," she breathed heavily.

Sylvia introduced herself, opened the door, and followed Dolores inside.

When they were shown to their table, Dolores tossed her over-sized, cracked, faux-leather purse onto the booth seat and sidled in with a heave of relief. "Why I lug that thing around . . . you'd think I needed it," she said. Sweat was collecting on her flushed forehead and neck. She dug into her purse, pulled out a dingy gray handkerchief, and wiped her neck and brow. "Exercise sure ain't a habit of mine!" she guffawed.

That's exercise? Crossing the parking lot? Sylvia blinked in disbelief. How would Dolores ever make it up and down the stairs to do laundry? And Steve—who said he was grossed out by his own belly—would be grossed out looking at her every week. Dolores made him seem fit.

Nevertheless, they were here, so they ordered breakfast. Dolores got pancakes, with whipped cream and strawberries, and sausage. Sylvia ordered a veggie omelet and a side of fresh fruit.

While they waited for their food, Sylvia briefly reviewed her list of tasks, while Dolores hammered her with questions. "How do I pay for groceries? Do I have to use my car? Does Steve help with chores? Does he eat three meals a day? Is he ever violent? Does the job pay?"

Sylvia wanted to give it up right there, but the food hadn't arrived yet, so she went through the motions, inquiring about Dolores' previous care-giving experience. She never got a straight answer. *Good riddance, Dolores.*

That afternoon, Sylvia met with a psychiatric nurse, who looked to be in her early thirties. She had a hot body, wearing a provocative, low-cut silk blouse that accentuated her large, firm breasts, tight jeans, and strap heels. She had hot pink toenail polish, acrylic fingernails to match, long blond hair, and heavy make-up. Steve's fantasy personified: the Playboy Bunny. Her credentials were promising, but she was too pretty.

The following morning, Sylvia met candidate number three, a middle-aged man, a nurse practitioner at the local VA hospital, who never cracked a smile. This no-nonsense, Vietnam vet was used to dealing with damaged souls and knew what they needed. As he described it, "In short, to be kept busy with regular chores, eat balanced meals, early to bed, early to rise." *The military approach,* Sylvia thought. *Steve's fears about men brought to life.*

Sylvia was beginning to wonder if she'd have to live there indefinitely. And then, the biggest surprise. When Steve asked about the interviews, Sylvia told him she didn't like anyone so far, but she'd keep trying.

"Well, I know you probably won't let me," he began. "But I was wondering if I could live independently." Social worker speak.

Sylvia was taken aback. "I never thought about that," she said.

"I think I could try," Steve ventured.

Sylvia had to process this. Was he able? Better equipped now? Was this possible? "Maybe I'll speak to Dr. Nora about that. And Marcie, your new living specialist." They'd met Marcie soon after the library interview. Steve seemed to like her, probably because she was pretty and young—a pleasant surprise for him. "And I'll call Scott," Sylvia said.

"Okay. I like being here by myself."

"I bet," she agreed. "I have to say I like it better with no one else here, too."

30

September was hot and humid, and the locusts hadn't stopped buzzing since August. Sylvia recalled the stifling classrooms in grade school. It didn't help that she wore sweaters and wool pleated skirts with knee socks, because she couldn't wait to wear fall clothes. How silly. Like not wearing white after Labor Day. Sylvia longed for October weather, when the air was crisp and cool, but she'd be back home in Los Angeles by then. And it'd be hot there, too, through November. After ten years, she still couldn't get used to that. Thank god the home in Ohio was air-conditioned. She stayed inside most of the time, unless she went to the lake—a great comfort.

When Sylvia told Scott about Steve's request to live alone, he was as surprised as she was. "Oh boy, that seems a reach. But kind of good that he'd even ask. Shows gumption," he said, using one of their dad's favorite words.

Sylvia laughed. "It does. When I checked with Dr. Nora and Marcie, his new living specialist, they both thought it was a good sign and worth a try."

"What's a living specialist?"

"They don't call themselves case managers anymore," she said. "Anyway, they said that the optimal situation is to live independently."

"Sounds like psychobabble to me," Scott said.

"But if we lay down some conditions for Steve, it might work," Sylvia said.

194

"Like what?"

"Like we set up a housekeeper to come several times a week, to clean and do laundry, to check that his med tray is filled—stuff like that."

"Where do you find one?"

"Marcie said that Medicaid can provide an aide fourteen hours a week, so it's free."

"That's great. But wouldn't you have to train the person?" Scott asked.

"Of course. Maybe another condition should be that he has to take his meds to live here on his own," she said.

"For sure. But we'll never know if he has."

"We've never really known. All he wants is to live by himself. His heart is in it."

"But it takes consistency, which we can never count on," Scott said. "It seems like more is needed to make it work."

"We'll only know if we try," Sylvia replied. "But I'm hoping you can be more involved."

"I'm not sure how I can with work and all," Scott said begrudgingly.

Why wouldn't he know how? Sylvia wondered. In her mind, this was a family situation that required close monitoring by both of them. She needed Scott to be there for her *and* for Steve. "Right now," she suggested, "it seems an occasional trip here, with me, would be what I'd need from you."

"Yeah, I s'pose so," Steve relented. "It's just hard with a young family."

Scott's daughter was ten years old, an only child. She was a gem— never a problem. Sweet-natured, lovely, a good student, and eager to please. Why would it be so hard for Scott to come to Ohio for a few days, once or twice a year? And his wife didn't work, so she was home and super dedicated to raising their daughter with good values, activities, and community involvement. After what Sylvia went through as a single parent for twelve years, working full-time, she couldn't imagine why Scott couldn't manage this small request. "I don't see why it would be so hard," Sylvia said. "I thought you might want to."

"I do want to, sort of. You know how I hate going back there. Too many bad memories when Steve went off the grid. And I also just started a different career, which takes a lot of time."

Scott had quit modeling full-time to train as a stockbroker. He was burned out from traveling and bored with the scene. He said he didn't want to go back to chemical engineering, his first career, so he took his chances and started over. More money in brokerage, he'd said.

Sylvia tried to understand. She knew how Scott's life had changed overnight after Steve's first psychotic break, and it only became worse throughout Scott's high school years. Scott had lived through it all, and Sylvia hadn't. But now more than ever, it seemed to her an unavoidable responsibility that they should share. "Well, I hope you'll try for my sake. And you won't be here by yourself," she offered. "You'll be with me." Scott had visited Steve twice without her, but it hadn't gone well, even though Nancy was there, too. One never knew with Steve—mood swings were inevitable.

"I'd only be there when you're there anyway. Steve is always better with you." He sighed, "You know I'll do my best."

"That's all I ask."

The next morning, Sylvia made bacon, scrambled eggs, and English muffins for breakfast. She and Steve sat together at the dining room table, and she told him the good news.

Steve was elated. "Really? You'll let me live by myself?"

She chuckled. "Yes." She explained the basic conditions, and he seemed amenable. "We'll meet with Marcie this afternoon to talk about the arrangements."

"What time?" Steve asked.

"One o'clock."

"Can I go to Pizza Hut now? I'll be back by one."

Steve actually showed up ahead of time. He was sweating. "It's so hot out!"

"Why don't you wear shorts? And a short-sleeved shirt? You'd feel better," Sylvia said.

"My legs are too white." Steve headed to his room.

Marcie arrived, and Steve joined them in the living room. He'd changed clothes—short-sleeved shirt but not shorts.

Sylvia began to outline the conditions, mentioning that the housekeeper or aide should come three times a week, for two hours.

Steve balked. "I don't need someone here that much. I can do that stuff."

Here we go, Sylvia thought. *He's already digging in his heels.* "No, we have to keep the house in good shape. You don't do your laundry."

"Oh, right."

"Or dust or vacuum or wash dishes, change sheets or—"

"Okay, okay," he relented.

"These are the conditions we already discussed for you to live independently," Sylvia reminded him.

"Who's going to come?" he asked.

"I'll arrange for someone," Marcie said. "It'll probably take about ten days before someone can start." She looked at Sylvia. "Will you still be here?"

"I'll be here until mid-September."

"It might be close," she considered. "It takes time to get it processed. And, Steve, you need to be here while the aide is here."

"I do?"

"Yes. It's the law. She'll come at exact times, so you'll know when you have to be here to let her in."

This was news to Sylvia, but it made sense. She couldn't imagine that Steve would keep track of a schedule. He never had one. Except for his one hour at the library, one day a week. "Can someone call him the night before to remind him? Like they call to remind him to take his meds?"

"That's changing," Marcie said. "Steve hasn't answered the phone when they've called, so they won't continue to remind him of his meds anymore."

"Oh dear. No med reminder call anymore?" Sylvia wondered if *she* should call him about his meds. A big undertaking.

"I don't need a call about my meds," Steve said. "I always take my meds."

"Well, sometimes you fall asleep and forget," Sylvia said.

Steve rolled his eyes. "I take them, Sylvia."

"But the aide can call to remind you when she's coming," Marcie added.

"That'd be great," he said.

"And how will he get groceries?"

"The aide can do that, but she'll have to have access to money to buy them," Marcie said. "Steve should probably go with her."

"I'd have to go to the store? With the aide?" Steve was getting agitated. He got up and started to pace. "I don't even know how to buy groceries."

"The aide will know how," Sylvia reassured him. "And I'll make a grocery list. All you have to do is be there to pay for it."

"And how will I do that? Can I have a smoke?"

"Sure," Sylvia said. "Go ahead. We'll discuss how to do this."

Steve left for the garage while she and Marcie continued the discussion.

"He'll have to go with her to the store," Sylvia said. "There's no other way. I can't trust someone to have access to funds."

"I agree," Marcie said. "He'll just have to get used to it."

"Can you come by to monitor this for a while?"

Marcie hesitated. "Well, it's not really part of my duties, but I'd be willing to come once maybe."

Sylvia was pissed. Not a part of her duties? Then what was? Driving Steve to appointments? She sure wasn't like Ted, the last living specialist. The situation was getting more complicated by the minute. "Will the same aide come each time?"

"I'll try to arrange that."

"That's paramount here," Sylva said. "I must have the same person come each time. Otherwise, it'll be a nightmare. Steve needs to get used to people."

Marcie nodded. "I understand. I'll make that a contingency."

"Good." *At least that will work out,* Sylvia thought. "So you'll let me know as soon as possible when she'll start? It has to be a woman, by the way. And not a black woman. Steve has a problem there. I know it's not

PC, but that's the way it is with him. And for no reason that I know of. Maybe he's just stuck in the sixties."

Marcie laughed. "No problem. Many are like that." She got up to leave. "I know this is more difficult with you living so far away, but it will be fine. I'll do my best to come at the beginning, after you've left. And I'll keep in touch with you."

"Thank you," Sylvia said. "I need that."

After Marcie left, Sylvia decided she'd *have* to be here when the aide came. Even if she had to change her flight, again. The logistics were sounding more difficult than she'd imagined. Mostly the grocery shopping. She'd have to insist to Steve that he had to shop with the aide, otherwise it wouldn't work. But she could imagine him telling the aide that he didn't need anything, just so he wouldn't have to go. Her head was spinning, so she sat down at her desk in the family room and began to make two lists: one of food items, one of household tasks. At least that made the situation feel manageable.

31

Adam arrived two days before the wedding. Sylvia was waiting in the driveway to greet him. He practically dove out of the car to embrace her. "I've missed you so much. I keep thinking about our trip to the French River, sitting on that boulder, watching the Northern Lights that night, swimming naked."

That night Adam had said a prayer to his sister who died of lung cancer eight years before. They were very close to each other. He'd prayed that she 'speak' to him, and the Northern Lights appeared soon after. He said it was her answer to him.

"Seems ages ago. I still can't believe we saw them. It's like a dream."

"I want us to go away again, soon. You need it more than ever," he said.

She kissed him. "I love your thinking."

Steve came outside. He looked down and turned.

"Hey, Steve. Come here." Adam reached to hug him and Steve hesitantly hugged back.

"Didn't want to break this up," Steve smiled.

"You're not," Adam said.

"Can I get your bag?"

"No, I'll get it. Thanks." Adam grabbed his overnighter, and they all headed into the house. "How about a swim?"

"Perfect," Sylvia said. "Steve, do you want to join us at the lake?"

"Naw, you guys go," he said, heading toward the garage.

"How about steaks on the grill tonight?" Adam asked.

"Sounds great," Steve said. "I haven't had a steak in years!"

Sylvia looked at Adam. "Not true," she whispered.

"Then it's time you had one," Adam called out to him.

"Let's drive to the lake. Too hot to walk," Sylvia said.

"Fine with me."

They got in their bathing suits and left. After a quick dip in the lake, a wind kicked up, so they took a Sunfish—a small sailboat available for members of the village—out for a short sail. When they got back, Adam left to go to the store for the steaks.

The phone rang. It was her son, Trevor. "Guess what, Mom?"

Sylvia held her breath for a second. Even though he'd held it together for two years, she never knew what might come next with him. First clean and sober living, then modeling. It was nothing short of amazing that her son was now following in the footsteps of Scott. After his first job with Abercrombie & Fitch, he'd been working nonstop. "Honey, what's going on?"

"I'm going to Paris!" he exclaimed.

"What?" Sylvia gasped.

"Yep. My agent wants me to hook up with an agent there. I'll be doing a runway show and more."

"I'm thrilled!" Sylvia could hardly believe it. "I wish I could go."

"Me, too. You can speak the language. Now I wish I'd taken your advice and learned French."

"You won't even need it," Sylvia reassured him. "When do you leave?"

"In two days. I can't wait."

"Do you know for how long?"

"No, it depends on how much work I get," he replied. "It could be months."

"I wish I could see you before you go." Though, honestly, Sylvia's relief over Trevor's sobriety, and his ability to support himself, made up for the ache of missing him. This was more than she ever dreamed possible for him. And for her.

"I know. Me, too," Trevor said. "I'll keep you posted."

"I know you will. Mommy do."

"Son do."

This sweet code emerged long ago, when Trevor was little. Instead of writing "I love you," they'd signed notes to each other with "Mommy do" and "Son do." And so it carried on.

—

The wedding was held at the home of a childhood friend of Nancy's, in a colonial-style mansion with white pillars, a circular drive, immaculate gardens, and a patio in back. Nancy and Martin were standing out front as cars pulled up. Valet service was provided by the owner. Adam and Sylvia got out of the car to greet his sister and Martin. Nancy squealed as she hugged Adam with all her might, while Sylvia stood there wondering what to do with herself. She approached Martin with a smile and gave him a brief hug, congratulating him. Then she quickly moved to Nancy to avoid any awkward conversation with Martin, but her earlier dread of seeing him soon dissolved. The occasion and Adam's presence diffused any unpleasantness. She knew she'd make it through the evening, maybe even finding it enjoyable. The ceremony was casual and touching, and she honestly hoped that Nancy and Martin would stay happily married. Sylvia hung out with Nancy's youngest son, Kyle, whom she'd always liked. His marriage was in jeopardy (he'd met someone else), which was no real surprise to Sylvia. His wife was a micromanaging control freak. Still, they had two young children.

His situation was not so different from Adam's and hers, actually. She'd reconnected with Adam at their high school reunion, when he was still married. His children were very young, and his wife also an angry control freak. Adam left the marriage and married Sylvia after a three-year, long-distance courtship—Adam in Los Angeles, Sylvia in Oregon. And here was another long-distance relationship culminating in marriage. Nancy and Martin fell in love through letters, neither was married to someone else, nor did they have the heart-wrenching complications of young children. And they were older than she and

Adam, which accounted for their desire to move quickly. *None of us knows what's around the corner, nor should we judge anyone else.* Sylvia saw this, especially now.

Adam had many old family friends to meet and greet, and at her request he'd included her at every turn. Guests dwindled after the cake was cut. The festivities were over, but the couple who owned the home wanted Sylvia and Adam to stay longer. So they did. Nancy and Martin, and Lisa and her husband stayed, too. Not what Sylvia had anticipated. She was ready to go home.

The three couples gathered in the kitchen around an enormous marble-top island, drinking champagne or beer or whatever the well-stocked bar had to offer. Adam became the center of attention, as usual, telling funny stories about his first job after college, selling Hoover vacuum cleaners door-to-door in London, where he'd lived for five years on a houseboat on the Thames. That year the annual appliance expo, which the Queen customarily attended, had a circus theme. Adam, holding a lion cub, was dressed like a ringmaster, in red coat tails and black top hat. As the Queen slowly approached his station, the cub let loose all over Adam's pants, exuding a most horrific smell. Somehow, Adam anxiously managed to remove his pants and stand behind a washing machine nearby as the Queen passed and greeted him. Adam told a story like no one else, and this one left his audience roaring with laughter.

Nancy hovered near her brother and began to regale the group with more of Adam's escapades from when he lived with her family in California in the seventies. Sylvia, who had heard these stories more than once, tried to look amused but she wasn't. Tired of it all, she decided to sneak out back to have a cigarette. Just as she was backing away toward the door, Martin appeared next to her.

"Those two sure like to hang on, don't they?" he asked, sounding defeated. "You look as ready to leave as I am."

Sylvia sighed. *Now he wants to make small talk with me? What rotten timing.* "Yeah, they could go on all night."

Martin shifted his feet, then blurted out. "Nancy probably wants to go all night, after the news about Danny." He looked down. "Thought you should know, so you could tell Adam."

"What about Danny?"

"Car accident. He's in hospital."

"Oh god. When did this happen?"

"Three days ago. She's been to see him every day, of course."

"How bad is he?" Sylvia asked.

"He's in a coma, and the doctors don't know how it'll go."

Bursts of laughter filled the room. Sylva looked over at Nancy who was in tears from laughing, or maybe not. Sylvia knew all too well how laughter could dissolve into tears of anguish. Still, Nancy had somehow managed to put on a brave face for her day.

"I'm so sorry. What timing."

"Bad news never has a right time," he said. "Nothing to do but wait and see."

"Is she still going to leave with you?"

Before he could answer, Nancy and Adam joined them. Finally, they were all ready to call it a night. Nancy was hanging on to Adam's arm like she needed him to hold her up. She was definitely beyond tipsy. Who could blame her?

They all headed for the front door, and Adam handed Nancy over to her husband. "She's all yours! Good luck with her tonight," he joked. Martin helped Nancy into the car, while Lisa and her husband climbed into the backseat. They waved their good-byes and drove off.

———

No sooner than she settled into the car, Nancy promptly dozed off.

"It went off without a hitch, considering," Lisa said.

Nancy hiccupped awake. "What? Where are we?"

"We're going to Lisa's," Martin said. "How's my new wife?"

"I think I'm going to be sick," Nancy said.

They pulled over, and Martin got out to help her, holding her while she heaved. "That's what you needed, my girl. You'll feel better now, and we'll get you into bed straight away."

Nancy cried the rest of the way back. "What am I going to do? How can I leave him? It's all gone up in smoke."

"We'll talk about it tomorrow," Martin said. "It's another day, love. I'll be with you no matter what."

32

END OF SEPTEMBER 2002

Steve sat in the garage and waited for the new aide to show up with his case manager, Marcie. "Oh yeah, living specialist. Why did they change that?" he asked himself. The aide's name was Gloria. Sylvia was still here, so he wasn't as worried about having to be with them by himself. She would explain everything. "What'll I do when she leaves?" Now he wasn't so sure that living independently was such a good idea. "What will I eat? I don't want to go to the store with her. I wish Nancy was still here." He smoked one cigarette after the other, got up, sat down, wandered out to the driveway then back again. A car drove up. They were here.

Steve watched Marcie get out of her car then the aide, Gloria. She looked middle-aged, but sort of classy. She was well-dressed, which he always appreciated, with dark, short, wavy hair. She wore make-up and earrings, and she was smiling. She was kind of pretty, not overweight like him, but a little plump and fairly tall. *No Playboy Bunny,* he snickered.

She came right over to him. "Hi, you must be Steve. I'm Gloria."

Steve stood up and shook her hand, "That's me. So you're going to be my aide, I guess."

"Yes, Gloria's going to come here three times a week, Steve," Marcie said.

"That much?"

"For a few months anyway," Marcie said.

"We'll be fine, Steve," Gloria said. "I can help out wherever you need me to."

"I don't know what to tell you to do. But my sister is still here. She can tell you."

"Should we go inside?" Marcie asked.

"Oh, right. I'll get Sylvia."

They entered the house through the garage, proceeding to the living room. Sylvia greeted them, inviting them to sit down.

"Do I need to stay?" Steve asked.

"Yes, Steve. We all need to talk about what Gloria's going to do, and you need to hear that. And then to check the med tray to be sure it's filled."

"I don't think I need Gloria to come three times a week," Steve said.

"That's the deal we made." Sylvia spoke the words carefully.

"I didn't agree to it," Steve protested.

Marcie tried to explain why it was necessary, but Steve still balked. Gloria promised she wouldn't get in his way while she was there, assuring him it was only for two hours.

"Two hours?" Steve complained. "Why so long?"

Sylvia was exasperated. "Do you want to live here alone?" she asked.

He rolled his eyes. "You know I do. I don't need someone here all the time."

"It *isn't* all the time. This is how it has to be. Take it or leave it. If you leave it, I'll find someone to *live* here!"

"Are you mad at me?" Steve often asked her this when she spoke firmly. He looked sheepish.

"I'm frustrated," she responded. Sylvia worried that Steve wouldn't remember to be home to let Gloria in the house, or that he'd pretend he'd forgotten she was coming. Worse, since Steve was being so difficult, she was afraid Gloria might bail. She acknowledged to herself that Steve's reluctance with any new situation was the norm. The best approach was to move forward with the next step.

"What?" asked Steve.

"Let's set up the time of day that works best for you," Sylvia said.

"I like afternoons. It takes me a long time to wake up."

A small window was opening, and Gloria picked up on it. "How does two o'clock sound?" Her tone was matter-of-fact, like it was just the two of them setting up a prearranged business deal.

"That's good for me," he said.

She nodded and winked. "Great. And which days would you like?"

"None," he laughed at his own joke.

"Monday, Wednesday, and Friday would be ideal," Sylvia said. "Definitely before and after the weekend. Things tend to get piled up."

"But I work on Friday," Steve said. "For an hour. From eleven to twelve."

"Perfect," Gloria said. "Because I won't come until two."

"Oh, right," Steve smiled at her. "That would work."

"So, I think we figured it out, Steve. You and I can decide when to get groceries. I'd like to know what you like to eat. Maybe I can prepare a meal for you, too."

"I love sloppy joes and chili and Hamburger Helper."

"Those are easy for me to make," she said.

He hesitated. "But what if I don't like . . . um . . . ?"

Sylvia had been here before with Nancy, so she knew what he wanted to ask. "I'll give Gloria Mom's recipes for sloppy joes and chili, and a grocery list of your favorite foods."

"See? We're all set," Gloria said.

"I guess we are," Steve said. "Can I leave now?" He looked at Gloria. "I like to go to Pizza Hut a lot."

"I love their pizza," Gloria said.

"I just drink iced tea there. Sometimes I get pizza, but I don't like to spend the money."

Gloria chuckled. "Maybe I'll pick one up sometime and bring it here."

"Wow. That'd even be better than sloppy joes!"

"So you're off to Pizza Hut?" Sylvia asked.

"Yes. I won't be long. Probably an hour or two." Steve stood with a confident, relaxed air. "Nice to meet you, Gloria."

"Nice to meet you, Steve. I'll see you next week."

With a self-assured stride, Steve went out the side door.

Sylvia leaned against the sofa. "Whew. That wasn't looking promising, but you sure brought him around, Gloria."

"It's understandable that he'd be wary of a stranger. And I've done this before, mostly with the elderly. They can be just as resistant."

"Another thing that's very important," Sylvia said. "You'll need to check that his med tray is filled and maybe check his pill vials for out-of-date empties. He tends to keep all of them, which I think can confuse him."

"Sure. I can do that," she agreed, "but I'm not allowed to check his actual meds."

"I understand that. I'll be here for your first visit to show you the ropes, but after that I can only hope he lets you in."

"We'll work it out. Do you want me to call the night before I come? To remind him?"

"I couldn't ask for more," Sylvia said.

33

A t the dining room table, Steve sat patiently next to Sylvia while she explained how to use a debit card.

"I don't get it. Where does the money come from?"

"The card automatically deducts it from our joint checking account."

Steve went blank. "Really? But how?"

"It's all done through computers."

"I don't understand computers. I'll never use one."

"You don't need to. The card will be easier for you to buy groceries with Gloria. Easier than writing a check, don't you think?"

"Oh. Right. It'd take me too long to write one. And people would be standing in line. What if I made a mistake and had to write another one, and they'd have to wait? I always make mistakes."

"Me, too. So, a debit card is much quicker once you get the hang of it," Sylvia said.

"It might take longer than once. Like when Jack, across the street, showed me how to pump gas. And he said he'd go with me as long as I needed him to, so I could remember how." Steve had only bought gas at the one local station where there was still full service with attendants. When they changed to self-service only, he called Sylvia and told her he didn't know how to pump gas. The light on the dash had been on for several days, and he was worried he'd run out, so he didn't drive. Sylvia had called the neighbor to ask if he'd help Steve.

"And now you know how, right?"

Steve laughed, "I do!"

"See? It just takes practice."

"Nancy always bought the groceries. Can't Gloria do it?"

"Not with her own money, and I don't want her to be on our bank account."

"Oh, yeah." Steve contemplated this. "She might steal our money. Maybe I should hide the checkbook."

"I don't think you need to worry about that," Sylvia said.

"Dad always said I was a worrywart. And Nancy. She said I worry too much."

"I worry, too. About lots of stuff."

"You have kids and a husband and a house and . . . you have a lot to worry about."

That's an understatement. Sylvia smiled, "Anyway, Gloria will help you with the debit card if you forget."

"I think I like Gloria," Steve declared.

"That's good," Sylvia chuckled. "So you'll let her in the house?"

He furrowed his brow and scowled at her. "Why wouldn't I?"

"That was a joke."

"Not very funny," Steve shook his head.

"Back to the debit card," Sylvia redirected him. "You'll need a PIN number to use it."

"A what?"

"Four numbers you won't forget, so the card will work. Do you know your Social Security number?"

Steve rattled it off.

"Use the last four numbers for your PIN."

"2-3-7-8."

"Good. That's all you need to remember when you slide the card through the machine at the checkout register."

"Will you write this down for me?"

"I already did." She showed him the index card. "I'd take you to the store to show you how it works, but . . . "

"Slow down," Steve said. "I want to read this first."

Sylvia waited until he looked up. "The debit card won't get here before I leave, but put it in your wallet as soon as it arrives in the mail."

"Okay."

Sylvia told him she would buy lots of groceries before she left, so he'd be well stocked. Stouffer's frozen dinners, luncheon meats, Chunky soups, Kraft cheese slices, Oatnut bread, Miracle Whip, peanut butter, jams, cereal (Cheerios, Grape-Nuts Flakes, Sugar Crisp), Ritz crackers, bananas, apples, pears—all the things he liked and didn't have to cook, since he was afraid to use the stove. Luckily, Steve knew how to use the microwave.

"When do you leave?" he asked.

"In three days, but our minister is coming to bless the house Monday afternoon, and you said you'd go to church with me tomorrow." The family had attended the Silver Lake Church, a hub of social activity in the community, throughout their childhoods, and both Sylvia and Steve were confirmed there.

"I know. I promised. Do I have to wear a tie?"

"No, a sport jacket though."

"And my oxblood tasseled loafers. Why is the minister going to bless the house?"

"To ask God to watch over our house and you, now that you'll be living alone," Sylvia replied.

Steve thought about this. "That's nice, Sylvia. Was that your idea?"

She nodded.

"Is anybody else coming?"

"Maybe Marcie, your case manager, Gloria, the housekeeper, maybe Amy next door, and our friend, Karen."

"Karen's *your* friend." Karen and Sylvia were the same age, three years older than Steve. They'd gone to school together since first grade, and they became best friends in high school. Steve still saw Karen as "Sylvia's friend," as if the age difference still mattered. But Karen had known Steve before he became ill, and she wanted to help wherever she could, especially now that he'd be living alone. Karen was her rock, one of many unexpected blessings in Silver Lake in the form of old family friends, friends of their parents, those who knew Steve when. Solace came with old ties.

"Yes, she's my oldest friend, but she hopes to get to know you better, so you'll feel comfortable to call her if you need anything."

"Oh," he smiled. "I probably won't."

"I'll leave her phone number anyway."

"You must be glad to go back home," Steve said, looking hopeful, like he wanted her to be ready to leave.

"You bet I am," Sylvia said.

"I don't bet."

"I know, I know. It's just an expression. And you're ready to have the house to yourself, aren't you?"

"I am," he sighed. "I don't mean I don't want you here . . . "

"No, I understand. It'll be quieter for you," she said.

"That's it," he nodded. "I like it quiet. Nancy was noisy." He looked puzzled. "Isn't Nancy married now?"

"Yes, to Martin."

"And she's moving to England?"

"Right. It all worked out for her. She seems very happy and I'm glad for her.

"Did she take Sammy?"

"No, she couldn't. He's with a friend of hers."

"I can't believe it. She gave away her dog?"

If he only knew about Danny, but there was no need to tell Steve that. Nancy needed to move on with her life. "Her friend loves Sammy, and he knows her well. He'll be fine."

"Can I go to Pizza Hut before you go to the store?"

"I'd rather go shopping now before the crowd. Okay?"

"Yeah. I'm too tired anyway. I'll take a nap."

"Good idea."

———

The day after Sylvia left for LA, Steve was more than relieved. It was a warm sunny afternoon. He walked around the backyard and picked up a few dead limbs that had dropped from the giant pin oak trees his dad had planted before he was born. "It's my turn to look after the place. I'm almost happy. I haven't said that in years." He talked to himself and hummed a tune as he strolled. "Maybe my luck hasn't run out. I'm finally getting my wish—to be left alone!"

—

2005

Though Steve told Sylvia he felt lonely at times, he felt free of the pressure to behave properly for someone else. Sometimes he forgot Gloria was coming, and he wasn't home on time to let her in. Sometimes he listened to old cassettes that his parents had recorded and reminisced: Mantovani, Strauss waltzes, trumpet solos, Christmas carols. But his favorite thing was to watch old movies on TCM. It reminded him of earlier days, when he and Sylvia watched movies from the forties together. Sometimes he called Sylvia to tell her about the movies he'd watched. "I don't turn the sound up," he said, "but I can figure out what's going on." He'd name actors like Cary Grant, Jimmy Stewart, Greta Garbo, and then relate the story lines, or as much as he could figure out. He and Scott called each other. Steve might ask when Scott could come visit and Scott said he'd visit in the summers when Sylvia was there.

But there were also numerous problems. "How do I turn on the A/C? The garage door won't open. My car is stuck in the snow." Steve worried about using too much water or electricity or spending too much money on groceries. Probably a good thing. Gloria stayed for over two years and then left to get married. Many aides came and went. Sylvia traveled to Ohio three times a year, training different aides, some okay, some not. One just sat on the front deck with Steve and smoked, barely doing the laundry, avoiding the necessary cleaning. But Steve adapted to them all. He never complained. He knew the conditions: you can stay in the house as long as you take your meds and have a housekeeper. Sometimes he missed meds, skipped the library volunteer job, or canceled the aide, which was only evident when Sylvia came to check on things. But Steve managed. Who would've thought Steve could live by himself? Could pay some bills, end up buying groceries by himself, keep all of his medical appointments and volunteer at the library, increasing his time from one hour to two? But he did. His desire to be independent was a stronger force than his siblings could have imagined. Of course, they managed a lot. Family needs to be the advocate. And when there's no family? God help them.

—

There's an old story about a father with a mentally and physically disabled child. He asked a reverend, "How could God do this? How could He bring a child into the world who must struggle daily to be accepted, to live normally? If God is perfect, where is His perfection?" One day, the father and son happened to see the neighborhood baseball team playing a game as they passed by. The son had never played on the team but wanted badly to play. The father asked the team captain, who knew the boy, if his son could join in. The captain called a huddle with both teams to make the request. It was the last inning of a tie game. The teams agreed to let him in to bat. The pitcher lobbed the ball so the boy could manage to hit it. The opposing players purposefully threw the ball in a direction that let the boy get to first base, then second, and then home. The boy won the game for them, because both teams let it happen. They lifted the boy on their shoulders. He was a hero.

"And the answer to your question," the reverend said, "is when God brings a child like this into the world, the perfection that He seeks is in the way that people react to this child. That's the perfection He seeks."

ACKNOWLEDGMENTS

I want to acknowledge those who spurred me on with accolades, constructive criticism, and strong editing: First, my writer's group (my second family) since May 2013—Margaret Karlin, Christina Alex, Kathrin Segal, Ellen Ruderman, Lindsay Lees, Kim Gottlieb-Walker, Jovita Jenkins, Madelyn Norman, and Alexia LaFortune, who led me to Brooke Warner, editor and publisher of She Writes Press. Collectively, they are responsible for the completion of this novel. Second, my husband, Jeff, who never wavered in his belief in my work and was patient and understanding about my extensive trips to Ohio—the source of my material! And finally, my loving brothers, Gary and David, and our devoted parents, who gave us a joyful childhood in Silver Lake, Ohio, my treasured oasis. How grateful I am to all of you.

ABOUT THE
AUTHOR

Joan Jackson was raised in Ohio. After teaching French for a time, she went on to manage a French-Tahitian export company in Oregon. She is the author of the novel *Voluntary Chaos* and has published several magazine articles and written a collection of short stories. Jackson spends ten weeks annually in her childhood home in Silver Lake, Ohio, caretaking and managing the home for her schizophrenic brother, who lives alone. She and her husband reside in Los Angeles, California.

ALSO BY JOAN JACKSON

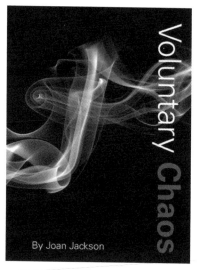

VOLUNTARY CHAOS
2010 New York Book Festival Honorable Mention

A stay-at-home mom becomes entangled in a passionate love affair. Unable to reconcile her duty-bound commitment to the husband she's outgrown and her devotion to her two young children, Sylvia wrestles for years with the moral dilemma to stay married or divorce. Under the shadow of Mt St Helens, everything blows apart. We see her best friend advise her to stay married but 'live separate lives', her return to work teaching French, her parents' despair coping with her younger brother's schizophrenia, and her endearing children struggle with their parents' inability to avoid chaos. From Oregon to Europe she gradually learns to face the inevitability to find contentment within herself.

SELECTED TITLES FROM SHE WRITES PRESS

She Writes Press is an independent publishing company founded to serve women writers everywhere. Visit us at www.shewritespress.com.

Stella Rose by Tammy Flanders Hetrick
$16.95, 978-1-63152-921-4
When her dying best friend asks her to take care of her sixteen-year-old daughter, Abby says yes—but as she grapples with raising a grieving teenager, she realizes she didn't know her best friend as well as she thought she did.

True Stories at the Smoky View by Jill McCroskey Coupe
$16.95, 978-1-63152-051-8
The lives of a librarian and a ten-year-old boy are changed forever when they become stranded by a blizzard in a Tennessee motel and join forces in a very personal search for justice.

The Rooms Are Filled by Jessica Null Vealitzek
$16.95, 978-1-938314-58-2
The coming-of-age story of two outcasts—a nine-year-old boy who just lost his father, and a closeted young woman—brought together by circumstance.

A Drop In The Ocean: A Novel by Jenni Ogden
$16.95, 978-1-63152-026-6
When middle-aged Anna Fergusson's research lab is abruptly closed, she flees Boston to an island on Australia's Great Barrier Reef—where, amongst the seabirds, nesting turtles, and eccentric islanders, she finds a family and learns some bittersweet lessons about love.

Shelter Us by Laura Diamond
$16.95, 978-1-63152-970-2
Lawyer-turned-stay-at-home-mom Sarah Shaw is still struggling to find a steady happiness after the death of her infant daughter when she meets a young homeless mother and toddler she can't get out of her mind—and becomes determined to rescue them.

Tasa's Song by Linda Kass
$16.95, 978-1-63152-064-8
From a peaceful village in eastern Poland to a partitioned post-war Vienna, from a promising childhood to a year living underground, *Tasa's Song* celebrates the bonds of love, the power of memory, the solace of music, and the enduring strength of the human spirit.